MW00577076

BLOOD OF THE SEVEN SUNS

To: Dr. Schlueter,

Thank you for your care—

Peace & Good,

[illegible]

BLOOD OF THE SEVEN SUNS

A Medieval Novel Based on Real People & Events

H. G. WATTS

Septizonium ◈ Media

This is a work of fiction and should not be construed as biographically or historically precise. This story is primarily a product of the author's imagination.

Septizonium ◈ Media

ISBN 978-1-7336239-0-2

Cover Photograph: Simone Martini, Agnese di Boemia © Photographic Archives of the Sacred Convent of the Basilica of St. Francis in Assisi, Italy.

TO:

God
Author of My Life

M.D.W.
Love of My Life

Family
Joy of My Life

Franciscans
Touchstone of My Life

CONTENTS

PROLOGUE
The Jacoba Letters

"His feet. I will never forget his feet. Bloody. Battered. Beaten. I unwrapped them with care and kissed them. My tears fell upon his lifeless body as they mingled with the fragrant water of this final corporal cleansing... I went about my dreadful task of bathing him while knowing that no more would I see or touch or hold the earthly form of this man I so loved. "

So begins a 13th Century letter from Lady Giacoma dei Settesoli also known as Jacoba Frangipane. She was one of very few women with whom Giovanni Bernardone allowed himself any genuine familiarity. While there is no official record of professed love between them, Jacoba dei Settesoli was the only woman allowed to be with him when he died… and the only woman whose remains share his crypt.

The story of Giacoma and Giovanni may seem like an unremarkable medieval tale of love and loss to those who read her letters except that Jacoba wasn't an ordinary woman. She was a beautiful, powerful, wealthy Roman noble. And Giovanni wasn't an ordinary man: He was Francis of Assisi, the sinner who became a saint.

The discovery in 1977 of various documents related to Jacoba and their eventual translation from Medieval Latin into modern English may be worth a volume in themselves. However, for now, I will share what I gleaned from the content of these parchments that lay undisturbed in an ancient Perugian villa for nearly nine centuries.

I have devoted the better part of my life to meticulously finding accurate yet contemporary words to convey to the modern world this remarkable woman's story as well as piece together how this great love story may have evolved.

Throughout this volume, I have interspersed Jacoba's actual correspondence and pertinent letters authored by others in the hope that you will find her story as fascinating and inspiring as I have.

– H. G. Watts

INTRODUCTION
Epoch of Blood

Jacoba dei Settesoli (Jacoba of the Seven Suns) was born into a world not unlike ours today – full of turmoil, violence, greed as well as extremes of abundance and scarcity.

The Middle Ages in Europe were turbulent and strange. Conflict abounded, and Italy was not exempt.

It was the time of major Crusades. However, war was waged not only against invading Saracens and monarchs determined to expand their realms but also between walled hill-towns that dotted the Italian landscape. In addition, within those town walls seeds of rebellion were starting to sprout as a new, middle class of wealthy merchants began to emerge and challenge the role of nobles and the feudal system itself.

For Rome, upheaval and chaos were constant. It was a city at war with itself. Its skyline was dominated by hundreds of towers built solely for combat. Its strange appearance would have made Rome unrecognizable to its ancient inhabitants as well as those born in the Renaissance.

Rome in the 11th, 12th, and 13th Centuries was a jumble of different structures built over, around, and within the ruins that blanketed the city. Early monumental structures that escaped devastation from time, war and looters had been transformed into palaces for the rich and powerful.

However, their magnificence was often hidden by the countless humble dwellings alongside them.

Leadership of the city vacillated greatly depending upon which families were in power and to whom they owed their allegiance. Loyalty could be achieved with bribes, violence, or marriage. It was seldom attained through diplomacy alone.

The Middle Ages were also an era of pilgrimage. Rome – as the heart of Western European Christendom – hosted many visitors which brought both blessings and problems.

Popes of the Middle Ages played pivotal roles in the secular world as well as in the spiritual lives of Christians. Although the Catholic Church was a uniting force that helped propel Europe out of the Dark Ages, many of its leaders, and much of its flock as well, had grown overly focused on temporal matters at the expense of spiritual concerns.

The seat of the Church remained in Rome, but its popes were sometimes forced to leave the city temporarily due to the volatility of powerful families like the Frangipani as well as threats from outside Rome's walls.

Death perpetually hovered over medieval people in their prime. It could come from birthing a child or at the blade of a foe or from the dreaded disease of leprosy not to mention accidents.

Despite all the ugliness of the period, or perhaps because of it, the Middle Ages produced the chivalric code, troubadours and courtly love as well as religious reforms. It was also an era of hope and progress. And Jacoba was in the thick of it.

A Communiqué

From Aldruda Frangipane,
Countess of Bertinoro
To her son, Rainerio II Frangipane
Summer, 1184

All is well in Astura. Duchessa Maria gave birth to a healthy female child. The baby will be called Jacoba. The plans your late father and I made for the family's future have been assured. I will return to Rome before the next moon. Be strong. Take heart.

A. F.

Chapter I
Birthing Blood
1184 – Torre Astura, Latium Coast, Italy

The screams began shortly after sunset. Intermittent. Intense. They ended just after midnight when the baby's head crowned. The urge to push the tiny body through the birth canal was overwhelming. No more screams of pain, just grunts of effort mixed with groans of resolve. The mother's labor was soon over, and tears of joy streamed down her face with the child's first wail. Her baby was alive. She herself was alive. They had both survived childbirth – one of life's greatest risks. It was what she hoped for, what she prayed for.

Covered in blood and meconium, the newborn was quickly seized by one of the attendants, brought to a waiting table and gently cleansed with a mixture of rose water and salt. The servant swaddled the child with strips of linen and headed back to the birthing bed to put the newborn into the arms of the exhausted, waiting mother. However, before this mission could be accomplished, a wizened woman wearing fine garments intercepted the servant and snatched the bundle. The old woman had flung open the door to the room and marched in grandly within minutes of hearing the child's first cry.

"Male or female," she said in a way that was a demand rather than a question. "It's a baby girl, Contessa Aldruda," the servant deferentially responded. "Very good," Aldruda said, adding under her breath, "I knew the predictions of a son were wrong!"

The aged aristocrat placed the newborn in the hand-hewn cradle that was waiting in the darkest corner of the room. "Bring some candles closer," she commanded as she briskly loosened the baby's swaddling linens. Two maids scurried to give the countess more light.

The ancient noble began counting fingers and toes. Only after she was satisfied there were ten of each did she more closely assess the overall appearance of the baby. Aldruda Frangipane, Countess of Bertinoro, spoke aloud to no one in particular: "Yes, she will do. Her hair is dark and thick. Her head will be well-shapen. Her legs are long."

When the baby reflexively gripped her tiny fingers around the gnarly little finger offered by the old lady, Aldruda smiled and murmured, "She will be strong as well as beautiful. She will make the perfect bride for our Gratien."

Now content the newborn would eventually be physically worthy of joining the Frangipane family, Aldruda moved away from the cradle and motioned to the attendants to take the child to its mother.

After giving Maria dei Normanni a moment to hold her daughter, Aldruda approached the birthing bed. “What will you name her, Duchessa Maria?” Her tone was brusque, but that wasn’t unusual for Aldruda. She was more comfortable shouting an order to a knight in battle than addressing the mother of a newborn.

“Giacoma,” Maria responded without taking her eyes off the precious bundle in her arms. “Vincentius and I were informed I was carrying a boy, Contessa. The alignment of the planets at conception foretold it. And when the drops of my blood sank rather than floated in the spring water, a male birth was confirmed. We had selected the name Giacomo many months ago. Did you know it means ‘follower of God?’ Well, anyway, a son for us obviously wasn’t in God’s plan, but we will, nevertheless, name our child after St. James,” Maria added. Throughout her profuse reply the young duchessa’s gaze remained fixed on her baby. She was enthralled by the little person in her arms.

“Hmmm…” Aldruda burbled. “Giacoma’s patron saint is Jacobus? … You’ll have to forgive me. I’m not used to these vernacular versions of traditional Latin names.”

Aldruda motioned to the wet nurse to get the child. “It’s time for your new daughter to get some nourishment… and for us to speak candidly.”

Aldruda continued: “Since you bore a daughter and not a son, we are agreed then that Giacoma will marry my grandson Gratien when she is of child-bearing age.” The contessa delivered the statement in a tentative tone that made it sound more like a question.

“Of course,” Maria answered softly while never shifting her gaze from Jacoba who was now on the other side of the room with the wet nurse. "Giacomina and Gratien will wed. If my baby had been male, he would have wed your granddaughter. Vincentius discussed this with me before he left for Marino. We agreed it would be best for the Normanni and the Frangipani…you know…in order to reinforce our blood ties."

"Very good then." Aldruda said matter-of-factly. In a more enthusiastic tone she added, "The bonds of our families will be sealed for generations to come.

"Now, I am going to take my leave, Duchessa. May God bless you and Giacoma." The old woman kissed Maria on the forehead and gave an uncharacteristically loving glance toward the baby now sucking at the wet nurse's breast.

"Oh… and just one more thing, Duchessa," Aldruda said as she glanced back to the birthing bed. "I hope you might indulge an old woman's whim. I have always been deeply fond of the more ancient form of your daughter's name; so, I and my family will call her Jacoba."

Aldruda didn't bother to wait for a response from Maria before heading for the door. She exited as vigorously as she had entered. Aldruda's assertive manner suited her. She was a warrior princess who ranked among other fighting female nobles of her generation. These included Eleanor of Aquitaine who went on Crusade as well as Petronilla, the English countess who fought with rebels against Henry II.

It wasn't the remarkable heartiness of the elderly woman that was so surprising. It was her very presence that astonished. To the world, Aldruda Frangipane, Countess of Bertinoro, died a decade earlier. Only a handful of people knew she was alive. The crags in her face included not only the deep wrinkles of advanced age but also scars from combat.

As her servant undressed Aldruda for bed, the old woman's mind drifted to events of the night: the cries of the mother's labor, the live birth of a girl, the naming of the child. In her mind, Aldruda asked why she much preferred the baby be called Jacoba.

Once alone in her bed chamber, she began a soliloquy under her breath, *"Of course, names are important. They are our destiny. It's a good thing I remembered my Latin. Jacobus. Yes. The supplanter. That's the Latin meaning of her name.*

"We must always call the girl Jacoba. It's so much stronger than Giacoma – That name belongs to someone who should be living in a convent not a fortress. Our Gratien will need a forceful and clever wife. Someone who can help the family defend and expand its holdings outside Rome and supplant the Pierleoni for power in Rome.

"Jacoba. Yes. She will be our "supplanter." She will follow in my footsteps"

Aldruda fell off to sleep confident that with her guidance, the newborn would live up to the name Jacoba. Once married to Gratien, she would step into the shoes of Aldruda and the other Frangipane women to accomplish what mattered to the family – retaining its power and increasing its holdings.

ꕥ

In her bed chamber one level below Aldruda, Duchessa Maria's thoughts in those early morning hours were also focused on the newborn now back in her arms.

Maria thought it odd the way things worked out. She always pictured her baby being born in the family's palace in Trastevere or perhaps in their summer residence in Nettuno. It seemed coincidental if not ironic her daughter's birth took place here in this fortress that belonged to the family of the child's future husband.

Maria looked around the spacious room. It was cool – a welcome relief from the scorching heat of Rome in summer. It was richly decorated – especially for a fortification. It was safe. This last attribute was most important to her.

Although attacks by Muslim pirates had somewhat waned in the Tyrrhenian Sea since the Normans began their conquest of Sicily, the barbarous assaults nevertheless proved fatal for those who were unprepared. When sightings of a Saracen ship approaching the area reached Nettuno three days earlier, nobles and gentry sought refuge in the Frangipane tower.

The pirates ultimately targeted another coastal town for their lethal foray, but Maria was encouraged by her husband to remain in the Frangipane fortress while he was away. She was thankful she did since the Frangipane's servants were more experienced than her own as far as delivering babies.

"Giacomina," Maria whispered to her sleeping child, "Someday you shall be a great lady and rule all of Rome with Gratien Frangipane. You shall have joys. You shall have sorrows. Your father and I will do our best to prepare you for the life you will lead."

A few moments later, little Jacoba was asleep. One of the maids carried her to the cradle that had been moved from the darkest corner of the room closer to the Duchessa's bed at Maria's request. The mother watched the sleeping baby for a few moments before she herself succumbed to exhaustion

A Letter from Jacoba dei Settesoli

To an Anonymous Relative

July, 1205 – Rome

My Dear Cousin,

I hope my letter finds you and your family well. It is unbelievably hot here, and being with child makes the Roman heat even less tolerable. I'm fond of remembering our earliest summers in Nettuno – before the responsibilities of life took away our innocent delights, when the sun brought warmth rather than discomfort.

The children and I hope to join you in the country next summer. I want them to know summers are different beyond our city's walls.

I am anxiously awaiting Gratien's return from the Marches of Ancona where he was assisting an ally. I'm also somewhat apprehensive. There is now talk of another crusade, and I worry I will lose him to battle one way or another.

As you know too well, being the wife of a feudal lord makes one fearful your spouse will not return from one of his "little wars." Yet when My Love returns, I fear I am nevertheless losing him because the fighting changes him in small ways. When he has lived war day in and day out, it takes him several days to adjust to the peace of our home. The children will grow up not knowing what a joyful man Gratien was before all of these skirmishes took control of him. This makes me sad.

I am thankful for my needlework. I do it almost daily, and it keeps me sane. With Gratien away more than he is here, I must run the household down to every detail. It is more taxing than I ever imagined, and I have gained a new respect for my dearest mother. I now know what most of her days are like when my father is busy defending property and family.

I am feeling shame as I admit to being thankful for the current battles near Florence. The quarrel there involves the Pierleoni not the Frangipani or Normanni. With the attention of our Roman adversaries drawn north, we have enjoyed a few months of relative calm here.

Because of this unintended truce among our Roman families, it has been safer than usual to travel our city's streets. I have used this time to my advantage to visit the holy churches within Rome and have even ventured outside the walls. Each sanctuary brings me a different inspiration.

I need to tell you about an odd event on one of my excursions several weeks ago. My loyal servant Sabina and little Johanna accompanied me – under the protection of our Frangipane family guards, of course – to the tomb of St. Peter. I had not been there since the births of Johanna and Jacob. I wanted to pray and give alms for my beloved Gratien's safe return.

The church was crowded — as always — with pilgrims and beggars. However, it wasn't as you would have remembered it when we were children. Nothing in Rome is as it used to be. Many of those in this holy place were talking loudly; some even laughing and gesturing rudely. Few were praying. Even fewer were giving alms. Given my condition, I scolded them with my eyes only. I probably should have also used a few well chosen words. Instead, I quietly dropped my offering through the grate as I have in the past and moved off to the side to say my prayers away from the buzzing swarm.

My own silent reflection was interrupted when I heard the loud clatter of coins deliberately being tossed into the grate. The fellow making this racket was dressed in fine clothes and appeared to be a gentleman – perhaps a noble on pilgrimage. He should have known better. Yet, he did this a number of times – purposely creating a lot of noise and looking around to make sure others noticed.

I approached the man to urge him to show consideration when he abruptly moved toward a beggar sitting in a dark corner of the church not far from where I was trying to pray. The well-dressed man motioned to the beggar and then spoke to him. I could not hear his words, but I saw the beggar's eyes grow wide soon followed by a nod of agreement between the men.

Both began disrobing. I should have looked away, but I didn't because it was such an oddity. After they stripped, they exchanged clothes. The now well-dressed beggar walked off while the fellow who initiated the clothing exchange assumed the beggar's position.

With eyes downcast and hand outstretched, he began to plead for alms – even though just moments before he had made a clattering show of giving away many coins.

Something moved me to walk past him on my way out. As I approached, I could hear his low voice asking for alms. He was speaking in French! I couldn't believe it. I tossed a few coins into his open palm. He said thank you but never raised his eyes to me. I wanted to see the eyes of this man who behaved so strangely and find out why he acted in such an odd manner. So, although I should not have, I spoke to him. "Beggar, why do you not look at me?" I asked.

His eyes were still downcast when he replied: "Because I know you are a woman, and I know I would see great beauty. And in great beauty, there is great temptation."

There was something peculiarly familiar about his voice. I knew it from somewhere and desperately wanted to see his face. I told him, "You have no need to worry about either because I am no beauty, and I am already wed. My only charm is this growing belly since I am with child. I just want to ask a question, and I want to see your eyes when you answer."

The beggar slowly lifted his head. His eyes startled me. It was Giovanni – Giovanni from Assisi – the cloth merchant's son who goes by the name of Francis. Giovanni was the same yet quite different. His eyes were still big and watery. They were piercing, sad and joyful at the same time.

Do you remember me telling you about him? He was my "summer friend" when I visited Assisi as a child. He was and always will be my first and special love . . .

ജ്ഷ

Jacoba's mind suddenly flooded with memories more than a decade old yet as vivid and warm as the Roman sun. She let her writing quill rest in the ink horn as her mind flashed back to her first trip to Assisi, recalling a summer many years earlier when she was away from her family and from Rome.

Chapter II
Young Blood
Summer, 1192 – Rome & Assisi, Italy

Jacoba had no idea things she saw, people she met, and feelings she experienced during the summer of her eighth year would impact her life for its entirety.

It wasn't the fatiguing heat that delivered the child of Maria and Vincentius dei Normanni to a small hill town in the Umbrian hills. It was Roman violence.

Jacoba was too young to comprehend what was going on among the families fighting each other for power, for property, for pride. All she knew was she would be taking a trip to a small hill city with Cecilia — her mother's most trusted servant and Jacoba's favorite – and they were going to play a little game during the time she would be away.

Jacoba's mother told her she had to pretend to be Cecilia's niece and keep the family's surname and noble heritage a secret. She told Jacoba the two would stay with the Bombarones, and Jacoba was obliged to say the family was related to Cecilia.

"If you carry out this small pretense and do a task for me, Jacoba, there will be a wonderful surprise for you when you get home." Duchessa Maria explained there was a cloth merchant in this town – a friend of Signor Bombarone – who regularly traveled to France to buy beautiful fabrics for clothing as well as quality linen for household needs.

Jacoba's mother did not share the true reason for the little charade: The child's life was in grave danger. The Orsini and the Frangipani Families were once again in conflict in Rome. Jacoba's Norman family was aligned with the Frangipani, and the Orsini showed no mercy – even to children.

Maria dei Normanni wanted Jacoba to have a happier childhood than she did; so, her explanation to Jacoba was that she longed to have some gowns and cloaks made from fine French cloth because they would remind her of her homeland. She said she would love to select it herself but she had to be in Rome the next several moons.

It would be the responsibility of Jacoba with the help of Cecilia to select the most beautiful fabrics. Some of the plain textiles would be made into chemises by the cloth merchant's associates in Assisi while the most costly fabrics such as velvets and brocades would be brought back to Rome so Maria's seamstress could make gowns not only for herself but also for Jacoba.

"If you play the 'pretend game' well, Jacoba, I may even have one of your gowns trimmed in fur. Would you like that?" Maria faked a convincing smile as her heart ached.

She didn't want her daughter to be so far from her but knew it was best for the child.

The eight-year-old's eyes lit up at the thought of being given a special task by her mother as well as having a beautiful new fur-trimmed gown for herself. She liked many things in her life including fine clothes.

To make the trip even more of an adventure, Maria told Jacoba she would be leaving very, very early the next day. Maria and Cecilia had already packed the things Jacoba would need for the journey and her indefinite stay.

ꟸ

Jacoba was excited, apprehensive and happy at the same time. She thought she would never fall asleep and was surprised when she felt her mother's hand gently awakening her. Cecilia was also nearby, ready to dress her young charge for the long ride. It was still dark, and Jacoba recalled never being awakened in the night for any previous journeys. She knew this was going to be an adventure like no other.

The horses were ready — their hooves digging the ground and their nostrils flaring. They looked immense to little Jacoba who was accustomed to riding smaller mounts. The four horses were laden with nothing that would draw attention to the travelers, tempt thieves, or slow their pace. Their only cargo would be Jacoba, Cecilia, and three armed guards whose weapons were secreted under coarse wool tunics similar to those worn by most commoners.

Without speaking, one of the guards gently pulled Jacoba from her mother's side and placed her on the horse with Cecilia. After mounting his own black horse, he gave a hand signal for the entourage to go. Jacoba's mother traced a blessing in the air to Jacoba and the group, then blew a kiss to her daughter. Jacoba blew a kiss back and waved good-bye.

Six Normanni soldiers who were transporting necessities for Jacoba's extended stay provided a more likely target for potential robbers; so, they left Rome separately in the dead of night, well in advance of Jacoba. Both entourages were well beyond the dangers of the city by the time dawn broke.

Jacoba recalled never venturing outside of Rome except for trips to Ninfa where her family retreated when the weather or warfare in Rome became unbearably hot. So, Assisi and everything en route were new and exciting. The 33-mile journey took much of the day since the horses' gait varied between trotting and walking.

As Assisi emerged from a hazy horizon, Jacoba was surprised at its small size and its great beauty. Perhaps because she was seeing Assisi from a distance, Jacoba thought its walls wrapped around the hill town like a mother's arms in contrast to the inhospitable walls of Rome. Although the latter were crumbling, they remained foreboding.

The expanse in front of the hill town was awash in a mixture of greens, browns and colors provided by its assortment of olive groves, vineyards, poppy fields and patches of sunflowers. The variety of the shades of green alone made her feel like she was approaching an enchanted realm.

Reality set in for her as they entered Porta San Giorgio. Although not as crowded as Rome, Assisi appeared to be just as filthy. The odor of rotting refuse and raw sewage near the city gate made Jacoba instinctively put her hand over her nose and mouth.

"It will get better, little one," Cecilia said in a reassuring voice. "We are staying farther up the hill where there is no stench and where you can see for many miles."

They arrived at the home of the Bombarones, located up the hill from one of the town's piazzas. Jacoba and Cecilia would be staying with the family for most of the summer. Jacoba's father knew and trusted the elder Bombarone from some previous business and military dealings. Because of a significant and undisclosed favor performed by Jacoba's father, the Bombarones felt indebted to him and willingly offered to host Jacoba and Cecilia in their spacious home for the summer. The three Normanni soldiers would remain with the Bombarones for Jacoba's entire stay. They would, however, masquerade as transient laborers hired to work in the family's stables and on Bombarone land.

The head of the Bombarone household and his wife were the only people in Assisi who knew Jacoba's true identity. Their four children knew nothing of Jacoba's noble lineage. Even if they did, they wouldn't have cared. They seemed happy at the thought of a new playmate to share in their games and pranks.

Upon arrival, Jacoba's first "task" from her mother was to present Signor Bombarone with a letter and a key to a strongbox that had been transported by the earlier retinue. He immediately broke the seal on the letter and silently read the words. Jacoba could tell by his eyes and the smile that crossed his lips that he was pleased with the words. He did not open the strongbox but asked a servant to put it in their safe room while he carefully placed the key in a pocket inside his surcoat.

Later, Jacoba asked Cecilia what the box and letter were for. Cecilia said she didn't know but guessed there was probably a great number of gold coins from her father to take care of expenses during their stay.

"Can we go to the cloth merchant's house now to see his fine fabrics?" Jacoba inquired with enthusiasm while unsuccessfully trying to hold back a yawn.

Cecilia laughed. "That will have to wait until tomorrow, little one. For now, it's time for bed. You've had a long journey and a long day. There will be plenty of time since we will be here for many weeks."

Just then Jacoba realized she would not be back in Rome for a long time, and her mother's loving hands would not be tucking her into bed. Her sudden pang of homesickness was quickly eased by her sleepiness. The last thing she remembered before nodding off was a kiss on the forehead from Cecilia and a soft blanket being pulled over her shoulders.

The night passed quickly for Jacoba. Sunlight streaming into the room combined with muffled sounds from a more distant part of the house gently woke her. She knew she'd had dreams but couldn't recall them no matter how hard she tried. The space around her was unfamiliar, and it took her a moment to remember she was in the Bombarone home in Assisi not in her own bed chamber in Rome.

A sudden rap on the door startled Jacoba, but she was soon reassured at hearing Cecilia's voice accompanied by whining iron hinges as the door slowly opened. "Are you planning to sleep all day, mademoiselle?" Cecilia asked playfully. "I'll help you dress. Your new playmates are waiting to meet you."

Jacoba had never been in a home like this. It was much smaller than her palace in Trastevere or even their summer residence near Ninfa.

She could hear laughter and the voices of children drifting down the stairwell from the upstairs kitchen. Jacoba was eager to meet her new friends since her mother told her there were several children in the Bombarone household. As an only child, Jacoba's interactions at home were primarily with adults unless out-of-town cousins were visiting.

Excited by the prospect of playmates, Jacoba bounded up the steps following the trail of laughter until she found herself in the kitchen – the point of origin for the giggles and guffaws. There she discovered children of various ages and genders gathered around a table, making funny faces at each other with every spoonful of frumenty they ate.

One youngster put a dab of the wheat porridge on his nose and was giving it a cross-eyed stare to the delight of his audience. Not to be outdone, another little boy created a frumenty mustache for himself by intentionally abandoning his wooden spoon and putting the lip of the bowl directly to his mouth. Again, laughter. Parents were nowhere in sight, and the cook paid no mind to the morning foolishness.

One child in particular caught Jacoba's eye because he was not participating in the breakfast amusement but was eating by himself at the end of the table while reading a small parchment.

All of a sudden, a hush flooded the room as the boisterous brood took note of Jacoba's arrival. They scurried over to her and began self-introductions. "I'm Adelasia, but just call me Alasia," said the long-haired outgoing five-year-old. "I'm Giuseppe, and I'm the youngest," said the four-year-old boy with the porridge on his nose. The "mustachioed" youngster who looked all of six-and-a-half bent forward deeply from his waist while saying: "I'm Ferrante . . . at your service."

Barely looking up from the parchment he was reading, the youngster in the corner introduced himself as Elias. The 11-year-old said he was pleased to meet Jacoba, but his body language didn't show it. He added coolly but politely that he would be accompanying Jacoba and her aunt to the cloth merchant's shop. He didn't add that he was "assigned" by his parents to be Jacoba's "friend" for the summer.

Elias was given the task because he was smart and sensible. Signor Bombarone was confident his eldest son would watch out for their guest and help make her stay a happy one. Elias and his friends were not as mischievous as many other children; so, Signor Bombarone believed Elias would make certain Jacoba wouldn't find trouble. Most important, if trouble happened to find her, Elias would know what to do. He was tall for his age and rather muscular. So, Elias could provide Jacoba some physical protection should the need arise.

After Jacoba introduced herself, the kids began bombarding her with questions. *How old are you? Where are you from? Why are you here? What games do you like to play?*

Just as Jacoba started to answer the flurry of queries, the matron of the Bombarone household entered the kitchen and clapped her hands twice. Suddenly silence. “Please allow our guest to eat now since she has a busy day ahead,” the mother snapped, adding, “Did you say your morning blessing?” The children bowed their heads sheepishly, crossed themselves in unison and recited a brief prayer.

Before long, Jacoba and Cecilia were on their way to the cloth merchant’s shop. Elias was two steps ahead, leading the way. It was a brief walk from the Bombarone residence to Pietro Bernardone’s cloth shop.

It was there that she first laid eyes on Giovanni Bernardone, the merchant’s son – the one they call “Francesco” – Francis, one of the people who would change her life forever.

Two years Jacoba’s senior and Elias’s best friend, Francis wasn’t as classically good-looking as Elias. However, there was something about Francis’ piercing dark eyes and charismatic smile that made him exceedingly attractive to nearly everyone he met. In addition, Francis was always on stage. When the little entourage entered his father’s shop, Francis tried to impress the group by greeting them in French since few Assisians beyond his own family spoke the language. To give his salutation a bit more pizzazz, he accompanied the words with an overly dramatic flourish of his right hand and a slight bow.

Francis’ look of self-satisfaction at his superiority quickly changed to surprise when Cecilia returned the greeting. It changed to utter dismay when little Jacoba not only said hello and introduced herself but began asking Francis about the fabrics, the store, himself and his family in rapid-fire, fluent French. Although some French was spoken at home, Francis’s command of the language was no match for Jacoba's; so, his only response was to tell her that his father would arrive momentarily to answer all questions.

Elias, who usually found Francis's self-importance to be charming and annoying at the same time, found it totally amusing at the moment. Elias also felt a sudden affection for Jacoba after watching the Bombarone's little-girl-guest unintentionally outshine his pompous pal. It also gave Elias pause to wonder who this little girl was since he had no other childhood acquaintances who could speak fluent French as well as Latin which was the language of the Bombarone household. His amazement and amusement faded when the head of the Bernardone household entered the shop.

Pietro Bernardone was a force of nature when it came to his cloth business or anything else that involved making money. His shop was stocked with a variety of fine fabrics that he knew would appeal to Assisi's "majores" or nobility – the customers he most valued – and to the wealthier members of city's up-and-coming merchant class. "Minores" or peasants almost never came into the shop unless they were picking up a package on behalf of their lord or lady. Pietro, who himself was technically among Assisi's "minores," had by this time accumulated enough wealth to make him part of the city's emerging middle class.

Pietro was affable with all prospective patrons and had an uncanny ability to quickly size up the social rank and economic status of customers based upon their dress. He would then display the cloth he speculated would be most appealing and affordable to them. "Why waste time? Time is money," he would often say.

"Hmmm," Pietro thought to himself as he quickly assessed the two females, *"The child is dressed in fine wool beautifully seamed, and the tunic has some embellishments. The woman's clothes on the other hand are simpler and not so well made. Perhaps this is an indulgent mother who foregoes her own desires in order to make sure her daughter has the best or perhaps…."*

Before Pietro could continue his silent musings, little Jacoba – speaking in French – introduced herself and her "aunt," then asked to see a bolt of sendal (taffeta) or brocade in crimson with some gold threads, please. "And do you have fur trims – perhaps otter or ermine?" she quickly added.

Pietro was taken aback at her precociousness as well as her expensive taste, but he was also intrigued. This was no ordinary youngster. So, the merchant decided it would be best to accommodate her since it could result in a profitable sale. Scratching his head as if it would help him to better remember the contents of his storeroom, Pietro said he would check to see what he had in crimson sendal and disappeared behind a door at the back of the shop.

While Pietro was gone, Francis and Elias began talking about their plans for the day. Too old for playing the games their younger siblings found enjoyable, the two friends often just rambled around Assisi seeking out others their age who were also looking for amusement. Sometimes, they would explore beyond Assisi's walls, up Mount Subasio or down into the valley where their fathers owned properties. It wasn't uncommon for a few other kids their age to join them.

There were times the group would make believe they were knights and have mock sword fights with tree branches or pretend they were troubadours and compose little songs or poems for noble ladies. Other times, they would hunt small game in the forest or take a dip in the river. However, what Francis and Elias most liked to do was search for hidden treasure.

It was rumored that when the Romans and earlier civilizations populated the area, some of the town's wealthier inhabitants would hide articles made of gold and other precious metals and gems in secret caches outside the walls. In the event of an attack, these ancient Assisians could focus on escaping with their lives instead of staying to fight for their homes and possessions. With portions of their wealth stowed in various hideaways in the surrounding forests, they could flee quickly knowing that all would not be lost — they could start over somewhere else if they had to.

The legend of hidden treasure was bolstered by several stories passed down through many generations. One involved a peasant who was turning over a field when his plow struck a mass of metal. It turned out to be a Roman strong box with gold coins bearing the image of Emperor Tiberius.

Another story entailed a young man who was hunting small game on Mount Subasio when he discovered a leather pouch with many silver coins of unknown origin. It was lodged in the knothole of a large ancient tree that had blown down in a storm.

The most astonishing story was one handed down for centuries about a chest of gold goblets and precious jewelry supposedly found by a Roman soldier toward the end of the Empire. It was thought the coffer's priceless contents belonged to an ancient Etruscan king.

Francis and Elias believed all the tales of treasure and never tired of trekking around Mount Subasio in search of hidden hoards.

For more immediate gratification, the duo would go to *Colle d'Inferno* – Hill of Hell – an immense old garbage dump where they could almost always find something interesting if they looked hard enough and were willing to withstand the stench. Besides waste material from Assisi's households, the dump would sometimes offer them little "treasures" like broken cups or discarded building materials. One day they discovered that if they dug a little at the base of the hill farthest from the city, they could find relics from ancient Rome's occupation of the area. Although their discoveries of pottery shards from amphora and clay oil lamps may have been of no monetary value, they enjoyed the hunt.

To get to the Hill of Hell, the boys would leave town via a small ancient Roman gate on the west end of Assisi. Nicknamed the *"Portello di Panico"* or *"Panic Hatch,"* it was located in a destitute area of town where most Assisians seldom ventured. Once beyond the portello, Francis and Elias would walk along the old Roman wall to a place where they could safely negotiate a ravine separating the trash hill from the city.

One day as they were climbing up the "dump-side" of the gorge, they happened upon a broken Roman fibula covered by verdigris. Most likely, it had been unearthed by erosion from recent rainstorms. They thought it was a wonderful treasure, and it served to whet their appetite for further exploration.

They kept secret their adventures to the Hill of Hell. They knew if their parents learned of their exploits, the two would be forbidden to go there. True, the place was still used for dumping refuse, but that wasn't the only reason it had garnered the name of Hill of Hell. It had also become the site for Assisi's public executions.

"Whatever we do, Francis, I have to bring *her* with us," Elias said rolling his eyes toward Jacoba. Francis gave a small sigh at the thought of having a girl tag along on their exploits. It wasn't that they objected to girls being included in their activities, it's just that Jacoba seemed too delicate to fit in with them, their activities, and their other friends. Both assumed she would never enjoy doing what they liked to do.

"My father made me promise I would stay with her whenever she left the house," Elias added.

"That means no trip to the 'hill' this week?" Francis didn't try to hide his disappointment. "Can we ditch her along the way somewhere?"

"Francis…He made me promise." Elias particularly emphasized the word 'promise.' "My father said it was very important that she be kept safe. So, for the next six weeks I can't go anywhere without her. I'm sorry, Francis."

"I promise not to be a burden," Jacoba insisted. They looked at her in astonishment. She obviously overheard the last part of their conversation; so, not only were they embarrassed but they now felt "trapped" into taking her along. She quickly added she could ride a horse and was learning to hunt and would love to meet their friends and be happy to do whatever they liked to do.

Just then, Pietro returned with two bolts of very fine wool. “I’m afraid this is all that I have in crimson,” Pietro said, adding, “But I leave for the Fair of St. Jean next week, and I will bring back whatever it is that you and your aunt would like. You’ll have it within six weeks, the good Lord willing.”

Jacoba quickly described the type of elegant fabrics she wanted. Pietro looked at her intently trying to make mental notes, but he knew he couldn’t remember it all. So, he soon grabbed quill and ink and began scribbling on a piece of paper. When Jacoba was finished, Cecilia told her she could go off to play with the boys since Cecilia herself would handle the details of the order.

The trio of children left the shop together and so began their lifelong love triangle.

Chapter III
Blood Oath

Assisi

At first Elias and Francis were simply resigned to the presence of their younger "fifth wheel." However, within a few days they began to take pleasure in her company. She wasn't like their sisters or other little girls they knew. She was smart for her age and unafraid. She was also curious and observant. And she seemed to genuinely enjoy doing the things the boys did.

It also probably didn't hurt the blossoming friendships that Jacoba was pretty. Elias and Francis took no specific notice of her grey-green eyes, long neck, or flawless light-olive skin. And since Cecilia usually loosely braided Jacoba's chestnut hair or tied it up in ribbons, the boys never realized how shiny it was even when it would accidentally fall in loose curls below her shoulders. While Elias and Francis may have instinctively found Jacoba physically attractive, it was something they never actually thought about or talked about.

The quality in Jacoba the boys most admired was the way she made them feel. She looked upon Francis and Elias as the older brothers she didn't have. They were her protectors and teachers as well as her friends. Although their parents, their peers and their siblings treated Francis and Elias like the ten-year-olds they were, Jacoba deemed them elder and wiser … as well as fun to be with.

When Jacoba was with them, Francis and Elias saw Assisi and Mount Subasio through her fresh eyes. For Jacoba, spending time with the boys gave her a sense of freedom to experience an existence far different from her life in Rome. They ran through the fields and trekked about the forests. They explored the caves and coves of Mount Subasio. They roamed the streets and alleyways of Assisi itself.

Just as the boys took no conscious note of Jacoba's good looks, she likewise saw neither their physical features nor their flaws. Elias was especially tall for his age but was muscular rather than gangly. He was a good-looking boy who inherited the strong facial features of his father including an aquiline nose and deep-set, dark eyes. His thick jet-black hair and smooth olive skin came from his mother. Elias never thought about his appearance nor did he ever suspect that some young females – cousins as well as playmates – harbored secret "crushes" on him.

Francis, on the other hand, was obsessed about getting everyone to like him. He was neither tall nor muscular. He looked a lot like a youthful version of his father, who was not a particularly handsome man. Francis's nose was thin and relatively straight. His hair was brown and not so thick as Elias's or many of the other boys in Assisi. Francis's eyes were brown, too, with one slightly larger than the other. While Elias's dark eyes studied you, Francis's eyes danced with you. They smiled at you and invited you to join him. They were framed with thick lashes – a birth gift from his mother's side of the family.

Whatever Francis may have lacked in physical appearance, he made up for with his expansive personality. He was generous with his smile and strove to make others happy. He flattered with compliments … entertained with witticisms … and amused with antics. He made those around him – the young, the old and those in between – feel good. That made him feel good.

Francis was the reason Elias and Jacoba would quickly do their respective chores in the Bombarone household early in the morning. When the work was finished, they would meet Francis on the piazza, then sit on the steps of the temple of Minerva as they determined the destination for their daily adventures.

On this particular day, they would be party to something that would haunt them for decades to come.

Francis had overheard his parents whispering about a rare occurrence in Assisi – the public execution of a murderer. Most of Assisi had not even been aware of the discovery four days earlier of a female corpse just outside the southernmost town wall near the ancient Roman cistern.

The unknown woman had been bludgeoned to death. While no one witnessed the crime, several of the minores who regularly begged near the crime scene said they had seen a stranger – a Gypsy – arguing with the victim – also a foreigner – the day before the body was found. So, it was assumed the Gypsy was the culprit.

The beggars told Assisi authorities they had reason to believe the man was hiding in one of the caves on Mount Subasio. A search party was quickly organized. Although it took the better part of a day, they found the stranger. There was blood under his fingernails, and he made no effort to deny the murder accusation. The woman was his wife. It was apparently a crime of passion.

The murderer was quiet and somewhat repentant; so, it was determined that he would be hung by rope rather than face one of the more excruciating forms of execution such as being sawn in half or buried alive. The town, thankfully, had disposed of its breaking wheel a decade earlier.

It was also determined the murderer's death sentence would be carried out on the Hill of Hell. Since the site was a garbage dump, there was no need to consider what to do with the corpse. It could be left on the gibbet so that birds, insects and rats would handle its disposal.

It was doubtful many Assisians would be present to witness the execution since both the victim and perpetrator were unknown in the town – even to the poorest of the poor. Few, if any, of the merchant class would be there since they were busy with last-minute preparation for extensive travel to the various summer fairs in Italy and France. Assisi's majores had no particular interest in this case since the murder didn't involve a noble or any of their serfs … nor did it take place within the city walls.

Francis said he had overheard his father tell his mother that the execution was to take place at noon on this very day. Francis concluded his "report" with a question to Elias and Jacoba: "Do you want to go to the Hill today?"

"I've never seen an execution," Elias said in a rather enthusiastic tone that was somewhat tinged with revulsion.

"I haven't either," Francis countered with animation and no hint of disgust, adding, "I've never seen anyone die. I wonder what that would be like."

"What about you?" Elias asked as he looked at Jacoba. "It would be your chance to finally go to the Hill of Hell. We've never taken any of our other friends there. But you'd have to promise not to tell a soul about this!"

In an uncharacteristically hesitant voice, Jacoba responded by saying she would go with the boys because she was curious about seeing the Hill of Hell since she had heard them talk about it, but she didn't really want to watch the execution.

She added in a quiet voice, "and …. Yes. I have seen someone die."

The boys jaws dropped simultaneously and they demanded to hear the details. She said she would tell them, but not right now. She was visibly upset upon recalling the death; so, the boys assumed she was talking about a close relative.

They didn't push her for the story – not because she was obviously distressed; but rather, the boys wanted to get to the Hill of Hell in time to watch the execution. To do that, they would have to leave the piazza immediately.

"You don't have to watch it, Jacoba!" Elias said.

"But you may change your mind once you're there," Francis added.

The trio hurried down the narrow streets of Assisi. They decided to use the southernmost gate of the city and follow along the old Roman wall to avoid inadvertently running into anyone they knew. Just as they approached the gate, Francis suddenly halted and put his arms out to stop his comrades.

"We need to keep this secret…very secret," he said in a hushed voice. "It must never be shared with anyone or we will be in real trouble."

"Agreed," answered Elias. "What do you want us to do?"

"I think it needs to be an oath," Francis whispered "…a blood oath."

"Is that permitted by the Church?" Jacoba asked.

"I don't see why not," Elias countered. "This has nothing to do with our Faith. It won't hurt anyone. It will just be the three of us making a promise."

Elias pulled out a small knife he always kept with him. It was a gift from his parents when he turned nine. He used it mostly to cut wild herbs and greens to bring home from the forest. He had never drawn blood with it – not even the blood of a small game animal.

"Will it hurt?" Another question from Jacoba.

"Just a little prick. That's all," Francis reassured her as Elias put the tip of the blade to his own ring finger and pressed just hard enough to draw blood. Francis was next. Then, Jacoba.

They looked at each other and pressed their three ring fingers together so their blood would mingle.

With fingers of the three still adjoined, Francis said very solemnly, "Whatever events happen on this day, I agree to keep secret for my life."

"Now each of you must say it while our blood continues to blend." Francis instructed them with his eyes as well as his words.

After Elias and Jacoba intoned the sentence as directed, Francis looked up at them and said, "Brother Elias, Brother Jacoba, we are now sworn to secrecy with a special bond of blood that will keep us close to one another until the day we die."

Once their hands parted, the three put their respective fingers into their mouths to stop the bleeding. And they tore off to the Hill of Hell.

ꕥ

They approached the Hill surreptitiously so as not to be seen by anyone. Francis and Elias knew the hill well and sometimes approached it from this long, roundabout way when they wanted to avoid city lanes and people. Though it took them more time, they thought it was a wise decision. As a result, by the time the trio arrived, the execution was over.

The 39 citizens who came to see the hanging chose not to cross the little makeshift bridge that had been hastily constructed along with the gibbet on the previous day. Instead, the official witnesses and gawkers viewed the hanging from a small swathe of land just outside the Portello di Panico – the large hatch-type door that had been cut into the city wall. The portello, much smaller than a city gate, provided ancient and current Assisians with easy access to their garbage dump. It got its name of "Panic Door" because it also served as an escape hatch when enemies were storming Assisi's gates.

Besides the three children who snuck up the back of trash heap, the only people on the hill itself were the official executioner and two other men who had helped construct the hanging post. Once assured the criminal was dead, they, too, left the area. The corpse, however, remained … rotating ever so slightly with each gust of wind.

The boys stared with stone faces at the lifeless body. Jacoba unintentionally looked up and saw it. She reflexively turned away and buried her head in Francis's shoulder. He put his arm around her to comfort her and told Elias they should leave. Elias agreed and felt a twinge of jealousy the moment Jacoba turned to Francis instead of him.

As they silently began their descent down the backside of the Hill to cross the gorge at a more amenable place, Jacoba stopped suddenly. "Do you hear that?" she asked. "Where's it coming from?"

It sounded like someone was weeping loudly. The sobs were emanating from the vicinity of an old, small trash mound not far from where they were standing. Francis suggested it might be an injured animal and that it would probably be better for them to quickly go in the opposite direction. However, Elias and Jacoba over-ruled him.

So, the trio began cautiously walking toward the mound to investigate. As they got closer they could vaguely make out what appeared to be a young, raven-haired woman huddled there – her legs drawn up to her chin, her arms wrapped around them to hold them in place as she rocked back and forth. "We must help her," Jacoba said.

"But maybe she is a leper," Francis whispered. "I won't go near a leper!!!"

"She would have warned us," Elias tried to be assuring. "… But maybe we should ask her."

Francis – who stopped a good 15 paces away from the girl and well behind Elias and Jacoba — didn't hesitate and shouted rather loudly, "Are you a leper?"

She said nothing, but slowly shook her head *no*.

When she looked up, the children could see that her face was wet with tears. She wasn't anyone they recognized from Assisi.

Jacoba approached the hunched figure and asked in a gentle voice, "What's wrong? Are you all right? Are you hurt?"

Silence from the young woman. Her eyes gazed at nothing, her body shook, and she continued to rock back and forth while wailing.

"I don't think we can help her, Jacoba. Let's go before *we* get into some kind of trouble," Francis suggested in a nervous voice as his eyes scanned the surrounding area.

Elias remained quiet while his eyes darted from Francis to the crying girl to Jacoba.

"Let's stay here a moment. I want to find out what's wrong," Jacoba said as she got even closer to the girl. She bent down and put her arms around the older girl as best as she could and whispered something in her ear. The girl nodded her head very slowly in the affirmative.

Jacoba then looked at Francis and Elias. "She is lamenting. She must have known the man who died."

The stranger had stopped rocking, and her keening was quickly evolving into loud and jerky snivels as she attempted to speak. "He … was … my … father …," the words came out slowly and disjointed as she tried to catch her breath. "I … loved … him …"

"I'm so sorry," Jacoba told her as the boys looked on in silence and amazement.

"What is your name?" Jacoba continued.

"Prassede," the girl responded. "Can you help me?" she asked as she looked to Jacoba, then Elias and finally Francis.

"I don't know. What do you need from us, Prassede?" Jacoba inquired with hesitation in her voice.

"I need to bury my father. I watched him die. It hurt me so much to see that, but what I truly cannot bear is to know the birds will peck at him, and the rats will feed on him." The girl, who looked to be about 14 years old, had somewhat gained her composure and continued in a forlorn voice, "He was a good person most of the time. I don't think he meant to kill Castellana. He must have had strong drink. She must have provoked him. He must not have known what he was doing. He loved her. I know it. He loved me, too. But now, I am totally alone."

"Do you want to come back to Assisi with us?" Francis asked.

Prassede responded with an emphatic "NO!"

"Where do you live?" Elias asked.

Prassede gave a nod toward Mount Subasio and responded sadly and slowly, "I have no home … at least not one that would be like yours. I am not from here. For a long time I have been living in forests and caves – wherever my father and stepmother took me." She continued, "We went wherever my father could find work. I never knew my mother. She died when I was born. Because I'm half-Gypsy and because of my father's crime, I fear for my safety in this city. At any rate, I am used to caves and forests and am not afraid. I like being alone."

Between her grief and her pride, the young woman had trouble getting out the following appeal: "....But there is one thing I would like to ask of you. .....Would you help me cut down my father's body and bring him to a place where I can dig a grave for him? There is no one else I can ask."

She paused as the three children tried to absorb her extraordinary and bold request. Then Prassede continued: "I know that's a lot to ask of strangers, especially such young strangers, but I can tell you are kind. He was my father. I want to say prayers over him. Then, I will cover him with earth and stones so that no animals trouble him, and he can have the peace he never had when he lived."

They stared at each other. Then Elias broke the silence while looking at Francis and Jacoba: "If we are going to help with this grim deed and finish before sunset, we had better get moving." Elias went on to bark out orders without even waiting for a response from his friends, "Jacoba, you and Prassede find a place at the base of the hill — a place that can't be seen from the town gate. Find a place where the earth is soft and begin your digging."

Elias went on, "I have my knife, so Francis and I will cut the rope. Prassede, we may need your help to move him; so, come back up here when you are finished preparing the trough. Jacoba, you can stay there and start gathering stones – as large as you can carry. We need to proceed quickly."

Without any words, Jacoba extended her hand to Prassede to help her get on her feet. Wiping her wet face with her dirty hands, Prassede quietly said, "Thank you. Someday I will repay all of you for your kindness."

ഊര

Jacoba, Francis and Elias amazed themselves as well as Prassede. They accomplished their ghastly task well before sunset, cleansed themselves as best as they could in a nearby stream and hurried to the closest city gate. Prassede walked quickly in a different direction — toward the forest below town where she had stayed by herself the previous evening.

Once inside Assisi's walls, the children ran as rapidly as possible to their respective homes – hoping to arrive before supper since their absence at the evening meal would have raised questions they did not want to answer. They were blood brothers, after all, who vowed to keep the morbid activities of this day a secret forever.

That night, as Cecilia prepared Jacoba for bed, the child was unusually silent. Chalking up Jacoba's reticence to homesickness, the servant gave her a hug and helped her into bed. Cecilia had no idea of the life-altering events Jacoba experienced that day. How could she know?

Once tucked in, Jacoba said her evening prayers to herself. She thanked God for her family, for their love. She asked Him to keep her mother and father safe. Just thinking of them, however, made Jacoba painfully homesick.

She didn't dwell long on her own sadness since her thoughts involuntarily jumped to the events of the day. In her head, Jacoba relived what had taken place during the previous 12 hours: seeing the dangling corpse on the Hill of Hell … hearing the keening of Prassede … burying Prassede's father. While her mind replayed the events, Jacoba's heart stirred up the accompanying emotions.

Prassede was the immediate focal point of both her head and her heart. Jacoba felt a deep sorrow and tried hard not to imagine how dire Prassede's life would be from now on. The more Jacoba tried to block visions of what life would be like without a family … being completely alone … having no home, the more anxious she became. The mere thought of Prassede's plight made her miserable.

Yet, she remembered that when the group parted ways, Prassede seemed very much at peace despite the dreadful events of the day. Jacoba recalled that once her father's burial was completed, Prassede reverently recited the Lord's Prayer over the makeshift grave. Jacoba, Elias and Francis had looked at each other in astonishment when they learned the Gypsy girl had been baptized into the Church as a baby and that her father had taught her the basics of their Faith. Jacoba recalled that by the time Prassede finished the prayer, her aura of despondency had morphed into tranquility.

Even more astounding to Jacoba was that Prassede seemed unafraid to go into the forest alone to spend the night. Jacoba believed there was something extraordinary about this girl who was only a few years older yet was so fearless and serene at the same time.

Jacoba then realized she herself was a lot stronger and braver than she thought. She was proud she was able to help Prassede despite being repulsed by virtually everything she found herself doing.

When her thoughts drifted to Elias, Jacoba was struck by his practicality and leadership. He didn't come across as being sympathetic to the grieving Prassede, yet it was his swift, commanding decisiveness and capable direction that made the trio's compassionate deeds happen. Until the events of this day, Jacoba had not noticed the strength of Elias's personality nor his intelligence. She was deeply impressed by both.

Then there was Francis… She felt something special for him. He wasn't the same kind of leader Elias was, but he comforted Jacoba when she turned to him. Jacoba knew Francis wanted nothing to do with Prassede, yet he didn't run away. Jacoba was amazed he chose to stay and help.

In addition, it was Francis who surprisingly suggested the three "blood brothers" make contact with Prassede the following day to make sure she was all right. He said they should bring food in case her foraging efforts hadn't gone well. He himself would provide her with some discarded woolen cloth from his father's shop since the caves of Mount Subasio – Prassede's ultimate destination – could get unpleasantly chilly at night, even in summer.

Before falling asleep, Jacoba also gave thought to the promise that she, Elias and Francis made much earlier that day. She recalled how they sealed it by blending their blood. In the darkness, she could not see the tiny wound that bound them; so, she put the "wounded" finger into her mouth. Her tongue immediately located the little notch in her skin that confirmed their strange pledge.

Though her mind was reeling from all that had happened, Jacoba couldn't help but feel blessed that these two boys were now her "brothers in blood." She also knew the experiences they shared created an undeniable bond that would link them to each other and to Prassede for the duration of their lives.

Chapter IV
Blood Brothers

Assisi

Jacoba, Elias and Francis were in a hurry to finish their chores so they could furtively gather items to bring to Prassede. They planned to meet her shortly after noon in an expansive area behind the Cathedral of San Rufino.

They would rendezvous at Torrione – an ancient sepulcher located at the north edge of the large churchyard. The crumbling little "tower" was all that remained of a monumental sepulcher built by and for an important Roman official more than a thousand years earlier.

This ancient ruin – like the Hill of Hell – was a place the boys had visited many times but told no one about. Within the structure was the burial chamber of Publius Petronius. The now-empty vault's entrance was on the valley side of Assisi and was not easily accessible.

Most Assisians didn't give much thought to Torrione. Many weren't even aware it existed. The townspeople's proportion of interest in local Roman ruins – of which there were many – was directly related to how much brick and stone they could carry away for construction. Nearly all of the travertine had been stripped from Torrione many decades if not centuries earlier, and most of its limestone had been removed as well.

Although it would seem a perfect hideout for thieves and other outlaws, criminals unanimously preferred the caves of Mount Subasio. Torrione had only one tiny, dark chamber that was difficult to enter and – more important – to exit quickly. Besides, its location was much too close to Piazza San Rufino, the civil and religious heart of the city.

Francis and Elias accidentally came upon Torrione two years earlier when the duo inexplicably and simultaneously felt unwell during a rather lengthy afternoon service at the Church of San Rufino. Their respective parents suggested they leave to get some air. Since the families were standing on opposite sides of the church, they never knew or even suspected the boys had previously agreed to "feel sick" at the end of the priest's first reading.

While Torrione's size, poor condition and location made it unattractive for adults, it was totally alluring for imaginative boys who liked to play there or just hang out. It was also the perfect place for the blood brothers to meet Prassede since it was off the beaten path while still being relatively close to the children's homes.

Jacoba, Elias and Francis arrived at Torrione close to noon. Prassede was not yet there, but they didn't mind waiting. It gave Francis an opportunity to follow-up on a comment Jacoba made the previous day.

"Brother Jacoba," he said while the trio seated themselves as comfortably as possible on the dank ground, "You mentioned something yesterday about seeing someone die. Were you with an old relative who passed on? Or was it a stranger run over by a cart? Where did it happen? Were you with your parents or Cecilia or were you alone?"

Elias chimed in, "Francis, stop asking so many questions. Let Jacoba talk."

Jacoba hesitated a moment and cast her eyes toward the ground. The boys could see this made her sad, and Francis now wished he hadn't badgered her with his questions. She began to tell her story slowly and softly:

"There isn't a whole lot to say. It was sad. It was horrible. I was much younger, and I was very scared." She paused. She didn't look at the boys but kept staring at the ground as she resumed her narrative. "My parents brought me with them to some type of celebration in the home of people who I had never seen before. The head of the household looked old to me. He was a big man with lots of scars, so he must have been some kind of knight. I think his name was Cencio or something like that. There were other children running around the place, but they were older and didn't ask me to play with them. I was glad. The place was big and dark … and I just wanted to stay near my mother because I didn't really like it there.

"It happened late in the afternoon. There were many people in the room still at table, picking at what remained of what had been a huge feast. It was more food than I had ever seen at any meal with our family – even when my many cousins and their parents came to our house for a long stay. Anyway, some of the older boys went up to the old knight and asked to see his Egyptian lion. The knight laughed a little and said he would get him.

"I asked my mother why the man would keep a lion in his house. My father jumped in and leaned over to tell me the animal was a leopard – a type of large cat – that Cencio tamed and taught to help him hunt in the forest.

"When the old knight returned with his 'cat' named Pardus, I was amazed and scared at the same time. I climbed onto my father's lap. The animal was like no other cat I had ever seen. It was very large, rather frightening, yet quite beautiful. Its fur was a warm light-brown color that was covered with small, black, flower-like spots. Pardus wasn't on a leash nor did he wear a collar.

"He stayed at the old knight's side and seemed tame, yet his eyes had a sort of fire in them. You could tell they were taking in every little detail in the room as if he were in the middle of a forest surveying it for prey or predators. The boys wanted to pet him, but the old knight shooed them away. He told them although Pardus was his pet and was gentle, there was still some of the "wild" within him. It was what made him a good hunter.

"Just as the old knight was beginning another sentence, one of the servants accidentally dropped a silver dish that made a loud clatter on the stone floor. The startled leopard was across the room pouncing on the young woman before the old knight knew the animal had left his side. Everything happened so quickly. I heard her shriek as the leopard seized upon her. I was never so frightened by anything. The cat easily knocked her to the ground. She didn't seem to struggle with it for very long. Her screams were quickly muffled by the sheer weight of the animal on her. The old man ran toward the girl, but it was too late. She made no more sounds by the time he reached her.

"She was dead, and Pardus looked to his master as if the old knight would give him a reward for so quickly and deftly bringing down such large quarry. The old knight somberly led the animal out of the room while everyone else was too stunned to move.

"Did the lion eat her?" Francis interrupted.

"No. There wasn't a single bite mark on her. My father said the animal strangled her. He had been taught by his master to throttle prey, not eat it. The girl's face was only slightly bruised, and her eyes were open wide. I will always remember the look on her face." Jacoba paused, and just as she was ready to continue, a silhouetted figure appeared at the doorway of the vault.

ꙮ

When Prassede arrived, she was carrying a basket containing three knives, a piece of linen, a small cooking pot and some flints for making fire. After placing her only earthly belongings on the ground, she began her tragic narrative.

Prassede explained she was in the forest gathering mushrooms and roots to eat when some men from Assisi arrested her father. "I hid behind a large tree when I heard the men on horseback approach. I was terrified but inched closer to where our little campsite was so I could better watch what was happening," she said. The trio of children quickly forgot about Jacoba's narrative and became engrossed in Prassede's story.

"My father readily admitted killing my step-mother. I couldn't believe what was happening. I did not even know Castellana was dead. She was beautiful and passionate but uncaring. She was often cruel to my father in words and in her behavior. She was also cruel to me physically," Prassede added as her eyes shifted to a large, nasty-looking bruise on her left arm.

"It didn't surprise me that she had not returned to our campsite the night she disappeared. Shortly after we'd arrive outside a new town, Castellana would leave us and head off by herself to 'explore' it. Sometimes her visits to a new city would last a few hours. Sometimes she would be gone for several days. She usually returned disheveled and hung over. However, there were times when she came back to us bathed, smelling of violets, and wearing new clothing. Her absence always made my father sad, but it always made me happy. I didn't like her.

"My father never chastised Castellana – even after she got back from one of her questionable expeditions. The only time I ever heard him raise his voice to her was when she slapped me … I should say when he *witnessed* her slapping me. That was the only time I ever sensed him capable of rage. He told her if she ever lifted a hand toward me again, that would be the end of things. She laughed at him and walked away.

"Castellana hit me often, especially when I was younger and couldn't defend myself … and always when my father was away, working in the fields or in town. She would give me bruises in places that would not be visible because she knew I would say nothing. She was right. I was afraid of her; so, I never told my father of her abuse. I don't fear being alone in the forest because I learned early on it was always better to chance nature's possible dangers than face the certainty of Castellana's brutality. I would often go off by myself, especially when I knew my father would be away for more than a few hours." Prassede's eyes were filling with tears as she continued her story:

"I think he killed her because of me. I think her death was my fault," She spoke so softly, her young listeners had to move even closer to hear her.

"My father finished his work in the field by noon that day and came back to our campsite much earlier than expected. Castellana never saw him approach because she was in a rage. She couldn't find a trinket she brought back from her most recent foray to Assisi and accused me of taking it. She said I needed to be punished. Then, she picked up a heavy piece of wood destined for our campfire and came at me with it. I put my arm up to protect my face. I thought the blow may have broken my arm. She did, too. And when she saw that my father had witnessed her viciousness, she ran away as fast as she could.

"My father didn't go after her. Instead, he rushed over to help me. He gently felt the bone in my arm and said it didn't seem to be broken. Then he walked me down to the stream and had me put my arm in the cold water. The last thing I remember is him telling me he loved me and to rest at our campsite. He kissed me on my forehead and said he would make sure this would never happen again. That night was the night Castellana disappeared from my life forever."

"Sadly, she inadvertently took my father with her. I would have gladly put up with her mistreatment to have him back here … with me again." Tears were now streaming down her face as Prassede finished relating what had happened.

Jacoba had edged her way over to Prassede and put her arm around the young woman as best as she could. After taking a few moments to compose herself, Prassede continued,

"The men who arrested my father never saw me. I wanted it that way. I have become accustomed to being alone. Truth be known, I like being alone. I'm happy they don't know of my existence. They took our family's little cart which contained all of our belongings. We didn't have much anyway," she explained somewhat wistfully. "This basket is all I have now. I had it with me when I was foraging in the forest."

Prassede didn't harbor ill will toward the Assisians for taking the family's meager belongings because they had no way of knowing anyone else had been living at the campsite. Prassede had no clothing other than what she was wearing as well as the items in her basket. Her only possession of any value was a metal ring with a small red stone that she wore on the middle finger of her right hand. It had belonged to the mother she never knew. Castellana wanted it for herself and never forgave Prassede's father for allowing Prassede to keep it.

The children presented Prassede with the food and cloth they brought for her. Then, Elias suggested that Prassede come with them to the nearby church where some adult could surely help her and perhaps give her shelter.

Prassede's narrowed eyes and furrowed brow gave her response even before she spoke. She looked intently at the three children and solemnly told them she would not, she could not do that.

"I like you," she said as her dark eyes moved from one child to the next, "and I want to stay near you, at least for a while. I have lived like a hermit for much of my life, and I've come to value my solitude. Villages and towns have brought me nothing but pain and sadness.

"There are many small caves up there," she nodded her head toward Mount Subasio, adding, "and I have already found one that suits me. But I need you to promise you will tell no one of my existence. If you tell, I will leave … and I would like to stay …at least for a while."

The three children were puzzled by her request but nodded in affirmation.

Prassede continued, "You have been very, very kind to me, and I have no way to repay you except with gratitude and prayers." She reached into a coarse linen bag that hung at her side and pulled out three pieces of thin tree bark. Their edges were bowed, and the children could tell something was hidden within each. Prassede handed them out.

The children's fingers instinctively spread open the curled ends of the bark to reveal tiny purple wildflowers and little crosses fashioned of twigs lashed together with natural cordage.

"These aren't very good gifts, but they're all I can give you. I hope you'll think of me and remember people may seem rough on the outside … but there can be goodness within … and I hope you will pray for me," Prassede was now standing and preparing to make her exit.

"Thank you," Jacoba was the first to speak as she jumped up and gave Prassede a hug.

The two boys mumbled "thank-you's" awkwardly and also got to their feet. Then Francis said, "Let's meet you here again next week."

Prassede hesitated for a moment, shook her head in agreement and quickly made her way out of the tomb.

Chapter V
Tainted Blood
Assisi

The "Blood Brothers" met at the usual place on the piazza a bit earlier than normal. They wanted to take their time to explore – and play in – the valley south of Assisi. They had no desire to go back to the Hill of Hell and, indeed, would not return there for the rest of summer. The trio had agreed the previous afternoon they would do their best to make sure their excursion south of town would be a day-long event.

Before they reached the city gate, however, the plan changed dramatically. The sound of mournful chanting stopped them in their tracks. They looked at each other knowingly and without speaking a word immediately altered the focus of their outing.

The trio listened intently for a moment and then instinctively followed their ears to the source of the intonations. It sounded very much like the "Dies Irae" of a funeral service, but they discovered it was coming from near the blacksmith's home in the lower part of town.

Elias was the first to speak up. "I, uh, think it might be the ritual for the living dead."

"The living dead?" Jacoba asked. She was totally perplexed.

"You know. Lepers," Francis interjected somewhat matter-of-factly.

Services for the dead were routine in Rome as well as Assisi. The mortality rate of the medieval world in which the "Blood Brothers" lived was high. Young women died in childbirth. Children didn't survive beyond infancy. Strong healthy men were killed in wars. Pestilence and mishaps of daily living proved fatal for anyone of any age. Jacoba had been to numerous funerals for deceased relatives and servants during her eight years of life, but they had always been in churches or in the small chapel in their palace. She knew nothing about the "living dead" so, she was intrigued.

Francis and Elias, on the other hand, believed they knew everything about lepers and were more than happy to share their "knowledge" with her.

"You mean you've really never seen a leper, Jacoba?!" Francis' voice was hushed but conveyed his emphatic disbelief at her naiveté.

Keeping their voices low so as not to attract attention, the boys took turns "educating" Jacoba about lepers and why they were pariahs. Elias started the muted tirade: "Lepers are unclean. They have big, ugly sores all over them. Some of them have claws for hands."

Francis chimed in, "If they get close to you — let alone touch you — you become one of them. You'd have to leave your family and go live in a leper house or maybe in some hovel all by yourself in the middle of nowhere. Then you die."

Francis and Elias made clear their hatred of lepers. They told Jacoba they had always kept their distance when they heard the bell or the clapper warning them one of the "living dead" was approaching. However, they once inadvertently got close enough to see a leper's face. "It was not only covered by large nodules but the tip of the man's nose was totally gone," Elias explained with great gusto while rubbing his finger on his own nose as if to make sure it was still there.

"He was hideous!" Francis quickly added, then went on to explain how they once observed a leper whose hands were so devastatingly deformed that he struggled to hang onto his begging bowl using the two frightful appendages.

While Francis and Elias seemed to know a lot about lepers, they had never personally known anyone who got "the sickness" nor had they attended any leper rites. So, today morbid curiosity propelled the two boys forward, and Jacoba followed them.

The small gathering of people assembled in front of the blacksmith's humble dwelling began to walk slowly toward the city gate that led to the valley between Assisi and Rivo Torto. The "Blood Brothers" watched the goings-on from a little distance behind the mourners, scurrying from passageway to passageway so they would not be noticed.

They dropped even further behind and hid themselves as best as they could when the funerary procession left the city streets and walked solemnly into the open valley. After travelling nearly a mile from the city gate, the tearful entourage stopped at a tiny stone hut that had been hastily built. The leper was apparently the wife of the blacksmith, and this hut was to be her new home.

Elias, Francis and Jacoba stealthily approached the group, taking cover behind trees and bushes, until they were close enough to hear as well as watch what was happening.

The woman was still wearing the white sheet she had been given earlier in the day at her parish church during the Mass of Separation. Underneath the white cloth the woman wore a new black, hooded garment that distinguished her as unclean. It would be her only attire for the rest of her life.

The leper carefully stepped down into what looked like a small shallow grave. She stood there as the priest recited a list of parameters for her new life:

"I forbid you to ever enter a church, a monastery, a fair, a mill, a market or an assembly of people. I forbid you to leave this house unless dressed in the clothing of the leper that has been blessed and given to you. I forbid you to drink at any stream or fountain unless using your own barrel or dipper," he intoned.

The three children strained to hear the priest's words, their eyes wide in astonishment and disbelief since they had never seen a rite like this. The priest continued, *"You must make every effort to avoid those who are not lepers like you. You must use this clapper to warn others of your presence.* He blessed a small wooden contraption on a stick that had been placed on the ground near the woman. The priest continued: *If you encounter anyone on the road who speaks to you, you must make sure you are down-wind of them before you answer. You may not enter any narrow passage so that passersby will not bump into you. You are forbidden to touch any child or give them anything. You may never drink or eat from any vessel but your own."*

The inventory of do's and don'ts seemed endless to the children as the priest continued blessing items that were laying at the edge of the symbolic grave with the leper standing in it. Even from a distance, the children could see the woman's fragile body shake as she sobbed. Her children were crying, too. Her husband looked on stoically as if in shock.

The rite eventually ended, and the group that had gathered around the grave began to slowly disperse. Francis, Elias and Jacoba quietly skedaddled to the closest grove of trees where they hid themselves until everyone had left the scene except the woman. The eyes of the young trio were fixed on her.

The leper pulled back the hood that had been concealing her face. She gave her head a little shake to loosen her hair that had been matted under the head covering. Then she stepped out of the little hollow in the ground, removed the white sheet that was covering her black garb, and picked up the items that had been left for her. Slowly and sadly she walked from her emblematic grave to her living tomb. She was now a walking phantom – no longer to be seen by family, friends or the community. Her only human contact from now on would be with other "living dead."

After the woman disappeared into her residential sepulcher and closed its door, the children continued staring at the place in silence even though they sensed the leper would not be reappearing in the doorway anytime soon. The gloomy spectacle they spent their day watching had overwhelmed them, and they seemed transfixed in their own thoughts.

It was Francis who jolted them from their daze: “Did you see the spots on her face?” He didn’t even try to disguise his disgust.

“You couldn’t miss them,” Elias chimed in. “Ugh!”

“Do you think her children will ever get to see her?” Jacoba seemed distraught. She realized in the moment that she herself was homesick and wished she could be with her own mother and father.

“I doubt it,” Elias said. “I’ve heard my parents talk about lepers. Her husband might visit her once in a while, but she probably wouldn’t want her children to be tainted.”

“I can’t imagine what that would be like…to know that you won’t ever see the people you love for the rest of your life…” Jacoba’s voice trailed off. She was on the verge of tears.

“My father says they bring it on themselves,” Francis picked up the conversation. “Their souls are unclean, and they’re paying for their sins.”

“You’re crazy, Francis!” Elias said, shaking his head. “I’ve heard of leper children who are barely old enough to walk. You can’t tell me that those kids are sinners! And if lepers were such big sinners, the Church wouldn’t be doing special Masses for them, would they?”

“Well, I’ve never seen leper kids. Where do they go? They can’t live alone,” Francis said in a challenging tone of voice.

“They go to that place for lepers in Arce near Rivo Torto. I’ve heard my parents talk about it. I think it’s called

San Lazar or San Rufino. It's named after some saint, and all they do there is care for lepers. It's like a parish for the living dead." Elias responded with some authority and once again impressed Jacoba with his knowledge.

What Jacoba saw today would linger in a corner of her mind to the end of her life. While the boys were taken with how repulsive the leper looked, Jacoba was overcome by the sadness of the woman. Jacoba didn't dare share her feelings with the boys because she knew they wouldn't understand. She wasn't filled with disgust in the same way they were. She was filled with pity not only for the leper but also for the woman's family.

Jacoba had not been particularly shocked by the boys' vivid descriptions of lepers' physical manifestations. In Rome, she had seen many people with deformities during her brief lifetime. Beggars — who positioned themselves near the entrances of Rome's churches in order to maximize donations from pilgrims — displayed a great array of physical abnormalities.

Jacoba also knew knights and nobles, including some family members, whose limbs were deformed or totally absent as a result of combat. Her own father's loving arms bore ugly scars from the swords of adversaries. And one of her family's oldest servants lost his left eye and much of his cheek in some sort of mishap that involved an explosion and fire.

No, it wasn't the physical appearance of the leper that frightened Jacoba. What deeply bothered her was the thought of having to give up your family…your possessions…your very life and being forced to live alone forever. She thought about Prassede, but that was different.

Prassede had chosen her solitary life, and she could change it if she wanted to.

Jacoba was troubled and wished she could talk to her mother or father or even Cecilia, but she knew that would only get herself and her "Blood Brothers" into trouble. So, even after returning to Rome at the end of summer, she never brought up the event that so deeply moved her.

Chapter VI
Norman Blood
1197 - Trastevere, Rome

Duchessa Maria was troubled. She hesitated before bringing the issue to her husband but decided not to wait.

"Vincentius," she called his name softly as she approached him from across the veranda located on the highest level of the palace. It was late in the day, and the lord of the manor was staring out across the river at Rome's skyline. The veranda was the only open area other than arrowslits that was exposed to the outside world. Every other window and balcony in the enormous structure faced the palace's inner courtyard.

"Maria, come see how peaceful and pleasing the city looks tonight. The setting sun has turned it to gold." He opened his arms to her, and she welcomed his embrace. Vincentius was tall with black curly hair and deep blue eyes.

His limbs were soldier's limbs – powerful, deeply tanned, and streaked with white mottled scars of combat. The contrast of Maria's porcelain skin against his was striking as was the dissimilarity her of light hair, delicate features and grey-brown eyes.

The couple had been married for 21 years. It was an arranged marriage.

Vincentius's family arrived in Rome several generations earlier. According to family lore, Vincentius's great-great-grandfather – Berard of Gascony – saved the life of Robert Guiscard during a battle in the Balkans. Using his arming sword like a broadsword, Berard hacked off the hands of Guiscard's attacker as the enemy combatant was preparing to plunge a sword into the Duke of Apulia's chest.

Guiscard was so impressed by Berard's loyalty and bravery; he presented him with new armor and insisted the knight ride by his side. While en route to Rome in 1083, Guiscard told great-great-grandpa that he would proclaim him duke of that city as soon as they could get King Henry IV to withdraw and free the Pope from Castel Sant'Angelo.

Unfortunately, the richest city in Europe was not destined to be grandpa Berard's duchy. Guiscard accomplished his goals all right: Henry retreated, and the besieged Pope Gregory was returned to the Lateran. However, there was little left of what had been the richest city in Europe after Guiscard's army of more than 30,000 warriors finished with it. Rome's streets and alleyways ran red as men, women, and children were slaughtered in a bloody spectacle that would have rivaled the ancient gladiatorial games.

Churches, palaces, shops, homes — nearly every building in the heart of Rome from the Palatine Hill to the Capitoline Hill — were on fire. The sobs of the suffering and the overpowering smell of the dead were everywhere.

Grandpa Berard had seen his share of brutality, but this was beyond the bloodlust of battle. When he saw Guiscard surveying the wanton destruction with a smile on his face, Berard decided then and there that soldiering was no longer for him. However, he was not so disgusted as to forget about Guiscard's promise of a reward.

Guiscard laughed a nervous laugh as Berard approached him. "It looks like Rome as it is right now would not be a good duchy for you after all. I'm sorry," Guiscard said solemnly and sincerely. "I never break a promise," Guiscard paused and looked around. "You can have that property over there, across the river … and the lands around it." He pointed to the Janiculum Hill in Trastevere. There was some type of large, ancient structure atop it, but the heavy smoke that enveloped them made it hard to see. "I give it to you and proclaim you 'Duke Berard.'"

Berard bowed slightly as a gesture of thanks to Guiscard and rode off through the blood and smoke that saturated Rome to claim his spoils. The two never saw each other again; but shortly before his death Guiscard gave Berard several deeds to lands south of Rome. With his new title and his lands, Berard married the daughter of a noble from Limoges whom he brought back to Rome.

From then on, marriages for Normanni males were always arranged to French noblewomen while Normanni females were wed to Italian nobles. The arrangements were often finalized while the betrothed were still in their cradles.

The idea that Vincentius dei Normanni actually descended from a robber baron never crossed his mind or that of anyone else. Although he was well aware of the family's history, the part always omitted was that Robert Guiscard had no authority to give Great-Great-Grandfather Berard either property or title. However, since his great-great-grandmother was a legitimate noble by blood, Vincentius's peerage was never in question.

So, befitting family custom, marriage was arranged early on between Vincentius and Maria, one of the daughters of the Duke of Brittany. For nobles, love was never a concern. Duty was everything.

Just like his father, grandfather and the Normanni men before them, Vincentius initially took pleasure in power and its trappings. Like his predecessors, he found battle exciting when he was young. However, now he much preferred the peaceful pursuits of life at the Normanni palace and its adjoining gardens and orchards. Most of all, he enjoyed time spent with his wife and their only child – Jacoba.

While Jacoba had tutors from whom she learned reading, writing, Latin, and basic mathematics, Vincentius himself taught his "Giacomina" to ride a horse. Maria instructed her in how a large household is run as well as coached her on the finer points of behaving and looking like a noblewoman.

Both parents taught her that no matter what life put before her, she must always keep her Faith and submit to the will of God and follow His commandments. They especially emphasized the fourth one: Honor thy father and mother.

Vincentius's time spent in the palace was precious to him and too brief. As a feudal lord, he was continuously summoned by the call of duty since his land holdings were extensive, and his vassals many. Not only did the Normanni Family have the palace and other properties in Trastevere – the area west of Rome's Tiber River – but they also owned numerous large fiefs in the area of Lake Albano and estates near the Tyrrhenian Sea.

Besides leading Normanni knights and soldiers into various skirmishes to protect his lands and the peasants who farmed it, Vincentius oversaw the regular collection of assessments from his vassals and dispensed justice when the need arose.

He networked incessantly with his allies – which included the various branches of the Frangipane Family – since relationships truly ruled Rome. A careless word or sideways glance could quickly transform a friend to a foe. He had seen it happen even more in recent years. Vincentius was thankful Trastevere was no longer considered a region of the City of Rome as it had been in ancient times, or he most likely would have had the additional responsibility of a papal appointment to the Roman Senate.

Management of the palace itself was left to Maria. She was nearly as tall as Vincentius with a slender build that made her appear more delicate than she was. Fortunately, she had a noble bearing that let everyone in the household know she was in charge. She never whined. She always commanded. She seldom needed to raise her voice since she could convey pleasure or displeasure through her eyes alone.

Running the palace and the family's other dwellings was more than a full-time job for Maria. The massive structure built on the "eighth" hill of Rome was their primary residence. It incorporated what was left of an ancient palace built by Domitian for his niece and lover, Julia Titi Flavia.

In ancient times, the area which their palace overlooked was the site of the Naumachia Augusti – an enormous man-made basin that provided a watery arena for naval spectacles. These mock battles which usually involved Roman prisoners condemned to death were even bloodier than the gladiatorial battles of the Colosseum (Flavian Amphitheater). It was reported this particular naumachia's inaugural "battle" involved 30 full-sized ships and more than 3,000 men. Because the basin provided virtually no room for the ships to maneuver away from each other, the event swiftly progressed to a bloodbath featuring gruesome hand-to-hand combat with few survivors.

The grisly games staged for Rome's amusement ended centuries before the arrival of the Normanni. While nothing remained of the death venue itself, the naumachia had ironically left a legacy of peace and tranquility in the form of a pine grove that grew over its ruins.

When Vincentius eventually tired of looking at the cityscape across the river, he shifted his gaze to the greenery just below and felt instantly refreshed.

"What is it, Maria?" he asked while he continued to embrace her. He looked into her grey-brown eyes: "I can tell something is wrong."

She sighed, and gazed deeply into Vincentius's eyes. Then, she said in a low, sad voice, "It's time, my lord."

"It's time?" Vincentius was puzzled.

"Yes. It's time," Maria responded in a more urgent tone. "You've been away a lot during the past year; so, you could not know. Giacomina has come of age. She has already bled three times. So now we must keep our promise to the Frangipani."

Vincentius let out a deep breath and heaved a sigh. He knew immediately what Maria meant, "She is so young. Do we really have to discuss her marriage right now?" There was concern as well as melancholy in Vincentius's voice. "Don't you think we can keep her with us awhile longer?"

"Vincentius, I love Giacomina as much as you do, but I am worried about 'things.'"

"What do you mean 'things?' What 'things?'" Now Vincentius seemed upset as well as puzzled. "The Frangipani don't know she is now marriageable, do they?"

"No, no, of course not!" Maria snapped back. Her voice then returned to a more gentle tone. "I have two concerns, my Love. The first is for Giacomina's physical safety. Today I received a letter from my cousin Giachet in Sicily. She wrote that Henry is on a rampage there against the Normanni. She fears for her life and that of her husband. Henry already arrested six Norman nobles. He is accusing them of plotting against him. Giachet thinks he will execute them all. He has already burned alive several associates of the late King Tancred. The 'mercy' that Henry showed Tancred's heir – the boy William – was to castrate and blind him before sending him into exile. And that was *after* the child and his family renounced all claims to Sicily! He didn't have to do that…William is just child!!!" Maria's emotions got the best of her, and she began to cry.

She continued in a shaky voice, "You yourself told me of the dreadful way he executed the Norman Count Richard of Acerra before the last Christmastide. It was shameful…dragging him behind a horse through Capua and hanging him by his feet to let him die an agonizingly slow death. How terrible! It was only by accident that a court jester, thinking he would please Henry, tied a large stone to Richard's neck which mercifully hastened his end. It's only a matter of time before Henry comes north to Rome. Giacomina would be much safer if she were a Frangipani rather than a Normanni. You know as well as I that they are more powerful at the moment than our family. They are able to make allies out of enemies whenever it suits them. And if any of their alliances fail, the Frangipani have the knights and arms to protect themselves. You've told me yourself that their fortresses are the strongest in all of Rome."

"You do have a point, my love," Vincentius interjected as he pulled Maria even closer to him and in a clumsily gentle way wiped some tears from her cheek with his sizeable hand. He quickly added, "But I don't think Henry will be at our palace gate tomorrow. There is talk that the Emperor is gravely ill and may not even last until this Christmastide. So, I think we can keep Giacomina with us a little longer." He tried his best not to sound patronizing.

"There's something else, Vincentius." Maria's tears suddenly stopped, and she spoke with firmness. "I noticed some '*things*' when Bombarone's son and his friend – the Bernardone boy – were guests in our house." She noticed

Vincentius's perplexed expression. So, she continued quickly, "It was around the time of the full moon. I told you they were coming, but you needed to be in Ninfa; so, you weren't here. They came from Assisi on behalf of their fathers to deliver goods Cecilia had ordered for us from them. Elias and Francis made the journey specifically for our household. Their horses were packed with goods for us, and they walked the entire way from Assisi to Rome. I remembered how kind the Bombarones were to Giacomina when she stayed with them that one summer; so, I made arrangements for our visitors to stay here and rest for several days before going home."

"Oh, yes. I remember you telling me they were coming," Vincentius lied since he seldom paid attention to the activities related to running the household. Maria noticed there was still a look of bewilderment on his face. She decided to save him embarrassment; so, she jostled his memory, "You met them both when you rode through Assisi on your way to Florence five years ago … you know … to personally thank Signor Bombarone and his family…Remember?"

Vincentius's face lit up as he now recalled meeting the youngsters five autumns ago. They were Giacomina's playmates who kept her safe and happy for the long summer she had to be away from her family. He would be ever grateful to them. He also remembered how she incessantly talked about them after she returned to Rome. He recalled that she had regularly exchanged letters with them over the years.

"So, how are Elias and Francis doing?" Vincentius asked in a jovial manner.

Maria responded in an uncharacteristically stiff way, “They have grown up, too.....just like our Giacomina.”

“Why are you upset, Maria?” Vincentius was again perplexed.

Maria started speaking a mile-a-minute: “I think Giacomina has feelings for him ... and he for her. I noticed it from the moment he entered the great hall. Their eyes locked on each other immediately. When they greeted each other, their little embrace was noticeably longer than it should have been. They always managed to sit next to each other at table, and his hand would ‘accidentally’ brush against hers several times during every meal. He would whisper something to her, and she would touch his arm and smile or laugh.”

Maria paused to catch her breath; so, Vincentius jumped in: “I’m sure they are just good friends, Maria. There is nothing to worry about.”

“They kissed! They were in the courtyard and didn’t think anyone was around. It wasn’t just an innocent little peck on the cheek. He had his arms around her, and she put her lips right up to his. I could tell this wasn’t the first kiss they had shared! Vincentius, this is serious. It can’t go on. It’s got to be stopped. She is promised to someone else. She is nobility. He is not. I won’t have her heart broken...”

Vincentius cut her off before Maria could go on: “All right, all right. There’s no need to work yourself into such agitation,” Vincentius tried to keep his tone as soothing as he could without sounding demeaning. “I will ride to Assisi next week and talk to Bombarone. He’s an old friend, and he will understand. I recall that Elias even as a boy cut a handsome figure; so, I’m not surprised that Giacomina might have a little crush on him. What surprises me is that Elias didn't know better than to indulge her."

"Vincentius, it wasn't Elias! It was Francis." Maria's voice was full of anxiety as she continued: "And this is more than a *little* infatuation.

"Do you remember when she was a little girl and would ask about whom she would marry, I would always tell her it would be a knight in fine armor who would care for her and protect her?" Maria asked this rhetorically and quickly resumed speaking: "I never named anyone but would say her husband would be older, wiser and stronger than she.

"Well, Elias happened to mention that Francis is going to become a knight. You know what that means!?! It's the only way that a merchant's son could even consider a relationship with a noble."

Vincentius tried to be calm, cool and rational: "Even so. How can a merchant from a small city afford to outfit a would-be knight?"

"Vincentius, you should have seen the clothes the boy was wearing – They were far more luxurious than anything I've seen on a young aristocrat here or any nobility period! Cecilia told me Francis's father is one of the wealthiest men in Assisi – much richer than any of the city's nobles, and he has ambitions for his son. He wants Francis to rise in social rank. He is willing to finance this folly at any cost! I'm telling you, Vincentius, the only thing that will end this infatuation is for Giacoma to marry Gratien Frangipane as soon as possible." Maria's tone now suggested mild panic.

Vincentius was silent and turned his gaze from Maria to the peaceful pine grove. Neither he nor she said anything for several moments. When he eventually looked back into his wife's eyes, she could now see uneasiness in them.

Vincentius quietly said, "I will speak to Rainerio Frangipane about the dowry the day after next."

Chapter VII
Promised Blood
Trastevere, Rome

By the next full moon, Vincentius and Rainerio had negotiated the dowry and set the date for Jacoba's marriage to Gratien Frangipane. It was early one evening that Maria and Vincentius talked to their daughter about her betrothal. Jacoba stared blankly upon hearing their announcement. She composed herself as quickly as she could and responded with two words, "I understand." She paused a moment and then politely excused herself.

When Maria attempted to follow Jacoba out of the room, Vincentius pulled her back. "Let her be, Maria. I'm sure this is a shock, but she will work it out in her mind."

"I'm not worried about that," Maria whispered. "Jacoba knows what's expected of a noblewoman, and she will do what is asked of her. I'm concerned about her heart. I could see great sadness in her eyes. I think she truly loved that boy from Assisi."

"Jacoba will be fine. She will come to love Gratien. He is a good man – not like so many of his cousins." Vincentius pulled Maria close to him and continued in a lighter tone of voice, "It seems to me that ***you*** yourself were in love with another when we were betrothed. And don't you think things have turned out quite well for us? Of course, I had to dazzle you with all the charm I could muster."

Maria looked up at Vincentius giving him a small, mischievous smile. He pulled her closer, tilted her chin upward with his hand and put his mouth firmly over half-open lips. They kissed deeply for a few moments. Then he said, "They will be like us. It will work out."

Ready to cry but not wanting to show disappointment, Jacoba had hurried to bed chamber, her thoughts racing more quickly than her feet. *"Gratien Frangipane...My parents have betrothed me to Gratien Frangipane. How could they do this to me? Don't they love me? Isn't he an old man? I thought I was supposed to marry a strong, brave knight who would care for me..."*

Jacoba quickly opened the wooden chest that sat at the foot of her bed. Her hands began to burrow through the various items of clothing until they reached a square of delicate white silk whose edges she had embroidered six years earlier with three letters: "A M A" – "loves."

She picked up the wedding veil and pressed it to her cheek. Memories rushed into her mind as swiftly as the tears that now flooded her eyes. She was back in Assisi reliving the summer day when she decided she was in love with Francis and convinced herself that he was her intended husband.

The playmates of Elias and Francis – mostly boys – varied from day-to-day as did their amusements. Jacoba got to know some of "the gang" better than others. Bernardo, Peter, and Angelo were most often part of the group. Two boys named Leo and Rufino, occasionally joined in play. The only girls besides Jacoba who joined them were Bernardo's sister Vanozza and Angelo's cousin Luchina. They were Jacoba's age and participated whenever they were "consigned" to the care of their older kin.

The kids loved doing anything that involved running, jumping, and "showing-off." In years past, when the little girls weren't around, the boys would dash off to one of the Roman ruins and have "stone battles." They would form two teams. Each boy would select 10 pebbles to give to a member of the opposing team. They supplied their "enemy" with its ammunition to make sure the pebbles with which they themselves would be pelted would not be overly large or sharp. Once their allotted pebbles were in their pockets, they would take cover behind pieces of the large fallen columns and start throwing the small rocks at each other. When everyone was out of ammo – or if someone accidentally received a cut and started bleeding – the war was over. They never really cared about who won or lost. They just derived great pleasure from throwing and dodging the stones.

This particular summer, the boys began a new activity they liked even more: pretending to be knights. Francis came up with the idea. He had been inspired by stories he'd heard from his older step-brother Angelo and his father.

The tales – probably somewhat embellished – were always relayed upon returning from their cloth-buying trips to France. Francis would take mental notes as his two elders talked about their encounters with Crusaders in armor on their way to the Holy Land. Francis was also fascinated by their descriptions of troubadours – the itinerant minstrels who entertained with music and verse.

Francis couldn't wait to begin his apprenticeship and go to France with his father. He wanted to see the sites and meet the people for himself instead of just hearing about them. For now, however, he had to be content with imaginary experiences. So, he came up with rather elaborate scenarios involving whomever his playmates of the day happened to be.

Although the pretend knights didn't have armor, four of them had simple wooden swords they themselves fashioned over the winter months. Elias was fortunate to have a "helmet." It was actually the remains of a very old corroded cooking pot he discovered on an expedition to Assisi's garbage dump. It just so happened to fit over his head, and oxidation had created holes in strategic places allowing him to see and breathe. Since the pot was too heavy to wear for more than 30 seconds at a time, Elias generally just held it and used it as a prop to make him appear more knightly.

Every boy wanted to be a knight, but you couldn't pretend to be a knight if you didn't have a sword. So, sword-owners Elias, Francis, Pietro and Bernardo would occasionally share their weapons with less fortunate playmates.

The preludes to the kids' mock conflicts were even more important than the "combat" itself. Boys who didn't have swords on a particular day were designated feudal lords, princes, or bishops and were given the task of dubbing the knights. Oddly, Francis never took on the role of noble or Church father. When he wasn't a knight, he preferred to be a troubadour and would make up short poems and sing them to anyone in the group who would listen.

Jacoba and the other girls were always nobles of some sort — usually princesses or ladies-in-waiting. In either case, they would make circlets of wildflowers to wear in their hair. Anyone without a sword – boy or girl – had to watch the mock fighting and cheer for their favorite knight.

Their play rituals grew more and more complex as the summer wore on thanks to Francis. He brought fabric remnants as well as odds and ends of ribbons and trims from his father's shop that were creatively used as banners for the knights, cloaks for the nobles, and "favours" to be presented to the knights by the ladies.

Vanozza took things a step further and suggested the "ladies" take home their pieces of cloth and embroider them. She took the girls aside and told them that she'd heard noble ladies always gave knights "favours" they themselves made like handkerchiefs, pillows, or scarves. Jacoba and Luchina initially weren't enthusiastic about the assignment, but went along with it since they were learning to do needlework and could use the practice.

Quickly seizing the largest and most beautiful scrap of cloth, Vanozza announced that she was going to make a pillow for Elias. Luchina grabbed two small pieces of cotton in order to stitch kerchiefs to give Bernardo and

Pietro. Both passed up a remnant of white silk which Jacoba reluctantly picked up. She looked at them and asked, "What do you think I should do with it?"

"Why don't you make a scarf for Francis?" Vanozza said in an innocently teasing way. "He likes you a lot. If you like him, you should put 'AMA' on it," Luchina added. Both girls giggled while Jacoba blushed.

Actually, Jacoba had already sensed that Francis liked her. She liked him a lot, too. She was especially flattered by his attentiveness to her. A few days earlier, playing the role of troubadour, Francis looked primarily at Jacoba as he performed his ditty:

My lady is the sun.
She makes my day so bright.
My lady is a bird.
Her song gives my heart flight.
My lady is love true.
She gives me life anew.
My lady I adore.
Amor. Amor. Amor.

Since the age of five, Jacoba had been often told by her mother that when she reached her 15th birthday, she would marry a fine knight who would take good care of her and make her very happy. After growing close to Francis during that summer of 1192 and knowing of his aspirations to knighthood, Jacoba was certain he was the person her mother was talking about. She also had no doubt the real reason her parents sent her to Assisi in secret was for her to get to know Francis. Jacoba was quite sure her parents must have already arranged her marriage to him.

With those thoughts in mind, she decided to put her heart and soul into making the scarf for him. She feigned illness for two days so she could stay in her room in the Bombarone house and complete the project in secret. It turned out to be her best needlework ever. She rolled and carefully hemmed the edges of the remnant. Then, she embroidered it using extraordinarily delicate and beautiful stitches. It was an exceptionally fine piece of needlework. Although Jacoba wanted to show the finished piece to Cecilia, she dared not.

Later that week, when the children were gathering at their usual place to play "knights and ladies," Jacoba asked Francis to step away from the group for a moment.

"Knight Francis," she said, "I have a favour for you."

In keeping with the role-playing of their ongoing game, Francis replied, "I am honored, my lady." He gave a slight bow.

Jacoba presented him with the piece of silk she had transformed into a scarf. He was taken aback seeing the letters AMA – vernacular for the word "loves" – embroidered along its edges. He was somewhat embarrassed but extremely elated by her gift.

"I fear this is truly too beautiful for me to carry into battle with these ruffians," he said as he held up the delicate, embellished fabric. "I think it would be better for you to keep this for me, Lady Jacoba" he said as he lifted it and stared into her eyes. "It shall be your wedding veil," he continued while gently placing it over her hair. "And I shall remove it on the day we are wed." Francis leaned in and swiftly kissed Jacoba lightly on her lips. Then he dashed off to join the other children.

She stood there momentarily dazed by what just took place. However, his actions totally reinforced her notion that Francis would one day become her husband.

Suddenly, Jacoba's mind snapped back to the present, and she was again asking herself how she could have been so wrong for the past six years.

Gratien Frangipane. He would be her husband. It was all arranged. It would not be Francis. It was never Francis. It was always one of the Frangipani. How could she break the news to Francis? Jacoba gently placed what she mistakenly thought would be her wedding veil back into bottom of the chest.

She went to the writing table in her room, took up a goose-feather quill pen, and dipped it into a little pot of carbon ink. She hesitated only slightly as she put the pen to the page of paper in front of her and by candlelight began to write:

My Dear Elias,

I trust you are in good health and your studies are going well. You have always been most comfortable with books and learning, especially compared to Francis, me, and anyone else I know. Please give my regards to your family.

I am writing because I have news that may be particularly disquieting to Francis, and I am seeking your help to convey it to him. I know it may be sometime before you see him, but I fear I shall never see Francis again.

I am greatly grieved because I am to be married to Gratien Frangipane. I still don't believe it myself. Unbeknownst to me, my parents finalized my betrothal last week. They informed me of it this very day. I am powerless to challenge my father's authority in this matter.

You know I love Francis beyond all measure, and he has expressed love for me. This was confirmed in the numerous letters we exchanged over the past several years.

Do you remember when you and Francis visited Rome some weeks ago? Francis and I went to the garden behind Santa Maria Cappella to walk together and listen to the lovely birdsong in that place. As we walked, we talked of a future with each other. You shall be the only person who knows it was there Francis gave me a token of his love – a silver and carnelian ring with Minerva's image etched in the red-orange stone. I readily accepted it and have until today worn it pinned to my undergarments, close to my heart.

Francis and I convinced ourselves that our destiny was to wed each other, but God's Will was otherwise. I must obey my parents and live up to the duties of my birth.

I wish I could be with Francis, look into his eyes and tell him myself about my heartbreak, but that is now impossible. It would be unseemly for me to see him, and my parents will permit me no more correspondence with him. So, I am beseeching you to be my surrogate and as gently as possible inform him of my situation. I must also give you the onerous task of returning the enclosed ring

on my behalf. Can you do these things for me – your "blood brother?"

I would ask one other favor. Please keep me in your prayers. I do not know what sort of person Gratien Frangipane is, but I am begging God that my new husband be a kind and faithful man and that I will learn to love him and be a good wife.

I have opened my heart to you, Elias, because you have always been a true friend to me as well as to Francis. I don't know when or if I shall ever see you or Francis again. I want you to know how much our friendship has meant to me.

With Great Affection,
Your Brother–Jacoba

Jacoba removed the ring from her undergarment, laid it on the letter, and folded the missive so the ring would not slip out. She took the beeswax candle from its holder on her writing table and held it at an angle that allowed the hot wax to drip onto the little paper packet where two edges met. She pressed the small lead matrix bearing her mother's family crest into the wax. She would give it to Cecilia in the early morning and ask her to put it into the hands of someone trustworthy who would soon be riding north. Since Cecilia would not yet have been informed of the wedding plans, the loyal servant would have no cause to question the correspondence or mention it to Jacoba's mother.

Chapter VIII
Roman Blood
1198 - The Abitato, Rome

The Frangipane Family tree was rooted in mystery and violence. Its coat-of-arms consisted of powerful lions standing on their hind legs facing each other defiantly while holding between them in their paws a single bread-round.

"Frangipane" in Latin means "broken bread." Some said this referred to the Eucharistic Prayer of the Catholic Mass – when the Host is consecrated – which includes the words "as Christ broke the bread." This link with the Church made sense because the Frangipani were intimately involved in papal politics for more than a century.

A more popular legend held that the first Frangipane – Pietro – was a rich merchant who distributed bread to the poor of Rome during Europe's great famine of 1016. He purportedly did his good deeds using a boat since the Tiber had dramatically flooded the city's streets at the time. "Broken bread" became "sharing bread."

The Frangipane themselves professed to be descendents of the ancient Roman plebeian family of Anicii. However, the first reference to them came around Pietro's time at the start of the new millennium. While the name itself appears to have been seeded in faith and good works, its reputation was nourished over many years by violence.

One of the early Frangipani was a canonized saint. Born in Rome in 1040, Ottone started dressing like a Benedictine monk around the age of 30 and began a 50-year-pilgrimage to many Christian shrines throughout the known world. Around 1117, he founded a hospice for pilgrims in Ariano Irpino, Italy, and ran it for several years until he became a hermit.

Eventually, he withdrew even more and began living like an anchorite, locking himself in a small cell next to St. Peter Apostle Church on the outskirts of town. In addition to praying and fasting, Ottone dug a grave in his cell to remind him not only of death but – more important – to live a holy life. He was credited with many miracles during his lifetime and afterward.

There are, however, few details of his earlier life as a knight – when he lived in Rome as a member of one of its most powerful families. He engaged in military action for more than a decade and without a doubt was involved in bloodshed. One might assume the sights, sounds and smells of hand-to-hand combat and death may have influenced Ottone's decision to pursue a lifestyle quite different from the rest of his family.

In addition, one might assume that another Frangipane – Cencius the First – was also inspired by his family's battles for power. A love-hate relationship between the Frangipani and the papacy developed during the latter half of the 11th Century. While Nicholas II was pope, Cencius gave the Church several castles and also helped Alexander II succeed Nicholas to the papal throne. Things changed, however, a few years after Pope Gregory VII ascended to the papacy.

Pope Gregory was praised by many for his extensive reforms in the Church such as enforcing celibacy for clergy and condemning simony. However, he was disparaged for his expansive use of papal power in the political arena. One of the people with whom Pope Gregory lost favor was Cencius I Frangipane. Cencius kidnapped the Pope during a liturgical service one Christmas Day and held him prisoner for a short time. Gregory was later beatified and canonized. Cencius was not.

The late 1100's was a strange, violent time in an even stranger violent city. Rome in 1198 was absurd and inimitable. The walls and the gates of the ancient city were nearly intact, but the magnificent structures that had been the heart of Ancient Rome were in ruin. Their beauty and strength were devastated over the centuries by natural disasters and human assaults. The ruins were like the keepsakes of an old widow desperately clinging to the memories of her dead beloved – fading reminders of what once was but will never again be.

The people of Rome, like its buildings, were also in ruin. There were now a mere 17,000 inhabitants within the walls that had protected one million during the city's glory days.

Noble families of "The Empire" had disappeared. The current ruling class seemed to have come out of nowhere. It was an unlikely mix of families. Some like the Frangipani claimed ancient Roman lineage while others like the Normanni were robber barons – the progeny of invaders from the north.

While the heritage of these new "aristocrats" was dissimilar, they shared a common desire for wealth and power which meant one thing: owning property in the form of land and gold. They continuously strove to acquire additional holdings while maintaining existing assets. They attained their goals through strategic alliances or brute force. Most often, they employed a combination of both.

These Romans lived and fought each other in what was called the *abitato* – the *inhabited* area of the city. It was a relatively small area in the midst of the ancient ruins along the Tiber near the river's bend. The only new construction of any consequence were fortress towers built hastily in a day or two by Rome's fighting factions who were continuously defending their properties or assailing the holdings of their enemies. At one point, there were nearly 200 of these tall, lean structures menacing Rome's skyline. Like giant stone saplings, the structures fell as quickly as they rose.

Between the abitato and the Aurelian Wall lay Rome's "disabitato" or "uninhabited place." The term was somewhat of a misnomer since it was populated during the day by grazing animals and serfs who tended the haphazard vineyards and small fields with various crops scattered amidst the ruins of the once great city. At night, one would find the area's occupants to be thieves, vagrants, murderers, and others trying to evade authority.

Within Rome's abitato, the most powerful families had appropriated the biggest and best ancient buildings for their own use. By the middle of the 12th Century, Cencio Frangipane had converted into his family's palace what was left of the Colosseum as well as the extensive complex of beautiful ancient structures on Rome's Palatine Hill.

Upon his marriage, Rainerio II (Aldruda's son) – was given the Frangipane's ancient palace at the foot of the Palatine, near the Circus Maximus. Known in the 1100's as the "Septem Solia," this grand structure would eventually become Jacoba's home. Its medieval moniker means "seven suns" – the name that would be forever linked with her.

In ancient times, the place was known as the Septizonium. It was built at the start of the third century by Emperor Septimius Severus at the southeast corner of the Palatine Hill.

Severus came from Rome's province of Africa, and it was said he built the stunningly beautiful building to impress visitors – especially those from Africa – approaching Rome from the south. The Septizonium's close proximity to the Circus Maximus meant masses of Roman citizens would also be able to view it with awe.

(The Circus Maximus – Rome's first and largest stadium – accommodated 150,000 spectators who watched chariot races, gladiatorial combat, and the martyrdom of Christians. The Circus had become a ruin long before the Frangipane came on the scene. It decayed centuries earlier through disuse. It was also quarried by many generations for building materials. The only remaining hints of its glory days were two large obelisks.)

The Septizonium's exterior of 1198 would have been unrecognizable to an ancient Roman. The place maintained considerable stateliness but lost all autonomy. Cencio Frangipane's acquisition of it in 1145 resulted in the total absorption of the Septem Solia into the family's fortifications which now covered the Palatine and beyond. An intricate system of tunnels linked the palaces of the various branches of the Frangipane Family.

Although Septem Solia's external grandeur was now obscured by towers, walls and other adjacent construction, its interior still retained some of its ancient opulence.

Some medieval Romans speculated the Septem Solia was originally a temple dedicated to the sun because of its incredibly intricate mosaics depicting planetary divinities as well as the seven days of the week. Others thought it had been a nymphaeum – a monument to water sprites – since at one time it boasted many spring-fed fountains as well as pools, though only a few remained. Most Romans, however, simply didn't care.

Gratien Frangipane was among those who "didn't care." To him the Septem Solia was merely home. He had grown up surrounded by 12th Century luxury, wealth and power. Likewise, he came to know its cost in terms of conflict, injury and death.

Like his father, Gratien took the stunning mosaics and other niceties of the palace itself for granted. He was more concerned about its functionality as a fortification. The 28-year-old was to be betrothed and would eventually be responsible for the safety of a wife – a very young wife.

Gratien was 13 years old when his parents told him a baby girl named Jacoba was to be his wife. They also told him that until their marriage, they expected him to behave like the knight and noble that he was. In other words, they trusted he would do his best to remain relatively celibate for the next decade-plus…or at least not find a love that would interfere with eventual marriage to "the child."

Despite his parents' encouragement to stay celibate until his marriage because it would make for a stronger bond with his bride, Gratien's older cousin gave him the opposite advice. *"Better to bed many before you wed since you may not have those opportunities after the vows are said"* is what his cousin Deodatus told him time and time again.

Perhaps surprisingly so, staying "relatively celibate" wasn't a terribly difficult task for the young noble.

Before his 14th birthday, Gratien was on his way to France to finish preparing for his life as the eventual head of the Frangipane Family. In addition to learning the art of warfare under the tutelage of a knight in Normandie, he also had an opportunity to live and study in a French monastery for several months. The latter provided him with an appreciation for learning, self-discipline, and hard work.

While staying in the monastery, he was love-struck by a beautiful dark-haired beauty whom he noticed while doing laundry in a nearby river. He volunteered to do laundry as often as he could just to glimpse her. After initially exchanging glances and eventually smiles, he approached the young woman on the pretense of needing advice on removing a stain from an altar cloth he was washing.

They began regularly engaging in conversation as they worked near each other on the river's edge. He learned that she was from a noble French family and was a temporary guest at a nearby nunnery. Her family brought her to the convent to protect her from unrest in the countryside surrounding the family's palace. They talked about how much they had in common. His attraction to her became overwhelming.

However, when he finally mustered enough courage to pull her close intending to kiss her, she recoiled and told him she was very fond of him but could never love him "in that way." She said her heart belonged to another. She never returned to the river's edge, and he no longer volunteered to do laundry.

Gratien's education lasted longer than that of most of the Frangipani clan. Surprisingly, he was allowed to study for several months at a school in Paris which would eventually become one of the premier universities in Europe. Gratien had a brilliant, curious mind and would have been outstanding at anything he pursued, but family pressure made him continue the way of knighthood. He would have liked to go to the University of Bologna for further study. Instead, he went to war.

At the age of 19, the young knight departed in one of the 52 ships that left from Pisa in April, 1189, for the port of Tyre in the Holy Land. It marked the start of the Third Crusade. He was actually looking forward to applying the art of warfare in battle. He also hoped to gain experience in the art of love-making since that had not been part of his education so far.

Although Gratien had participated in minor skirmishes in France as well as countless jousting matches, his previous combat experience didn't prepare the young knight for the bloodshed and brutality he encountered in the Kingdom of Jerusalem.

Gratien and his companions often turned to strong drink to not only douse the searing pain of their physical wounds but more important to blot out the memories of horrific carnage that burned in their minds. Some of the knights also sought refuge in the arms of prostitutes who roamed the camps, eager to provide solace in exchange for coinage.

One evening following a battle in which Gratien found himself standing in a pool of ankle-deep blood, he drank more strong spirits than usual. The two knights who had fought with him that day also drank with him that night. They convinced Gratien the charms of a woman were the only thing that could take his mind off of the killing field. In his drunken stupor, Gratien agreed. The two knights went off to find one of the female camp followers and bring her back to Gratien's tent. However, by the time the prostitute arrived, Gratien had blacked out and could not be awakened.

A few days later, following another bloodbath, Gratien's drinking buddies decided once again to hire some women to help them through the night. This time Gratien remained conscious and successfully "consoled" himself with the woman. He sought comfort several times after that with whichever woman his fellow knights chose for him.

Gratien and his comrades were unsuccessful in capturing Jerusalem from the enemy, and he returned to Rome tired and war-weary.

Gratien hated to admit it, but he was relieved to be finished with the Crusade. He had learned more than he ever wanted to know about warfare. And although he was always too drunk to remember his firsthand experience in lovemaking, he figured he'd learned enough from making mental notes on the bawdy stories of other knights who boasted of their erotic adventures in great detail.

Gratien did a lot of thinking on his trip home from the Holy Land. Somewhere along the way, he vowed to do two things: The first was to someday return to the Holy Land as a pilgrim to atone for the deaths on his hands and other sins he committed there. The second was to throw himself wholeheartedly into being committed to Jacoba even though he hadn't yet met her. He needed to resign himself that no matter what, she was to be his wife. He knew she would be young, and he prayed every day she wouldn't be repulsed by him because he was so much older. "*And God, if it please You, let her not be too foolish, too frail or too homely*" was always added to his prayer.

ꙮ

Surprisingly, Gratien was able to fulfill his first vow within the next several years. While the Third Crusade – in which he participated – didn't succeed in retaking Jerusalem, the Crusaders, nevertheless, had many victories elsewhere in the Holy Land. They successfully recaptured a number of key cities including Acre, an important port on the Mediterranean. In addition, a treaty had been signed with Saladin that allowed unarmed Christian and Muslim pilgrims to visit Jerusalem and other areas of the Holy Land.

Before setting sail for the Middle East, Gratien spent more than two-and-a-half years with his father visiting their family's holdings throughout Italy. It took him another six months of travel, but he reached Acre in the autumn of 1196.

For the next year and a half, he was a special guest in a monastery near the city. During his time there, Gratien prayed, visited holy sites and tried to atone for past sins by physically laboring to restore one of the area's Christian sites that had been ravaged by the Saracens. He also spent many hours contemplating his future and what having a wife would be like. His thoughts and feelings were ambivalent.

Sometimes he would recall his self-promise to totally commit to her, sight unseen. It was at one of those times that Gratien decided to commission a piece of jewelry for her from one of the region's finest goldsmiths. It was a small but sumptuous cross studded with precious gems that Gratien himself selected. The gold chain that held the cross was not as long as most, but it was more delicate and ornate than what he had seen in France or Italy. And its intricate clasp was beautifully embellished. Gratien was so pleased with the work of the jeweler that he asked him to make a special casket to hold the precious necklace.

Then, there were times when Gratien wanted to stay in Acre. He found peace there and thought perhaps he could find a way out of marrying "the child" so he could remain away from Rome indefinitely. He'd muse, "Perhaps if I sent her the beautiful cross with a message telling her she would be happier if she married someone she truly loved…"

Just as he was seriously mulling the potential of this latest scenario, two of his father's couriers appeared at his door. Although he already knew why they were there,

Gratien broke the wax seal and read the communiqué to himself: "*Jacoba has come of age. You are to be betrothed as soon as possible. Arrangements have been made for your immediate return to Rome.*"

Chapter IX
Comingled Blood
1200 – Rome

Jacoba could hardly believe she had been married to Gratien for more than a year. The time had gone by so quickly. She couldn't pinpoint the exact moment she fell in love with him, but she smiled to herself as she lay beside him and recalled her tearful nights in the months prior to their betrothal.

She realized how silly she was to have wasted so much time pining for Francis and dreading the prospect of marrying some feeble old man she'd never met.

It wasn't until the betrothal ceremony itself in the second month of 1199 that Jacoba first laid eyes on Gratien. She was completely taken aback at what she saw. Gratien looked much different than the relic of a man she had envisioned. He wasn't decrepit, and his manner didn't strike her as being crude or dour like the other Frangipane men she'd observed in the course of her young life.

Nearly a head taller than Jacoba, Gratien's slim, muscular build and perfect posture made him look like a 20-year-old. His angular face and strong chin were clean shaven and framed by dark hair that was shoulder length and slightly tousled. She was most struck by Gratien's nearly perfect teeth and his piercing dark eyes. The only blemish on his otherwise smooth olive complexion was an inch-long scar on his right temple, a permanent reminder of his months on Crusade.

Although she remembered being aware a great many people had come to the Septizonium's chapel to witness the noble couple's betrothal, Jacoba's eyes were focused solely on her future husband. She remembered how her voice quivered as she put her hand into his and repeated the words of the priest who solemnized the noble couple's promise to marry.

What was most clear in her memory was what happened after the solemn ceremony. As family and invited guests chattered and made their way from the chapel to the great hall for the celebratory feast, Gratien grabbed both of Jacoba's hands and pulled her away from the throng into a small, dark niche where no one could see them. Her back was against the wall, and he stood even closer to her now than when they took their vows at the altar.

The nearness of this stranger's body to hers stirred sensations within Jacoba she had never before experienced. Jacoba recalled feeling both slightly terrified of and extremely smitten by Gratien. She wasn't sure what to think about this knight and noble who was to be her husband. He had no physical resemblance to the hideous-looking ogre she had so often conjured in her mind while crying herself to sleep.

Gratien was a real man – not a boy or an adolescent. He was strong and powerful, unlike the gentle, lighthearted boy from Assisi who – until that very moment – she considered her singular forever love. She now felt confused and guilty about being so physically attracted to this man she'd only just met.

Suddenly, Gratien was looking directly into Jacoba's eyes and drawing her hands up to his lips. He gently kissed her left one and then her right, telling her gently in French, "All will be well, my dear one. I will love you, and I hope you will come to love me. We will take our time." Jacoba thought he would kiss her mouth the way Francis had done several times. She surprised herself by feeling disappointed when he didn't.

Instead, Gratien took a small, elaborately decorated box from his pocket. "I have brought something for you from the Holy Land. I had it made just for you," Gratien said while presenting her with the ornate gem-studded gold cross and chain he had commissioned in Acre.

He went on to explain the five rubies on the cross stood for the wounds of Jesus. The two large sapphires were meant to symbolize Jacoba and him. And the rare and precious pearl in the center was to signify their union in Christ.

Still somewhat dazed by what was happening, Jacoba simply said, "Thank you. It's beautiful, and I will treasure it." She remembered stuttering as she then asked him to do the honor of placing it around her neck.

"You are so young, Jacoba. You must think me very old," Gratien said as his manly hands fumbled with the chain's fastener. A slight smile crossed his lips as he continued, "Even though our families expect us to produce an heir nine moons after our wedding vows, I want you to know I will come to your bed only when you are ready to have me."

Her heart beat even faster as his fingers adjusted the cross around her neck, his left hand brushing her collarbone. He was looking deeply into her eyes, and she into his. She thought that now he would surely press his lips to hers.

Instead he went on to explain why he was now taking back the box that Jacoba was holding and returning it to his pocket: "I will keep this box on the table in my room. When you are ready for me to come to your chamber as your husband, you can let me know by putting the cross that is now around your neck into the box. Whether it takes a day, a week or a year, I will wait."

He then added in an almost matter-of-fact way, "I don't think you would have picked me for your husband, but I hope you may find we have more in common than you might imagine, Jacoba. Now, we'd better join our own celebration before a search party is sent out to find us!

ꙮꙮ

During the time between her betrothal and the wedding, Jacoba lived in the Septizonium with Gratien's mother, sister and other members of the Settesoli Branch of the Frangipane family. She had hoped to see more of Gratien to get to know him better before their marriage, but he was seldom there. As the family's sole heir, he spent most of his time with his father visiting the family's various fiefs and other properties outside Rome.

Life within the Septizonium was different than what Jacoba was used to when she was growing up in the Normanni palace. The Septizonium itself was huge and rambling. Besides countless gathering rooms, private rooms and passageways, there were several pools with ancient mosaics and fountains. She had never seen anything quite so magnificent.

There were also innumerable people who came and went throughout the palace day in and day out. They included guards, servants, stewards, knights and clerics in addition to Frangipani who belonged to other branches of the famous and powerful family.

The Frangipani wanted to make certain Jacoba would be well-prepared to take on her role as the wife of the man they were sure would one day rule Rome.

Jacoba was somewhat apprehensive when she understood what her responsibilities would be in terms of eventually running such an extensive household; so, she dedicated herself to learning all she could from the Frangipane women. She also knew she would have to play a role in helping to manage Gratien's various properties since she had observed and assisted her own mother in these types of tasks.

What was new and very different for her was learning what she would be called upon to do when a Frangipane property came under attack. She would need to fight. Jacoba had never experienced warfare nor did she want to.

Although she knew her own father was involved in many skirmishes, physical combat never came to the door of the Normanni palace in Jacoba's lifetime. She knew how to ride, and although she went on hunts with her father, Jacoba had never shot an arrow let alone wielded a sword, threw a spear or hurled rocks. Even during the make-believe combat games she played with Francis, Elias and the other kids during her summer in Assisi, she herself never picked up a pretend weapon or even threw pebbles.

"You will surprise yourself, Jacoba, with how fierce you will become when you find that your home and the lives of your family are threatened, especially once you have children," explained Gratien's mother. "Your build is too slight for you to hurl rocks, but you can learn archery if you let my son teach you." In a definitive tone, she added, "Gratien will return from Ninfa early tomorrow, and I will tell him to begin your lessons immediately."

ฉฌ

Gratien was ready and waiting for Jacoba by late morning of the following day, and the two set off on foot with a small retinue of guards and attendants. Although not particularly eager to learn to use a bow, Jacoba welcomed the opportunity to spend time with her husband-to-be. The two had begun walking next to each other in awkward silence but were soon talking and laughing as if they had known each other for years.

As soon as they reached an open area between some ancient ruins, Gratien quickly dismissed the small retinue, instructing the attendants to leave the supply of arrows and the basket of bread, fruit and wine … and return to the palace. He used the pretext that Jacoba would be uncomfortable with onlookers since this would be her first lesson. His real reason for sending away the entourage was that he wanted to be alone with his future wife for a few hours.

After helping Jacoba remove her surcoat so she could have greater mobility, Gratien demonstrated and then explained to her in great detail how to hold the bow and position the arrow. When she tried releasing the arrow, Gratien realized he needed to do a better job of walking her through the process. "We'll do this together, Jacoba, so you can get a better feel as to how far to draw back the string of the bow. Now, grab an arrow and position yourself as if you are going to shoot it." Gratian looked at her from the front and then the side in a calculating way. He adjusted her fingers on the bow. Then, he scratched his forehead. "Now hold the arrow the way I showed you and draw back the string," he continued explaining the technique while he positioned himself closely behind her. His body enveloped hers as he covered her hands with his. "We'll do this together a few time until you get a feel for it," he told her matter-of-factly.

Jacoba could feel Gratien's face against her hair and his breath in her ear as his hands directed her motions. The nearness of his body and the touch of his skin on hers were disconcerting to Jacoba. No one – not even Francis – had ever made her feel the way she felt in that instant. She hoped Gratien wouldn't notice that her heart was pounding and that she was short of breath. She wondered if he experienced anything similar.

Despite the distraction, it took no time at all for Jacoba to learn the basics of archery once he helped her get a feel for it. He took a few steps back and had her practice on her own.

When they decided to take a break, Gratien spread his cape on a huge flat stone that had once been part of an ancient pagan temple. Sitting side by side, they reviewed what they worked on for the previous two hours. When Gratien complimented Jacoba on being a quick learner, she responded by telling him that he was a great teacher.

She noticed an expression of melancholy flash across his face. "Did I say something wrong? Did I disappoint you in some way?"

"No. Not at all, Jacoba," Gratien's words came out in an uncharacteristically wistful voice as he shook his head.

"What's, wrong, Gratien?" She persisted.

He wasn't accustomed to having someone pick up on the subtlety of his facial expression…And if they did, they wouldn't dare ask him about it. On top of that, she seemed genuinely concerned, and he knew she wasn't going to let it drop. He felt flattered and very uncomfortable at the same time.

"I didn't mean to convey sadness, but your words about me being a teacher struck me in a strange way. While I know I have a duty to defend my family and those who live on their lands and the Church of course, I would honestly rather be a teacher than a warrior. I've never told that to anyone! The many years I spent in France away from Rome and away from conflict showed me a different way. I know I'm a good fighter, but I think I would have been a good teacher if I could have stayed in Paris . . ."

He stopped speaking suddenly when he noticed tears in Jacoba's eyes. Then, she finished his sentence: "…but you had to come back to Rome to marry me. I'm sorry."

"Giacomina, I didn't mean it that way at all." Gratien put his arms around her, pulled her close to him and gently kissed her hair. Then he looked her in the eye. "You believe in God, don't you?" He asked the question somewhat rhetorically but Jacoba nodded anyway. "Then, you must believe in Divine Providence. Things happen for a reason. 'Thy will be done.'

"You and I were born into certain families. And I believe some things were determined for us long before we were born. We have certain obligations, and it would be selfish not to try to fulfill those duties…

"When I lived in a French monastery for a while as a youth, the abbot – a very holy man – once told me that it's okay to pray for favors but you should be sure to tell God at the end of your prayer that what you truly want is whatever He wants for you.

"I'm sorry I didn't say that very well, but I think you know what I mean. You know that we have free will, right? I could have stayed in Paris, but I don't think that's what God wanted me to do. I think He wanted me to be right here with you right now. And I know He wants me to be your husband," Gratien still sounded wistful, and then his voice changed to cheerier tone: "And now I think it's His will that we see what the kitchen has put into the basket for us."

The two ate and talked and drank wine. They discovered they had a common love for books and for birds. Gratien promised to show Jacoba a small secret room in the family's Marino palace that was his personal library. "No one else has ever been in it," he said in a mock-serious voice then quickly added with a smile, "because no one else in my family likes to read."

Jacoba promised to take Gratien to a private garden near her family's palace in Trastevere where "the birdsong makes you think you are in heaven."

"Gratien, may I ask you something?" Jacoba got solemn all of a sudden. Without giving him a chance to answer, she continued, "Were you ever in love? Did you have someone in Paris that you left behind?"

Gratien's expression turned somber. He stared straight ahead and paused for what seemed like an eternity to Jacoba before answering. "'Yes, I think so' to your first question … and 'No, I didn't' to your second question." He went on to explain a 'serious infatuation' happened during his time at the monastery. It involved a young noblewoman studying in a nearby convent. He explained that he must have loved her because he made no further advances when she told him she was promised to another.

Gratien explained he had several interactions with various women while on Crusade. "I was not proud of my behavior there for things that happened on and off the battlefield. However, I can assure you, Jacoba, there was no love involved in anything I did over there. I went to confession, did my penance and will never talk about it again."

Gratien was visibly irritated by the conversation and decided to turn the table on Jacoba, "What about you? Has our betrothal '*interfered*' with a true love of your own?" She couldn't really tell whether he was angry, annoyed or apprehensive.

Without putting much thought into her response, Jacoba blurted out, "Of course I'm a virgin…if that's what you're asking!" She then launched nervously into a monologue speaking at a rate much faster than her normal pace:

"When I was eight years old, I spent many months in Assisi with a family there. I didn't know it at the time, but my parents had sent me there because they were concerned about my safety in Rome. I grew very close to three of my playmates, especially Elias, Francis and Prassede. They were like the siblings I never had. We knew back then that we would be lifelong friends.

"Over the years, Francis and Elias would visit me in Rome when one of their fathers had business here. Francis and I grew particularly close. He was kind and gentle and fun to be around.

"From little on, I was told by my mother that I would be wed to a wealthy knight who would be kind to me, protect me and love me. I had convinced myself Francis was that person. I thought the real reason my parents sent me to Assisi as a child was to get to know 'my future husband.'

"During his last visit, Francis told me his plans for knighthood were starting to gel since his father had purchased for him the best armor money could buy. He told me that after he became a knight, he would marry me… and then we kissed a couple of times."

Gratien was now looking intently at Jacoba. She went on, "The day after Francis and Elias left our palace following their last visit, my parents told me that I was to be betrothed…to you. I wrote to Elias that very evening asking him to break the news to Francis and return the token Francis gave me."

Gratien interrupted, "What did he give you? Tell me it wasn't a ring!"

"It was a ring, but as I told you – I don't have it anymore. And I have not seen Francis or heard from him since. I wrote to him a couple times in case Elias was not able to talk with him." Jacoba was now visibly upset and ready to cry.

Gratien said calmly, "You still love him, don't you?"

"Well…yes." Jacoba initially responded hesitantly but quickly added, "Francis will always have a special place in my heart." Jacoba's eyes were filling with tears. The words stunned and stung Gratien. He couldn't hide his disappointment nor did he try. Jacoba kept talking.. "But Gratien, after being with you, I know my love for Francis is very much different than my love for you," Jacoba bit her lower lip while trying to hold back her tears. She saw the look on Gratien's face and had not intended to hurt him the way she did.

There were several moments of silence before Gratien spoke. He was no longer looking at her. He just looked straight ahead. "Will you take this Francis man as a lover?" Gratien's tone of voice was somber, almost as if Jacoba's unfaithfulness after their wedding were a certainty to which he would need to resign himself.

Jacoba also looked straight ahead and nervously played with the cross around her neck as she responded: "Gratien, the vows we took three weeks ago, and the vows we will take when we are wed…Do they mean nothing to you? I made a solemn promise to you, and I will be faithful to you. I would never take Francis or any other as a lover!"

She went on, "You've not yet kissed my lips, Gratien, yet just being near you makes me feel like I've never felt before. Do you remember after our betrothal in church...You pulled me close to you in that tiny alcove and held me and kissed my hands?... Gratien, I thought I would faint. And just a little while ago, when you wrapped your arms around me to show me how to shoot the arrow, couldn't you feel my heart beating? I don't know what to say. I think more than anything, besides being your wife. I want to be *your* lover – your *only* lover." The tears she was trying to hold back were now trickling down Jacoba's cheeks. "Will *you* take a lover if you tire of me or find another who suits you better?"

Gratien moved closer to her and began to lightly brush away her tears. He gently lifted her chin, looked deeply into her eyes and without a word kissed her with an intensity that startled both of them. "Is this how Francis kissed you?!!" The words came out of his mouth like a demand rather than a question. He didn't wait for Jacoba to answer before kissing her again, pulling her even closer to him. After kissing her a third time and still pressing her against himself, he spoke in a tender yet firm tone: "From the moment I set eyes on you, I've never wanted another woman the way I want you…and I can't imagine anything could change that. You don't know me yet, Jacoba, but if you did, you would know that like you and unlike so many of my relatives, I keep the promises I make. I would not ever take a lover, even if you never grow to love me the way I already love you. You will be my one and my only love until I take my last breath! That is what I vow to you and to God."

When he leaned in to kiss her again, her eyes were closed but her mouth was slightly open as Gratien put his lips on hers. Without thought, he slid his tongue between her lips. Her eyes momentarily shot open, and Gratien was afraid perhaps he'd taken things too far too soon. But she didn't pull away from him. And when he kissed her again, her teeth were parted even more.

He whispered "I want to make love to you right now, right here…" Gratien passionately kissed her twice more then gently pushed her away and smiled. "But we need to stop or I'm afraid we will both have to go to confession." She smiled back at him, sighed and then rested her head on his chest for a long moment before they started back to the Septizonium.

They held hands as they walked. They didn't say much. But when they arrived at the palace, Gratien put his arms around Jacoba's waist, pulled her to him and said, "Someday I think I would like to meet this Francis and any other people with whom I have to share your heart." Jacoba looked up at him, smiled and kissed his lips: "Thank you, Gratien, for everything today." As they parted, she suddenly turned and added, "I love you."

ꕥ

Their wedding took place in early spring of 1199 at the family's palace in Marino located near Lake Alban. At the moment, it was safer to have major family gatherings outside Rome. Had they wed in the Septizonium or the Normanni palace let alone a church in Rome, they would have made themselves easy targets for an attack by their familiar enemies or those not yet known to them.

Besides, Marino provided a beautiful setting, and the family had not hosted any major events there in many years. Sharing their bounty with their vassals as well as noble allies was always a good move for the Frangipani politically and socially.

The ceremony itself came off without a hitch. Afterwards, Jacoba and Gratien distributed alms generously throughout the village as was the custom. The marriage celebration was extensive in the palace and throughout the countryside. The Normanni spared no expense when it came to providing the best of everything for Jacoba's wedding. Feasting tables were set up within the palace walls and beyond in strategic areas where commoners could also enjoy the bounty. Nobles and commoners alike found that the free flowing wine and spirits greatly enhanced the merry making.

The newlyweds participated in festivities into the early evening. However, as soon as Gratien saw that the couple themselves had ceased to be the focus of everyone's attention, he looked at Jacoba and noticed that she, too, seemed to be growing weary of the merriment.

He himself had very little spirits or wine to drink that day nor did she. He wanted to be able to consummate the marriage. He then recalled his promise to wait until Jacoba came to him and now wished he'd never made it.

His attention all day had been focused on his bride. From the moment he saw her in the palace chapel that morning, he wanted her carnally more than ever. She looked ethereal as she walked toward him. Her sinuous blue silk tunic embellished with pearls and gold threads glistened with her every movement. Her long shiny hair flowed well below her shoulders, and the narrow gold band atop her head that kept her small sheer veil in place reminded him of a halo. He had a twinge of guilt just looking at her as they stood facing each other and exchanging vows at the altar. He thought it must surely be wrong of him to feel uncontrollable lust for such an angelic creature.

Gratien couldn't get the day of her archery lesson out of his mind. He hadn't been able to spend any time alone with her since, and it was driving him crazy. He couldn't stop thinking about the way she felt in his arms and the taste of her lips.

When they looked into each other's eyes during the ceremony, he thought he saw the same fire that was there when they last kissed. And during the ensuing festivities, he noticed that she was often looking his way.

Although they sat next to each other during the feast, they had little time to converse since they were constantly barraged by well-wishers. Jacoba would occasionally touch Gratien's arm or hand, but Gratien worried maybe she was just trying to be "wifely." Then, all of a sudden, she leaned toward him and whispered, "Gratien, Do you think it would be possible to slip away now that everyone seems to be feeling quite merry? I think I would like to retire for the night."

Again, he thought about his promise to her and wondered whether she, too, remembered. Then, he wondered how many nights it would be before she would invite him to her bed. He would soon know.

"You leave. I'll stay a few moments longer so I can let the stewards know we have gone to our chambers but would like our guests to continue the festivities without us." Gratien wasn't overly optimistic about finding Jacoba's cross in the box on his table, but he wanted to give her some time to put it there. He had already instructed his servant to place one lighted candle near the box – the only thing on the large table – so it could be easily seen. He also left instructions the door between their rooms be unlocked but remain closed.

When Gratien went to his chamber a quarter hour later, he told his servant to immediately take his leave and go celebrate with his friends. Gratien said he would undress himself and also told the servant he could have the following day as a holiday. As soon as the servant closed the door, Gratien took off his boots and surcoat. He noticed the door between his room and Jacoba's was closed which made him certain she would not be inviting him to her bed. He slowly and glumly began removing his tunic as he walked to the table to check the box "just in case." He hesitated a moment, and then opened the lid of the ornate little jewel casket. It was empty. He heaved a sigh and said under his breath, "Perhaps another night…"

"Is tonight not good for you?" A voice came from a darkened corner of the room, and it so startled Gratien that he instinctively reach for the dagger he normally kept in his belt. Fortunately, today it was not part of his wedding attire.

Jacoba emerged from the shadows, looking as ethereal as she did in the morning. She was barefoot and wore only the floor-length translucent silk chemise she had worn under her bridal tunic. Her long, delicate arms were bare since her servants had already loosened all the laces of her sleeves except for one at each shoulder. Even in the dim candle light, Gratien could clearly see the details of her lithe figure through the filmy white fabric.

"Gratien, I forgot to ask my servant to unhook the chain on my necklace, and I couldn't unfasten it by myself. Will you please help me?" she asked as she turned her back to him. He stood closely behind her. To expose the clasp of the chain, he gently brushed her long hair over her left shoulder, running his fingers through it as he did so. However, instead of undoing the ornate fastener, Gratien began softly kissing her neck while his hands caressed her bare shoulders. Far from flinching at his touch, Jacoba melted into him, which inflamed his passion even more.

He buried his face in her hair, kissing her head, then her ear and her cheek as his hands undid the last two laces of her chemise. As she turned to face him so their lips could meet, her chemise fell to the floor. She threw her arms round his neck, and they kissed several times as they had on the day of her archery lesson. Gratien looked at her with love as well as lust. Then, he scooped her up into his arms and began carrying her to his bed. She whispered breathlessly into his ear, "I'm so sorry, Gratien. I know nothing about lovemaking."

He smiled and laughed a little as he said, "Giacomina, I don't think I know much more than you, but judging from the few moments we've had alone, I think we will enjoy learning together!"

ജ്ജ

The couple spent the next several months at each other's side. Jacoba traveled with Gratien to visit all of his properties. While he was busy adjudicating disputes among his vassals, she was involved in meeting with stewards and staff at the Frangipane's various palaces. Together, the noble couple would walk through their villages and into the countryside, talking with the locals and sometimes distributing alms.

When the two weren't on the road, they retreated to their favorite home — the Frangipane palace in Marino. They spent many hours together in Gratien's private library. Sometimes they would read together. Gratien had plans to improve the fields and orchards on their property in Rome's ancient Circus Maximus by setting up an irrigation system. So, he studied books and papers about farming he had collected over the years. Jacoba enjoyed just going through his library. While there were books and documents in the palace where she grew up, the Normanni collection was not nearly so extensive as Gratien's nor was the subject matter so varied. When she wasn't reading, Jacoba would sometimes do needlework.

When the two of them would happen to look up at the same time from what they were doing and their eyes would meet, they would instinctively and simultaneously put aside their pursuit and make love on the reading table.

The two also took several excursions to nearby Lake Alban where Gratien would try to teach Jacoba to swim. After dismissing the guards and servants, which he always did, the swimming lesson would soon end up as the married version of the archery lesson with the two of them not only kissing and embracing but making love in the water or on a grassy area near the shore. Whenever there was an opportunity to make love, they seized it.

ꙮ

And now, just a little more than a year after their marriage, Jacoba would soon be giving her husband a child. She lay in Gratien's bed smiling as she reminisced about their courtship and marriage. She absentmindedly began lightly rubbing her very swollen stomach when the child inside her began to kick. She then snuggled her back into her sleeping husband. A groggy Gratien gently put his arm over hers, and she placed his hand on the place where the little kicks could be felt. All Gratien said was, "Giacomina." Then he pulled her even closer to himself and began kissing the back of her neck.

Chapter X
Birthing Blood
1201 – Rome

The Septizonium was in an uproar. Lady Jacoba's water broke. The birth of the Frangipane child was imminent.

One of the largest and safest rooms in the palace had already been prepared as her lying-in room. However, servants continued scurrying about, seeing to last minute details. Extra chairs and cushions were being arranged around the room, and several tables were being stocked with various birthing supplies and sweet treats. The edibles, which included fruits and honeyed almonds, were there for the stream of family and invited guests who would be flowing in to see the noble newborn once the child had been baptized.

Fine coverlets had been placed on the bed where Jacoba would lay. Should the bed become uncomfortable for her ladyship, a three-legged birthing chair stood at the ready in another corner of the room. A beautifully carved wooden cradle had been placed in the darkest corner of the room several days earlier in anticipation of the noble birth since it was thought that bright light would damage the newborn's eyes.

Two mid-wives were on hand, and no fewer than five female Frangipane servants busied themselves checking and re-checking the chamber. The rosewater, the salt, the cloth for swaddling the newborn and an herbal salve to rub on Jacoba's stomach to ease her labor; everything was now where it should be. The only thing missing at the moment was the laboring mother.

Because death was so often the outcome of childbirth for 13th Century women and babies, Jacoba made her peace with God the moment she sensed labor was imminent. Two days earlier she had confessed to her priest at Santa Lucia before attending Mass and receiving the Eucharist.

Several weeks prior, Jacoba had given Gratien's mother a favorite cloak to be used to cover her corpse should the birthing experience prove fatal. Jacoba decided not to give the potential shroud to Gratien for safekeeping since she thought it might upset him.

Men – even those skilled in the healing arts – were never permitted in the lying-in room during labor and delivery. Gratien unilaterally decided he would change that practice. He was Jacoba's husband, after all, so he was already familiar with her body. And he believed his experiences with the blood, gore and chaos of combat had prepared him well enough for the birthing experience. He soon discovered he was greatly mistaken.

For a knight of medieval Rome, the lying-in room proved to be much different than the battlefield. What made a husband's attendance at childbirth a particularly agonizing as well as supremely frustrating ordeal was seeing the woman he loved face excruciating pain and possible death without being able to aid her in the slightest way. There was no enemy to slay or fend off, nor were there any prisoners to take. Any man – even a strong, muscular, commanding one like Gratien – was rendered completely powerless when it came to birthing.

After Jacoba's water burst, Gratien himself carried her to the lying-in room from his own bed, which she had shared with him every night since their wedding. After gently placing her in the birthing bed, Gratien took a chair next to it and held Jacoba's hand.

As labor progressed, the midwives asked Gratien to move out of the way so they could do what they needed to do. One began to rub Jacoba's abdomen with the soothing salve while the other placed a moistened cloth above her brow and spoke words of encouragement. Gratien's mother was in the room observing her son as well as Jacoba.

The labor pains were now coming with greater frequency as well as intensity. After more than two hours, Gratien could no longer sit and watch. He was now pacing back and forth across the large room. He could not bear to see his wife in any type of pain let alone this sort of agony. He also kept reminding himself this was his fault. He assumed God was most likely punishing him for his great lust for her.

When Jacoba's occasional whimpers caused by early labor pains evolved into earsplitting screams as the pains intensified, Gratien was convinced she would die. Now at wit's end, he began harassing the midwives. It was then that

Gratien's mother stepped in and firmly told her son he should go to the palace chapel and pray. "Right now, this is all in the hands of God … and your wife! Since she's in no mood to talk with you or anyone else at the moment, Gratien, I think it would be better for *you* to talk with God! Now, go!," Gratien's mother was adamant and opened the door for him.

She shut the door behind him, but the screams of his wife–his lover–followed him as he walked slowly along the lengthy corridor and down the long staircase. Once alone in the quiet of the chapel, he broke down and cried for the first time since he was a very young boy.

He initially fell to his knees in front of the altar but soon was prostrate on the cold, stone floor. The only light in the chapel came from a candle in the sanctuary lamp. He lifted his head so he could see the tabernacle, and he talked to God in a way he had never done before: *This is my fault. She's suffering for* ***my*** *lust. I've seen men die in many terrible ways by sword, axe, spear and arrow, but their pain did not go on and on, hour after hour. And how can this child–my very own seed–pass through her small birth opening without killing her? I should never have put her into this position. I'm the cause of her torture.*

If she should survive, she will surely never again want to share my bed. I don't blame her. If she prefers our marriage be a spiritual one from now on, I will take that vow and keep it.

Take my life in exchange for hers, God! I cannot live without her. I've never felt so powerless. I know 'Thy will be done,' but PLEASE, God, spare her. I will sacrifice anything for her life. I will do anything You ask of me if You just let her live.

Gratien lay on the floor for nearly three hours alternately sobbing and bargaining with God as he pleaded with Him for Jacoba's life. He was at the point of total exhaustion when his mother walked into the chapel. "Gratien, you may see your wife now," she said softly.

"She is alive?" he responded with hesitation in his voice. When Gratien's mother nodded affirmatively, he quickly added, "and she wants to see *me*?"

"Don't you want to see your new son? Now, pick yourself up and come with me." Gratien's mother replied to him while already making her way out of the chapel.

Gratien quickly got to his feet and began following his mother out the door. Suddenly he turned back to look at the tabernacle and in a very soft, sincere and solemn voice said, "Thank you, God! Thank you, God!"

As Gratien hurried up the steps and down the long hall to the lying-in room, his thoughts were on Jacoba. He assumed she probably wanted to see him to say she now hates him for what he did to her. He persuaded himself that she would no longer want to share his bed and that she may want to leave him to enter a convent. However, he hoped that when he told Jacoba of his willingness for them to have a chaste marriage, she would decide to remain with him at the Septizonium. "*After all,*" he thought, *"we now have a child to raise."* As if it hadn't occurred to him before, Gratien thought: ***"We have a child!"*** Now he couldn't get to her room fast enough.

He was astonished when he appeared in the doorway and heard Jacoba call his name in a weary yet cheerful voice.

He was totally flabbergasted when he saw her sitting up in bed holding a bloody little body and smiling. The linen of the bed was streaked with blood; Jacoba's hair was damp from perspiration; and she looked pale as well as tired. Otherwise, it was as if Jacoba had forgotten what she endured during the past six hours.

"Gratien, come meet Jacob, your son! I think he resembles you. Look at his dark hair and dark eyes," Jacoba was talking a mile a minute while staring at the baby. "I wanted you to see his strong limbs and beautiful little body before they swaddle him and hand him over to the wet nurse." Jacoba was still staring at the baby. "Isn't he the most amazing child you've ever seen? Do you want to hold him?" She finally looked up at Gratien.

Gratien hesitated. He'd done many different things in his life, but he'd never held a baby before. Jacoba thrust the baby toward him. Gratien had no choice. He awkwardly took the child into his arms and immediately fell in love with his new son. For several minutes, Gratien looked with awe at the tiny, bloody bundle of flesh that was part him and part Jacoba. His gaze never wavered as he marveled to himself about this little body from God that came out of their love for each other.

He would have continued his reverie, but one of the midwives told him it was now time for them to clean and swaddle Baby Jacob. The midwife congratulated Gratien on the birth of a male heir as she snatched the baby from his arms.

Baby Jacob would be baptized as soon as possible since it wasn't uncommon for babies – even seemingly healthy ones – to die within hours or days of their birth. Neither

Gratien nor Jacoba wanted their son to go to limbo in the event he didn't survive. Gratien's sister had been chosen as the godmother; so, she would carry the newborn to Santa Lucia's for the ceremony once he'd been swaddled and fed.

Everyone fussing around the baby guaranteed Gratien and Jacoba a few moments of private conversation before Jacoba took some desperately needed rest and before various family members, invited nobles, and clerics would start flooding in.

"Gratien, you haven't kissed me yet!" Jacoba's voice was tired, but he could tell her tone was mock-scolding. She continued, "While I can't share your bed, I hope you still love me. After all, Jacob will eventually need a little sister…or brother. I don't want him to grow up an 'only child' the way I did!"

Gratien kissed Jacoba gently on her forehead, sat himself on the edge of her bed and held her hand. Gratien was perplexed, and Jacoba could tell something was bothering him. "Gratien, what's wrong? You didn't kiss me on my mouth the way you usually do? I thought you would be happy that I gave you a son?"

"Giacomina, I am more than happy. It's just that I don't know what to say. I don't even know what to think," Gratien responded. "You showed me you are as brave as any knight I've ever known. You carried *my* seed for nine moons. Tonight you bled for me, endured hours of torment and almost died to give me our strong, healthy son. I love you for it," Gratien paused momentarily, "but I don't ever want to put you through this again.

"When you were close to death last night, I promised God that if He spared your life, I would take a vow to be chaste if you no longer want to share our marriage bed. When I walked in here a little while ago, I expected you to loathe me for the misery I'd caused you. Instead, here you are smiling and talking about having more children. You confound me, Jacoba."

Jacoba looked at him in disbelief as she began her own monologue: "Gratien, I don't think I was any closer to death last night than you are whenever you engage in one of your 'little wars' … or that every one of us in this room is right now. Since God can take us whenever and however He chooses, aren't we 'close to death' every moment of our lives?

"And as far as the pain of birth and the tribulations of carrying your child…You may find this hard to believe, but once I held our Jacob in my arms, I forgot about all of that. Think about it, Gratien: We are parents now. *He* came out of our love!," Jacoba emphasized the word 'he' as she momentarily shifted her gaze from Gratien to the table where their son was now being swaddled. She quickly added, "Our marriage is no longer about us alone."

She continued her postpartum speech: "The only reason I will not come to your bed is so I can heal. As she said the words, Jacoba glanced down at the bloody bedding as did Gratien. "The midwives said it may take two or three moons, but it doesn't mean that I *never* want to lay with you as your wife! Far from it!

"Need I remind you of your little lecture to me about following God's will? You were so sure it was His will for us to wed. Well, I don't think God wants you to turn into a monk now, and I *know* He does not want *me* to become a nun!

"Gratien, we serve Him best now by being married and loving each other in every sense of the word. I think it's His will for us to have more children…or maybe not. But we have to do our part." She paused, and then with hesitation in her voice added, "Is there some other reason you are talking as if you no longer desire to lay with me?"

"You misunderstand me, Giacomina," Gratien replied while bringing her hands to his lips. He kissed them tenderly and continued, "You know me better than that. If I could make love to you right now, I would!

"You mean everything to me, and the biggest sacrifice I could have offered God was to never again love you in a physical way," Gratien was looking into Jacoba's eyes as he added, "I'm not sure what to do now. I feel as if I truly owe God something major because not only are you alive, but you still have affection for me."

"Gratien, you should know better than to bargain with God, but since you feel you have to do something, why not do something to thank Him, something that will honor Him? I'm sure you will think of something important, but I'm sorry I'm just too tired to help you now." Jacoba could no longer fight her exhaustion, and her eyes began to close as she added in a faint voice and with a tired smile, "Just make sure whatever you come up with doesn't involve our marriage bed! …I…love…you...Gratien…" Jacoba barely got the words out before falling into a deep sleep.

Gratien kissed her on the mouth. Despite being exhausted himself, Gratien pulled up a chair and sat next to her bed for the next hour. As he watched her sleep, he thought about what significant thing he could do to honor and thank God … and please his wife.

Ideas flowed in and out of his brain: *Perhaps I should use my knightly skills and volunteer to go back to the Holy Land. Some of my allies from France have already responded to Innocent's call for a Fourth Crusade and have taken crusade vows. No, that would not be a good idea. My heart would not be in it. I'm not sure how pleasing it would be to God, and I know it would not please Jacoba. I need to stay here in Rome for her and my new son.*

Gratien's mind was galloping through idea after idea: *Maybe I could go on pilgrimage. Maybe I could help Jacoba at Santa Lucia's diaconia. Maybe I could give some gold coins to the poor. Maybe I could commission a piece of religious art for a church or our palace.* Unfortunately, as quickly as he came up with an idea, he discarded it.

Then, just as exhaustion was about to completely overtake him, Gratien was struck with inspiration. He would build a church! He thought it fit all of his criteria perfectly. A church would be a significant and lasting way to give glory to God and thank Him for His special blessings surrounding Jacob's birth. To honor Jacoba, the church could be dedicated to her most beloved saint – Lucia. It would be built–not in Rome–but in Marino, their favorite fief and the place where their son was most likely conceived. Gratien smiled to himself, satisfied this idea would please both God and Jacoba. He then rested his head on Jacoba's bed, closed his eyes, and welcomed sleep.

ജ്ഛ

Construction of the little church was overseen by Gratien with Jacoba's input and was completed in record time, by the end of 1202. The building project was more than a spiritual blessing for Marino's residents: It was also an economic boon. Skilled craftsmen were brought to the fief to work on the small gothic structure. In addition to spending a good part of their wages in Marino, the masons and artists took on locals as apprentices to help them get the job completed quickly.

Although the church was not so large or grand as Santa Lucia in Rome, it was a treasure for the people of Marino and the surrounding countryside as well as for Jacoba. The architect whom Gratien retained to design the structure also arranged to commission a number of small mosaics and frescoes as well as a large painted crucifix. Gratien Frangipane spared no expense with the project. *"After all, this is for God ... and Jacoba,"* he said to himself as he contentedly paid the bills.

From the day Santa Lucia's doors opened, Sunday Mass there was jam-packed. Most of the church-goers came primarily to gawk at the splendid little edifice and its contents.

Few of them could read, and few would ever be able to make a pilgrimage to Rome and see the stunning art of its churches. The peasants of Marino could, nevertheless, still learn their Bible lessons through the stories depicted in Santa Lucia's mosaics, frescoes, and crucifix. This made both Gratien and Jacoba very happy.

Chapter XI
Blood of the Innocents

Spring, 1203 - The Tiber River, Rome

A small crowd was forming along the Tiber's bank as Jacoba and her entourage crossed its narrow bridge.

"Sabina, what do you think is going on … I hope no one has drowned. Signal to the guards to take us there."

The servant seated across from Jacoba waved her hand out the carriage-like box poised on two poles powered by horses. One animal was connected to its front; the other to its rear. They had been trained to step at the same pace by the servants who rode them. A family guard walked next to each horse, and Jacoba's personal guards – Maffeo and Nardo – walked on either side of the noblewoman's luxurious little transport.

The entourage stopped near the growing assembly of onlookers. Jacoba could tell the people were agitated. Some in the crowd appeared to be servants on errands. Others looked like tradesmen. A few were probably pilgrims. Most were fishermen who'd just brought in the morning's catch.

People talked and gestured among themselves as they watched an old man lumber over the edge of his weather-beaten dinghy into the river's mucky edge. Grabbing the bow of his craft, he heaved it through the mud. Once the boat was secure, the old man took off his threadbare cap and held it over his heart. As he turned to the crowd, he shook his head slowly and pointed to his "catch." His tough, crumpled face was expressionless, but his watery eyes paled by cataracts betrayed deep sadness.

More prominent than fish in his net were three small human corpses. The sight of the dead newborns in various states of decomposition was sickening beyond description even to the most jaded observer. The old fisherman was at a loss for words. Women gasped or tsk-tsked. Men talked among themselves in hushed tones.

After a few moments, a lone voice was heard:

"Someone should get a priest."

"How about getting the Pope?" The response from one of the fishermen was markedly cynical. "These dead babies are from the pilgrim's whores. And the pilgrims keep coming because *'His Holiness'* wants them to! "

The crowd mumbled in disbelief as to how anyone could be so flippant, so disrespectful. Then they noticed the scornful fisherman wipe his eyes with the back of his hand and brush the sleeve of his shirt across his dripping nose.

"It's gotten worse." The insolent fisherman's voice was different now. Less harsh. More resigned. He scanned the faces in the crowd, then put an arm around the old fisherman and spoke loud enough for everyone to hear.

"You're not the first to net such wretchedness. It's happened to me twice in as many moons. I'd heard others say the same. It seems to be happening more these days."

Another fisherman reluctantly stepped forward. "I'm ashamed. I've netted some like this, too. When I'd see one in my net, I'd leave it in the water 'til I could maneuver my boat so no one would see me. Then, I'd slip the bloated little corpse away from the fish and back into the river before hauling my nets aboard. I never told anyone. I was afraid I'd get blamed for something."

Jacoba listened intently as several others told similar stories. Then she signaled to Sabina and the guards that she'd seen enough. It was time to move on. She gave her orders as dispassionately as always, but Sabina noticed tears in Jacoba's eyes.

"My appointment in Saxon Town is important, and I must not be late."

Jacoba had been invited by Innocent III to see "his" new hospital. The message from the Lateran indicated the Pope also had "important business" to discuss with her.

As the two women were settling into their conveyance, Jacoba suddenly stopped and snapped a different command.

"No, wait a moment, Sabina. Direct Maffeo to tell the fishermen the corpses will receive an appropriate burial. And order Nardo to respectfully place the babies into one of our empty traveling boxes." Jacoba pointed to the plain wooden containers under Sabina's seat.

"And here, give him my veil so he can wrap it around the bodies." She quickly removed the sumptuously-trimmed silk veil draped over her hair and handed it to her incredulous servant.

"But you're seeing the Pope." Sabina sounded panicked. "And we don't have another head covering for you."

"I think Lotar…" Jacoba caught herself before using the Pope's given name in front of her servant. "..I think the Pope will understand. We are not meeting him at the Lateran or St. Peter's or any other church for that matter, and today's circumstances *are* extenuating."

Sabina reached under her upholstered bench and took out the larger of two wooden boxes stored there. She thought her mistress had lost her mind but dared not question Jacobs's orders.

"What shall I have Maffeo and Nardo do with the box once it's full? It will, of course, smell extremely…uh…foul." Sabina had searched for a stronger word than foul but couldn't come up with one.

"Have them bring it to us and put it back under the seat. We will bring it to His Holiness. Oh…and tell Maffeo to also let the fishermen know we will make the Pope aware of their unspeakable catch."

Jacoba noticed the alarm on Sabina's face and tried to calm her.

"Sabina, I won't be banished from the Church for doing this. I promise."

The loyal servant lacked Jacoba's optimism but did as she was told.

ꙮ

As the entourage made its way to Saxon Town, Jacoba's thoughts focused on what she just witnessed. She assumed her presence on the bridge that particular morning at that exact time was no coincidence. *It was Divine Providence. God put me there for a reason. I'm meant to tell the Pope of this horrible thing. I pray His Holiness will know what to do.*

The horses clip-clopped through the narrow lanes relatively quickly, and soon Jacoba's mental deliberations were interrupted by Sabina.

"My Lady, we're here."

They had arrived at an entrance of the Pope's latest pet project: The Hospital of the Holy Spirit.

Years earlier, when Lotario dei Conti di Segni was studying theology in Paris, he encountered a devout man named Guy de Montpellier who had organized a group of lay brothers to care for the sick and the poor in Provence, France. He called the care-givers "Hospitallers of the Holy Ghost." In addition to tending the ill and injured, the Hospitallers took in orphans and saw to their education as well as their physical care.

When Lotario ascended to the papacy, one of his first actions was to officially establish Guy de Montpellier's brotherhood as a religious order that would answer directly to the pope – not to local church hierarchy. He summoned Guy de Montpellier to the Lateran and charged him with organizing similar services throughout Europe. Montpellier was to start in Rome by directing a new hospital that would be built in Saxon Town or Sassia as it was called. The Hospital of the Holy Spirit was to be the "mother" of the other institutions.

The new hospital under construction in Sassia was not far from St. Peter's. It was located on the site of the ancient Schola Saxonum, a place of hospitality that once catered to Saxon pilgrims. Originally named "Santa Maria" in honor of the Virgin Mary, the Schola had grown from a shelter set up in the 7th Century by a Saxon king into a rambling complex that included not only the shelter but also a church and various smaller buildings.

For four hundred years, the Schola provided physical and spiritual support to countless Anglo-Saxon pilgrims before it was gradually destroyed by fires and attacks by invaders including Saracens. The remnants of the Schola sat on land deeded to the King of England.

Although the ancient buildings were in ruin by the time Lotario dei Conti di Segni became pope, the endowments to support them were healthy. After convincing King John Lackland to donate the property, Innocent used the endowments and some of his personal wealth to finance the construction project.

The Pope invited the young, rich and influential Jacoba dei Settesoli to visit because he hoped she would play a role in its ongoing development as well as persuade her wealthy husband to add to its endowment.

The Pope knew the "Settesoli Frangipani" well and felt comfortable in their presence. He found them to be considerably more refined than their Frangipane relatives living in the palace at the Colosseum.

Lotario dei Conti di Segni himself was a well-mannered, articulate man who was extremely learned. Like Gratien, he had studied with theologians in Paris, although they were not there at the same time. Lotario was a decade older than Gratien.

The Pope knew Jacoba even better than Gratien. His nephew Stefano was Jacoba's cousin through marriage on the Normanni side of her family. Over the years, he and Jacoba sporadically saw each other at gatherings of their extended families. Lotario watched Jacoba grow from toddler to woman.

As a child, she impressed him with her intellect as well as her social skills. From little on, she was at ease with everyone – children, adults, even high-ranking clerics. He recalled Jacoba was never afraid to join in conversation with him or anyone else.

Quite fearless, she passionately articulated her thoughts extraordinarily well. Once Jacoba realized Lotario was a Cardinal, she began asking questions about the Faith and its practice. Her queries were often more challenging than those routinely posed by his subordinates or even the philosophical ones posed by his peers.

When Lotario ran into Jacoba at the Septizonium the year he was elected pope, he was surprised she was to be betrothed to a Frangipani. The Frangipani were somewhat beneath the Normanni in social status, and Lotario had hoped the "bright and beautiful little girl" would be matched to someone of her own nobility, intelligence and sophistication. However, once he came to know Gratien and saw how different he was from his Colosseum kin, Lotario changed his mind. Jacoba had married well.

A smile crossed the pontiff's face when an undersecretary announced Jacoba's arrival. The Pope's portable throne had been placed on a platform that was hastily constructed in a spacious room not far from the entrance to the hospital.

Jacoba appeared in the doorway, then walked slowly and respectfully toward the pope. His smile faded slightly when he noticed she wore no head covering. And he couldn't hide his bewilderment when a man unknown to Lotario entered behind her and stationed himself at the back of the room. The anonymous man held an unadorned wooden box. Lotario thought it resembled a common traveling container – not something a noble would present to a pope.

Jacoba approached the pontiff, knelt before him and respectfully kissed the large ring on his right hand.

"Your Holiness, Thank you for your invitation. How may I serve you and the Church?" She remained on her knees with her head bowed.

"Now that we've done with the formalities, please stand, Lady Jacoba. I appreciate you coming." In a quieter voice, the Pope added, "I would like the two of us to speak informally."

With a minimal wave of his hand, Lotario dismissed his guards as well as the undersecretary. He assumed Jacoba's man would also leave but he remained standing still holding the mysterious box.

"And who is this you've brought with you, Jacoba? I've told *my* guards to leave. Are you afraid of me that you did not also dismiss your man?

"No, of course not, Lo…tar…" She caught herself again. "Your Holiness!

"Maffeo is not here to protect me from you. He is carrying something I want to show you, but it can wait until you tell me how I may be of service to God and our Church."

The Pope stared at the box from afar. His curiosity was now aroused and wouldn't be sated until he ascertained its contents.

"Does it contain some of the sweet almond treats the Settesoli kitchen is famous for?"

"No, I left a box of those for you with the undersecretary when I arrived." Jacoba smiled, but her expression faded as she continued.

"Your Holiness, I'm afraid you will not be pleased by what the box contains."

Lotario could no longer stand the suspense. He sprang from his ornate chair and strode toward Maffeo until the smell from the box stopped him at 10 paces away. He recognized the stench of death and was momentarily shaken.

"Have you brought me a new relic?" His voice was muffled by the sleeve his arm instinctively raised to his face to protect his nose from the offending odor.

Jacoba shook her head back and forth.

"Woman, show it to me right now!" The Pope was adamant as well as abrupt. His red face indicated his curiosity had been overtaken by his impatience.

Jacoba nodded to Maffeo. He gently placed the box on the floor and removed its lid. Jacoba motioned to her guard to leave the room.

The Pope walked haltingly to the box. When he finally looked into the makeshift casket, he swallowed hard and turned to Jacoba.

"Jacoba, What is this?! Why have you brought me such a despicable gift? Why do you insult me so? What have I done to you?" His tone was restrained, but his anger was unmistakable.

"It's not a *gift* for you, Lotario." She forgot herself this time and didn't care.

"It's something I want you to see. It's something you *need* to see! *God* wants you to see this!"

"What are you talking about? I've seen hundreds of dead babies over the years, maybe thousands.

"Do you have any idea how many I've prayed over? How many families I've comforted? You know countless babies die along with their mothers in childbirth. And even the ones who make it often don't last through two moons." The Pope was fuming now.

"Your Holiness, I have no doubt you've seen many dead babies. But how many have you seen that have been murdered…smothered after their first cry of life then tossed into the Tiber…or worse – thrown living and breathing into a watery grave?"

"What are you talking about, Jacoba?"

With tears in her eyes, Jacoba relayed in great detail what she observed at the river's edge and what the fishermen said.

"Why have I not known of this before now?"

"The Tiber is a distance from the Lateran. How could these humble men transport such appalling catch through Rome's streets without arousing suspicion? They do not know you as I do. They were afraid to tell anyone. They say it has been happening more than ever.

"They say these babies are from the prostitutes here in Sassia. From the women who 'accommodate' Rome's pilgrims. They say *you* invite this problem by encouraging pilgrimages."

Pope Innocent – his nose now accustomed to the stench – had already lowered his arm and listened attentively but without expression to Jacoba. When she was finished, he motioned to her to go with him back to the other end of the room.

"This is sad but not shocking to you, is it, Jacoba?" The question was rhetorical. He wasn't looking for her to answer. As the two walked, the Pope descended into thought. He rubbed his chin with his thumb and forefinger. His eyes focused on the floor, and he spoke softly as if he were oblivious to Jacoba's presence.

"Sassia has always had women who sold themselves. Their sinful behavior causes disease and degradation. It's their own decision. They have misused their free will and suffer the consequences." The Pope shook his head in disgust as he stepped up to his papal chair.

Once seated, he looked intently at Jacoba who was now standing in front of him.

"What exactly do you think I should do? This is a place for the sick and the poor." The Pope made a grand flourish with his hand. "We are not here to reform the brothels of Rome."

"Your Holiness, the sins of the mothers concern me less than the deaths of the babies. How many hundreds of these innocents are at the bottom of the river? Surely you can do something…especially now that you have this grand building. Can you not spare a corner for unwanted babies?"

"Let me think on this. Let me pray on it. This isn't what I expected us to discuss today. I wanted to ask you to give some of your time to our new venture here…and to ask Gratien for monetary support."

The Pope chuckled slightly as he added, "And just like when you were a little girl, you challenge me."

"Your Holiness, I meant no disrespect."

"I know that."

"And when Your Holiness decides his new hospital will welcome unwanted newborns and see to their needs, I will enthusiastically accept your invitation to serve here. And I'm confident my husband will also be willing to provide financial support."

The Pope shook his head, smiled at Jacoba and blessed her. "Be on your way, Jacoba. You've had quite a day. And you've given me quite a day, too."

ഇഗ

That night as the Pope slept in his comfortable bed in the Lateran Palace, he had a discomforting dream. In it, he stood at the bank of the Tiber and saw fisherman after fisherman hauling in their day's catch. In every net, there were no fish; only the corpses of dead infants.

The following morning, the Pope told Guy de Montpellier that besides caring for the sick and the destitute, Rome's new hospital must also be a refuge for unwanted newborns.

ഇഗ

To further discourage infanticide, the Pope had a "Ruota degli Esposti" built into an exterior wall of the Hospital of the Holy Spirit. This "Wheel of the Exposed" was a device that allowed a mother to abandon her baby in complete anonymity. It had been used successfully in France for more than a decade. Jacoba suggested it after learning of a similar device from one of her French relatives, and Guy de Montpellier had seen one in action.

The baby hatch consisted of a large wooden disc divided into two parts by a wooden panel. One side of the wheel faced the street. The other faced the hospital's interior.

After the mother placed her infant on the street side of the disc, she would knock on the panel or ring a bell to alert the Hospitallers of the new arrival. They would spin the disc until the infant was safely within the building. Sometimes, a mother would include a coin, note, or small memento to be kept as identification should she return one day to claim the child.

After being fed by a wet nurse, the baby would be given a tattoo of the Hospitallers' cross on the sole of the left foot. Using a rose thorn to indelibly ink the mixture of red ochre, ash and honey on the infant's skin, the Hospitallers marked the baby as a member the hospital's family. The child would receive not only physical care but also education and preparation for him or her to become a productive Roman citizen.

Jacoba volunteered in the new hospital during the spring of 1203 and helped recruit others to serve. She wrote to one of her cousins in France that it was the most rewarding experience of her life.

Chapter XII
Blood and Thunder
Late Autumn 1203 – Rome

Not long after the birth of their son, Jacoba became pregnant with their second child. Jacob and Giovanna were born a little more than a year apart.

Gratien was euphoric. He loved being a father, and he loved being near his wife. While Gratien was still obligated to oversee the family's many properties scattered across the region, he tried to spend as much time as he could with Jacoba and their children.

He would take the family to Trastevere every week or two to visit Jacoba's parents. When Maria and Vincentius were in the presence of their grandchildren, they totally ignored Jacoba and Gratien. So, the two would slip away for an hour or so to visit a cloister on the family's estate where the birdsong seemed more divine than earthly. Gratien would steal kisses from Jacoba. However, because the garden was adjacent to a small chapel, Jacoba would not let him make love to her there. “I think we’re on holy ground, Gratien. We’d better not,” she would say. He would laugh and in mock dejection say, “I suppose I can wait until we get home.”

The honeymoon, unfortunately, didn’t last as long as the couple would have wished. Old war wounds took their toll on the health of Gratien’s father, and the responsibilities of managing the family’s holdings fell to Gratien – the only male heir.

Gratien struggled tirelessly to handle the accounts for the family’s many properties while Jacoba would sit quietly near him doing needlework. She could see by his continuously furrowed brow that Gratien didn’t particularly relish working with numbers. She, on the other hand, loved them. Her tutors told her she wasn’t like other little girls because she had a special aptitude for arithmetic. She was so quick and accurate with numbers that by the time she was 11 years old, her father had begun asking her to assist with tasks involving the Normanni family’s financial holdings.

She thought perhaps Gratien might welcome some help. So, one afternoon when her husband seemed especially frustrated with his accounting responsibilities, she quietly approached Gratien from behind and gently rubbed his shoulders. After a few moments, she leaned over him and in a soft voice asked if she could be of some assistance.

“Only if you can do arithmetic!” he snapped in an uncharacteristically abrupt tone. “Jacoba, I’m sorry. It’s nice that you want to help me, but this isn’t anything a woman can do, especially someone so young as you!”

Jacoba stepped back folded her arms and glared at Gratien. She retorted: "I didn't go to an advanced school in Paris like you did, but I had good tutors who taught me well, including arithmetic! They told me I wasn't like most other little girls because I actually *liked* numbers. And you know what? I still like them!

"There are a few things you don't know about me, Lord Gratien Frangipane, and this happens to be one of them. You also probably don't know that I not only helped my mother keep the household accounts for the palace but I also worked on accounts related to my father's massive holdings." There was a pause. Then she added, "And I did a great job!"

"Have at it, then! Try to make sense of all this…and make it add up!" In frustration with the ledgers and his wife, Gratien stood up and made an overly grand gesture toward a huge pile of papers indicating Jacoba should take his place at the work table. She gave him a little scowl, then sat down and got to work. He initially stood nearby, watching her and waiting for her to quickly give up in frustration. However, she immediately dug into the pile of notes and pieces of paper and began jotting down numbers.

Gratien noticed she was concentrating with great intensity, but she didn't give any hint that she was ready to give up. There was no expression of aggravation on her face nor in her body language; so, he sat on a chair and watched. She occasionally had a question for him about which account was associated with which palace or village…or why was a particular number attributed to a particular account. Other than that, she kept her face buried in the numbers.

Two hours later, she told him to please check everything just to make sure she had the correct figures in the correct places. She said there was no need to check the accuracy of her arithmetic since she had already done that, and it was perfect.

He smiled at her smugly as he began to review her work which he assumed would be laden with mistakes. His expression, however, gradually transformed into one of astonishment as he realized his young wife accomplished in two hours what normally took him two days to do.

“Giacomina, I don’t believe it! How did you do it?” Gratien was astounded.

“God gave each of us different talents. I can’t use a bow or throw a spear, but I can work with numbers. And truly, Gratien, I’d rather be working on the family accounts than stitching a piece of cloth. So, will you let me help you? It would make *me* happy!” Jacoba’s response sounded like a heartfelt plea.

Gratien smiled. “Anything to make you happy!” He neglected to tell Jacoba that her willingness to share this ‘burden of numbers’ made *him* even happier.

ꕥ

If the first few years of their marriage seemed like heaven to Jacoba and Gratien, the next several could best be described as hell. Jacoba and Gratien remained in love, but Rome itself was threatening their happiness. The probability of civil war now loomed over the abitato, so the couple had fewer opportunities to enjoy pursuits in Rome outside the palace.

Gratien was grateful that no "serious" fighting had yet broken out near the Septizonium since significant issues in his outlying fiefs needed immediate attention. He hated leaving his wife and family in Rome at this point but had no choice. With two young children in tow, Jacoba could no longer travel with him as she had their first year together.

When he left Rome, Gratien told Jacoba he would return after the full moon. However, he concluded his business a full week earlier and raced back to Rome alone on horseback. Gratien constantly worried about the safety of his family. Although he had posted guards throughout the palace and left more than a dozen additional soldiers with the family, he believed that he alone could provide the best protection for Jacoba and the children.

He had been away for more than three weeks and was thankful today to be returning to Rome early. He was comforted knowing his loving wife and their children would be there. He missed Jacoba more than he cared to admit, and he cherished his son and daughter.

In addition to the turmoil in various sections of Rome, the Septizonium itself was experiencing its own discord after the Frangipani had three months earlier welcomed some distant relatives from the north for an unspecified length of stay. The two families hadn't seen each other for many years, so the visitors were initially made to feel very much at home in the sprawling palace.

One of his most distant cousins tried her best to ingratiate herself with Gratien in particular. Occasionally she did manage to catch his attention. Antonia was a charming widow the same age as Gratien. She wasn't tall and graceful like Jacoba. She was rather short and sturdy with dark skin and dark eyes. However, she had an effervescence that seemed to spring up whenever a man walked into the room.

Gratien's family had made several visits to Antonia's family's estate when he was a child, and he vaguely recalled having had a boyhood crush on her. Over the past couple months, he and Antonia occasionally reminisced about the "old days" and the activities in which their families shared.

Antonia flirted coyly with Gratien whenever the opportunity presented itself. And she made those opportunities happen as often as she could by inserting herself into circumstances where she surmised Gratien would be present. With a smile and a look, a laugh and a wink his way, or a slight touch of his arm or his cheek, Antonia tried to hint to him in non-verbal ways that she wanted their renewed relationship to develop into an amorous one. Gratien liked her but only thought of her as that cute chubby girl he kissed once when he was eight years old.

Jacoba had noticed Antonia's flirtations and was greatly disturbed. She wasn't convinced that Gratien was forceful enough in fending off the woman's romantic gestures. Then Jacoba started wondering whether perhaps there were other women making similar advances when her good-looking, wealthy and powerful husband visited his various estates without her.

Jacoba felt sad and unusually helpless since she had no idea how to handle the situation. To make things worse, Antonia derided Jacoba to her face whenever Gratien wasn't present. When no one else was within earshot of them, Antonia would tell Jacoba about how wonderful Gratien's kisses were and that he loved Antonia long before Jacoba was even born.

The afternoon that Gratien arrived back in Rome, Antonia overheard one of the stewards telling a servant that the master just arrived, was currently in the stable, and would want to immediately bathe in his favorite small pool. She seized the opportunity to be alone with him before anyone else, rushing to the entryway closest to the stables. She was the first of the "family" to greet him. "Welcome home, my lordship," she said with a honeyed voice. "We have missed you so much," she gushed as she stood in front of him, blocking his way. Then she looked into his eyes, stood on her tiptoes and tried to kiss his lips. Gratien instinctively turned his dusty cheek to her, quickly pushed her aside and said rather flatly, "It's good to see you, too, Antonia. Now, I want to find my wife."

"You may not be happy with what you find, my lordship," Antonia said. Now there was sharpness to her voice, "Your wife is in her bed chamber with a young man!" Gratien stopped dead in his tracks and turned around, "What did you say?"

"I'm just telling you that you are rejecting me as your lover because you take the moral high ground yet you put up with your wife's infidelity," Antonia responded smugly.

Gratien turned away from her without a word. The thought of his wife in another man's arms let alone sharing a bed wounded him more painfully than any lance, blade or arrow ever did. He walked slowly and purposefully with his head held high to the nearest stairway that would take him to their chambers. Once out of the Antonia's sight, he took the steps two at a time and couldn't get up them fast enough.

By the time he reached the top of the long flight, he had convinced himself that Jacoba's lover must be Francis. He thought to himself that perhaps it's the reason she has not spoken of Francis since the day of the archery lesson.

Gratien took long, deliberate strides down the corridor to Jacoba's room, not exactly sure of what he would do once he got there. Her door was slightly ajar, and he could hear a man's voice. However, it was muted by the door's thick wood and its iron fastenings; so, Gratien was only able to pick up words here and there. He decided to listen for a few moments before storming in. He recognized Jacoba's voice. Even without catching every word, he could tell that she was excited and happy. Gratien heard the words "wonderful" and "thank you so much." He heard the man say something about her "beauty" and that he would return within three days. Gratien's heart sank. He couldn't face them at the moment because he wasn't sure if he would kill them or if he would break down and cry – something he hadn't done since the birth of Jacob.

He motioned to two guards at one end of the long corridor. They were at his side in an instant. He looked at one of the soldiers and said, "A young man will come out of that room. I want you to detain him and take him to the red room and hold him under guard there until I give you further orders." Gratien quickly added, "I don't think he will resist, but if he should pull a weapon, kill him." Gratien then told the other guard to let him know as soon as the young man had been restrained. He would be waiting in his chamber.

Within five minutes, there was a knock on Gratien's door, and the guard told him the man was now in custody. The thoughts that sped through Gratien's brain in those few moments ranged from "*perhaps I should not even bring this up so we can go on as we were*" to *"I myself will take on a lover to exact revenge for this"* to *"how could she do this to me, I thought she truly loved me."*

As it turned out, Gratien confidently walked into Jacoba's room and stood there unsmiling. The moment she saw him, she beamed and ran to him. She threw her arms around his neck and pulled him to her, and started to kiss his lips as vigorously as always after he returned from anywhere. But she suddenly stopped when she noticed his lips were not welcoming hers, and Gratien was now removing her arms from around his neck in a deliberately mechanical way.

"What's wrong, Gratien? Why are you so cold to me?" she choked out the words. She was confused, and tears were welling in her eyes."

"You had a man here in your bed chamber?" he asked in a dismal tone as he tried to calm down the feelings churning inside him. Before she had a chance to respond, he added, "I'm assuming he was '*your*' Francis!" She had never seen Gratien's eyes look at her the way they did at that moment. She couldn't tell whether they were full of fury or disappointment or a combination of both.

"Yes. Of course, there was a man here. You just missed him by a few moments. But it wasn't, Francis. I told you, Gratien, I've not seen Francis or heard from him since before our betrothal, since before I ever met you. The man who was here is named Giunta." Then, she added with a sigh of exasperation. "Your mother told you about everything, didn't she?"

It took a moment for Jacoba's words to sink into Gratien's brain. He initially thought to himself, *"Not Francis, not Francis, maybe this isn't as bad as it could be."* Then he realized it might be even worse and asked, "What on earth does my mother have to do with this?"

"She brought Giunta to me, Gratien! How could I have ever found him myself? I've never before had any reason to search for someone with his skills; so, I went to your mother. She's always been so kind to me." Jacoba's words were said so matter-of-factly that they pained Gratien even more. He couldn't believe the only other woman he loved – his own mother – would assist in this betrayal. He turned away from Jacoba, trying to think of what he should say or do next. This was an ambush in which his martial training was of no use.

Just then, there was a slight rap on the door, and Gratien's mother entered the room while asking Jacoba if Giunta had left. She told Jacoba she was sorry she had to take leave of them for a little while, but there was an issue that needed her immediate attention. When she noticed her son glowering in the far end of the room, she said even more cheerily than usual, "Gratien, you're home! Did you get to meet Giunta?"

Then looking back at Jacoba, Gratien's mother said, "You decided not to keep it a secret then?"

"I thought *you* told him!" Jacoba responded.

"No, of course I wouldn't tell him because I thought you wanted it to be a surprise." Jacoba's mother looked perplexed.

Gratien was totally baffled and now growing irate, "Tell me what?! That Jacoba has taken a lover and that you helped find him for her, Mother! You make it sound as if I should be pleased that I've been betrayed by the both of you!" There was disgust as well as frustration in his voice.

Although they tried to hold back their amusement, Jacoba and Gratien's mother looked at each other and smiled broadly. Gratien's mother spoke first. Although she was trying to hold back outright laughter, her tone toward him was somewhat stern, "You mean you thought your wife took a lover and that I helped her find this lover? After nearly four years of marriage and two beautiful children, I would think you would have more sense, my son! I've never seen your wife acknowledge any other man's glances let alone initiate a flirtation. I'm not sure I can say the same about you especially the past several months. Who told you Jacoba took a lover?....No, wait! I think I can guess. Was it Antonia?"

Gratien nodded "yes" in a sheepish way.

"That woman has been trouble since the moment she arrived. Her whole family has been a nuisance. They were the reason I wasn't here when you arrived, Gratien. The most recent issue with which I had to deal involved one of our visitors and your sister. Antonia and her family have generally been unkind to our servants, and I understand that Antonia has also said cruel things to your wife whenever you weren't present," Gratien's mother said, adding that it was time for their guests to go.

Gratien walked toward his wife and said, "I'll ask them to leave, Mother."

"No, Gratien!" Gratien's mother said firmly. "I'm going right now to *tell* them they *must* leave before tomorrow's sunset." She then added, "I think you need to clean yourself up. You're dusty from the road, and you smell like your horse. I'll tell one of the servants to start heating one of the small bathing pools for you. Right now, you need to stay here and apologize to your wife. Perhaps if you ask her nicely, she will help wash you while she tells you about her *'trysts'* with Giunta." Gratien's mother smiled and shook her head chuckling to herself as she left the room.

Gratien thought of something and called after her, "Mother, please tell the guards at the end of the hall to get word to the Red Room that I order them to release their detainee."

The old woman continued shaking her head while saying, "Gratien, Gratien, Gratien" as she walked down the long corridor.

Gratien turned to his wife and was speechless. When he opened his mouth to begin his apology, she put her finger to his lips to silence him.

She looked into his eyes and spoke softly, "When I saw the way you sometimes looked at Antonia and reminisced with her and laughed, I worried that I would lose you – if not to her, then to another. You've been apart from me so often lately, I was beside myself.

"Your mother saw my distress, and she came to me with the idea that an artist could do a small mosaic or a painting of my face that you could carry with you. She told me that you would like that and would look at it often. But I think she really thought it might help *me* feel better.

"She told me she knew of a young man from Pisa who was painting a crucifix for one of the cardinals here in Rome, and with my permission she would ask him if he'd like to earn a bit of extra money. She thought it would make a nice token for me to give you on the anniversary of our betrothal. She suggested it should be a surprise. Neither of us told anyone. She brought Giunta to my room twice to do sketches, and except for today she stayed with us the whole time and watched him work. Today, he brought the little painting he created. He was very pleased with his work, and so was I. He plans to come back here again, Gratien, within the next few days to drop off a small carrying box in which you can keep the painting."

Gratien was silent and just looked at her.

"Do you want to see it?" Jacoba asked, not quite sure whether her husband was truly over his snit.

"Yes, Giacomina…very much so," Gratien said softly.

She walked to the little table nearest her bed and brought the small piece of art to Gratien.

"Do you like it? Or is this something you really do not want?" Jacoba's voice hinted of uncertainty.

He looked at the picture. Then he looked at his wife. "It does not do your beauty justice, my love, but I *will* treasure it and keep it with me. Thank you." He put his arms around her, apologized for being dusty and smelling like his horse and then kissed her in the passionate way to which she'd been accustomed. "Just so you know. . . I've never needed anything to remind me of you because you are in my thoughts when I awaken in the morning, when I fall asleep at night, and almost all day long."

Gratien continued, "You said you sometimes noticed my eyes look upon other women. I think that's natural for men. I never think about it twice anymore because my glimpses of an attractive woman no longer stir anything sinful in my soul. What you don't see, my Giacomina, is what's *in my heart* when my eyes happen upon women. You've misinterpreted my notice of them with a desire for them.

"You do know I've seen countless men more than glance at *you*, Jacoba, and I could tell their gazes reflected lust in their hearts. But you never stared back, and I loved you even more for that."

The couple looked at each other wordlessly for a few moments. Then, as they were about to kiss, there was a loud knock on the door. "Master, the pool is ready for your bath," boomed the voice of Gratien's servant from the hall.

Gratien looked at Jacoba. "Will you join me, my ladyship?"

She responded with a smile, intertwined the long delicate fingers of her left hand into the strong brawny fingers of his right hand and pulled him toward the door. They didn't realize this would be the last relaxing moment they would share for some time to come.

Chapter XIII
City of Blood
Winter, 1204 – Rome

The struggle for control of Rome had been simmering for several years and was now on the verge of boiling over. Hostilities among several of Rome's dominant families and the newly installed "Conti Pope" began shortly after Innocent III's election in January of 1198, the year in which Jacoba and Gratien were betrothed.

The various branches of the Frangipane Family, including Gratien's, had often defended the supreme authority of the papacy. However, most of the Frangipani were less concerned about guarding the Pope's spiritual leadership than advancing his temporal power and influence – especially regarding governance of Rome. Besides putting their names and weapons behind the Church, some Frangipani even gave their lives protecting pontiffs from those who preferred to be aligned with kings or emperors.

They were especially protective of popes whose judgments benefitted the Frangipani in material ways.

On the day Pope Celestine III died, Church leaders gathered in the Septizonium to elect a new head. It was not surprising they chose to meet in this particular Frangipane palace since it provided safety as well as comfort. The Septizonium Frangipani had always opened their doors to men of the cloth – be they Church hierarchy or lesser clerics. More important, Gratien's family was less politically involved and more spiritually minded than other Frangipani, namely the branch of the family that called the Colosseum home.

Within hours of Celestine's death, the cardinals voted to make Giovanni dei Salerno pope. After the Benedictine cardinal promptly declined the "promotion," the cardinals elected 38-year-old Lotario dei Conti di Segni. Besides being selected Vicar of Christ in the very hall where Jacoba and Gratien later celebrated their betrothal, the young and rather handsome new pope also happened to be the uncle of Jacoba's first cousin – dei Normanni di Conti.

None of these ties mattered to other branches of the Frangipane Family. Whenever they perceived a threat to their power or fortune, they did not hesitate to act. So, when the family of the new pope flexed a bit of muscle by building a tower directly across from the Colosseum – the palatial home of Cencio Frangipane's clan – it was taken as a declaration of war.

The feuds among the powerful families of Rome erupted into all-out combat at the start of 1203. Terror and treachery continued on and off throughout that year and for the two years that followed.

While some branches of the Frangipane clan had temporarily switched allegiance from the Pope to King Henry, Gratien's father continued to support the Pope. This meant the Septizonium Frangipani initially avoided being drawn into Rome's conflict. The fact that Jacoba's cousin was the Pope's nephew may have also played a role in postponing the involvement of the Septizonium Frangipani. However, as various other Roman families got involved in the escalating conflicts, bloody street battles eventually found their way to the Septizonium.

Fortunately, two weeks before his family's palace came under attack, Gratien had wisely taken the children to stay with Jacoba's parents in Trastevere. At that time, he pleaded with Jacoba to go with them, but she said her place was with him and refused to leave. He argued that unlike his sister and mother, Jacoba wasn't born to fight and would be more of a hindrance than a help. "You're no Aldruda!" Gratien stated firmly. There was never any woman in the entire family quite like Gratien's warrior-grandmother. The late Aldruda genuinely relished physical combat. At the first hint of physical conflict involving any branch of the Frangipani clan, Aldruda immediately showed up to join in the fight.

Gratien's mother overheard Gratien's conversation with Jacoba and stepped in. She told her son rather sternly that Jacoba should remain in the Septizonium if she wanted to, "We will need her help to care for the wounded… and prepare for burial the bodies of those who will die."

Neither Gratien nor Jacoba said anything. Looking at Jacoba, Gratien's mother added, "It is decided then. You and your handmaid will work closely with Marco and Matteo. They will instruct you in caring for the wounded."

Marco, a distinguished man about 40 years old, was a healer from Salerno – a place noted for producing people who excelled in the healing arts. Matteo, his 22-year-old assistant who was also from Salerno, already had a good reputation for bone-setting skills as well as knowledge of herbs and healing potions. Gratien's mother had sought out the two healers a few years earlier to treat her husband Rainerio. She retained them ever since to not only meet the day-to-day medical needs of her huge household but also because she correctly anticipated that fighting in other areas of the abitato would eventually make its way to the Septizonium.

ꟸꟷ

Attacks on the palace of Gratien's family began in the early months of 1204. They were intermittent but deadly. The Pope himself had been assaulted by a mob the day after Easter of 1203. He escaped to France where he lived for several months until Rome cooled down. His Italian relatives, however, chose not to follow him but came in force to Rome to retaliate against the Orsini and Frangipani even though neither family had been directly involved in the Easter Monday fracas.

Within days of the attack on Pope Innocent, the Conti attacked the Colosseum. The street fighting there went on for many moons before it expanded to include the Settesoli branch of the powerful family. Three war towers went up across from the Septizonium. Under cover of night, Conti knights and less distinguished Conti fighters streamed into the strange "keeps" and made known they were "at the ready" although they initially merely kept watch on the Septizonium. Gratien's own armed forces guarded their family's palace and made sure the Conti fighters could see they, too, were at the ready.

Despite the many eyes watching each other, no one knew which side shot the first arrow. No one even knew whether it was an arrow that started the deadly skirmish; it may have been a spear or a rock. The hostilities intensified quickly and moved into the street between the makeshift towers and the Septizonium. While the initial clash was brief, it was bloody with both sides incurring numerous casualties and several deaths.

Jacoba never glimpsed the ferocious fighting at street level. She saw only its dreadful aftermath. Her post was in an immense room in the lowest level of the Septizonium, near the palace's two small bathing pools. Under Marco's direction, cots had been placed in the room weeks before in anticipation of probable casualties. Additional mattresses of straw were stacked in a corner should those casualties number more than anticipated.

Two large work tables were at the opposite end of the room. One was reserved for Marco, who was suturing flesh and muscle wounds, the results of arrows and spears. The other was where Matteo was setting the broken bones of men who had been hit with large rocks.

When Marco learned one of Jacoba's interests was needlework, he told her that she was to assist him. Sabina would help Matteo. The healer told the two women they would also need to quickly acquaint themselves with healing herbs as well as how to make potions and poultices. Jacoba was to supervise the work of several female servants assigned to work in the makeshift "ospedale." Four male servants served as the transport team, moving casualties and corpses.

The improvised pharmacy of this interim hospital was a room at the end of the long corridor. The place also served as the palace's temporary mortuary. In addition to shelves filled with jars containing crushed dried herbs and bottles of various liquid concoctions, the cavernous room included four large tables. One was for preparing potions and poultices. The other three were for preparing cadavers for burial. An elderly but physically robust and spiritually pious household servant named Felice was the overseer of this important and solemn task. Jacoba, Sabina and even Marco and Matteo as well as the servants were expected to assist her when they weren't tending to the living.

Jacoba was shaken to her very core when the first casualty was set down on Marco's work table. Since she had witnessed the death of a servant girl at her uncle's house many years earlier, Jacoba thought she was prepared to deal with the wounds of war. She was wrong.

The victim who lay in front of her was drenched in blood. Jacoba could not make out the man's face because a mask of congealed blood concealed much of it. There was a gash on his forehead. An arrow was lodged in his left shoulder. The right side of his body had been slashed by a sword in three places from arm to leg. Jacoba was in mild shock and ready to throw up. She swallowed her vomit and took a deep breath while saying a very quick prayer: "God help him. God help me."

Marco swiftly examined the patient, asked him a few questions and said calmly, "You're a lucky fellow. I think we can fix you up." Jacoba saw the whites of the man's eyes when they opened momentarily upon hearing the healer's voice. He quickly closed them since fresh blood was still trickling down from his forehead wound.

"Jacoba, help me clean the blood so we can stitch him up. It looks like mostly flesh wounds," Marco gave the order while examining the arrow that had gone through the man's shoulder. "Very good! The tip has already come out the other side."

Jacoba gently washed the blood from the man's eyes and face. She now recognized him as one of the squires. She called him by name and told him as calmly and confidently as she could that she would help care for him. He said something like, "My lady, how good of you" and then closed his eyes once more.

She helped Marco remove the squire's blood-drenched clothes and continued cleaning the blood from his limbs as Marco began stitching the gash on his head. "Come here, Jacoba, see how I do this," the healer said and quickly added, "I want you to do the other flesh wounds – the ones on his leg and arm – while I stitch his side and figure out how best to deal with his arrow wound." They worked simultaneously stitching the wounds. When that was done, it was time to tackle the arrow wound.

Had the tip of the arrow lodged in the squire's shoulder, the young man's chances of surviving would have narrowed drastically. Marco most likely would have put an ointment of honey in the wound and tried to remove it using a knife. Otherwise, he would have waited a week or so for the area to become infected in order to more easily find and dig out the little projectile. In either case, the patient's chances of survival would have been grim.

Fortunately, a small part of the arrow's shaft was the only thing lodged in the knight-to-be's shoulder. "Jacoba, please come over here and hold his hand while I pull this out," Marco was matter of fact in his tone, adding, "I have to save the opium-hemlock potion for amputations; so, your smile and soft hand will have to help ease this fellow's pain."

Marco turned the patient on his side so he could better negotiate the piece of wood from the exit wound. The doctor eased a strong wooden dowel covered by a bit of padded cloth into the young man's mouth. "This will hurt, young man, but only for a moment. If you bite down on this and look at her ladyship, the time will go faster."

The squire's eyes shot open the moment the doctor began yanking on the arrow shaft. Jacoba could see the agony not only in the young man's eyes but also in the way he clenched his teeth on the "biting stick" and tightened the grip on her hand. She lightly brushed his forehead with her free hand hoping to distract him.

It took Marco three minutes to remove the shaft – an eternity for the patient and Jacoba. Marco then proceeded to cauterize the wound, which caused the young man to faint. Jacoba thought the young man was dead, but Marco reassured her the squire would come around. "Now please have one of the servants carry him to a cot. I can do no more for him right now, and we'll need this table shortly for another."

The doctor was correct on both counts. The squire did come around, and there were three more casualties to "stitch up." Fortunately, there were no more arrow wounds.

The body of the first fatality was brought directly to the makeshift mortuary. When Felice saw how busy Jacoba was with the living, she whispered in her ear to come to the other room when she was finished.

Jacoba worked side-by-side with Marco late into the evening. Although totally exhausted, she went to the mortuary out of curiosity as well as duty. The sight of the corpse on the work table triggered her memory of Prassede's father and how as an eight-year-old she helped with his surreptitious burial.

Jacoba immediately recognized the lifeless body as that of a knight named Philip. He was in his mid-thirties and came from France. Jacoba was overwhelmed with sadness and wanted to cry. Of noble birth but not heir to the family estate, Philip had been in Gratien's service for several years and always fought bravely. The knight had suffered a relatively small but fatal head wound.

Felice explained to Jacoba that she had hoped to show her how to appropriately attend to a corpse. However, since it was getting quite late, Felice went ahead with her solemn task. "As you can see, I washed Philip's corpse with a solution of wine and a little honey while praying for his soul," Felice said, quickly adding that in other circumstances she would have removed the organs and washed the body inside and out with Aqua Vitae – a distilled concoction of grape syrup, rose water and various spices. "If he was going to be buried here, I would have cut him deeply here, here, here, here, and here," she said while pointing to his underarms, arms, groin, buttocks and legs. Felice continued, "Then, I would have put in some cloth I've been soaking in the Aqua Vitae along with some of the good-smelling herbs and spices." Felice nodded her head toward a shelf on the wall where the "aromatics" were stored.

"After that, I would have covered him with linen and wound some cerecloth around his body to keep out the air." Felice was talking as she walked to a shelf that held the winding fabric that had been dipped in wax. "Jacoba, here's where we keep the cerecloth in case you're looking for it."

"Normally, I'd have another servant put him in a wooden coffin, and we'd be ready for his funeral. However, Philip's squire told me his master wanted to be buried in France near his family. So, all I had to do was wash the body and pray for his soul. The monks of St. Gregory will do the rest," Felice said solemnly.

Just then, two Frangipane servants – Bindo and Duccio – appeared in the doorway and announced in a jovial way that they were ready to take old-Philip-the-knight to the monastery. With a scolding tone of voice, Felice reminded the young men to show respect for the fallen warrior. The duo simultaneously cast their eyes to the floor, muttered they were sorry, and soberly moved the cadaver to the stretcher they brought with them.

After they left with the corpse, Jacoba asked Felice about what more the monks would do. Felice answered her soberly with one word: "Excarnation." Felice could tell from Jacoba's face the young woman had no idea what it meant and added. "You know, prepare the remains 'German style.'" Jacoba now looked totally bewildered, so Felice told her to sit down and she would explain the process.

"You do know it would be very expensive as well as unpleasant and unsanitary to transport Knight Philip's body all the way to France if it wasn't prepared for the trip in a special way, don't you?" Felice continued in a matter-of-fact tone, "So, the holy monks will remove his organs and probably bury them on site. In some places, they burn them, but I'm quite sure the St. Gregory monks usually bury them.

"Then they will chop off his arms and legs as well as his head and boil the various parts in a vat of wine. They will do this solemnly and recite many prayers. Once cleansed of flesh and muscle, the bones will be dried, wrapped in linen or animal hide, and placed in an appropriate box for the long trip home."

For the second time that day, Jacoba thought she would vomit. Despite her Assisi experience with Prassede's father, she didn't realize how sheltered she had been from death and its aftermath. Felice saw that Jacoba's face had grown pale and suggested her ladyship get some rest. "I fear tomorrow will be no better than today. If you do not want to …" Felice was going to tell Jacoba she didn't have to return to the mortuary, but Jacoba cut her off in mid-sentence. "Thank you, Felice. I'll see you in the morning," Jacoba said after taking a deep breath and steeling her nerves. She took another deep breath and looked with an earnest expression at the old woman: "I really do appreciate what you do. I think not everyone could do it, but I think it is God's work…and I'm thankful you are willing to teach me. Good night, Felice."

Jacoba began crying as she walked slowly to Gratien's bed chamber. She was sitting on the bed sobbing and staring at nothing when he walked in a few minutes later.

"I'm sorry, Giacomina," he said softly as he sat on the bed next to her. He put his right arm around her and pulled her close. "I never wanted you to go through this." His left hand gently brushed her hair away from her face, and he kissed her softly on the forehead. "Marco told me you did great work today," Gratien said, knowing his words alone would probably not comfort her. He remembered the first time he himself was exposed to the carnage and death of combat. He vomited twice in the combat zone and drank himself into oblivion as soon as the battle was over.

"I just never knew it would be like this, Gratien, and I'm just on the fringes of it. I'm only seeing the dreadful results not the true horror of your combat." Jacoba said quietly. She continued, "Before today, the worst violence I had ever glimpsed was several years before we were betrothed. It was right before Lent was to start. I was with my parents. We were returning home from a visit to a cousin, and the road took us through the area below Mount Testaccio.

"Even before we saw the crowd, we heard people gleefully shouting 'Al porco' over and over again. It was the sound of great merriment. However, as our cart drew nearer to the gathering, my father told my mother and me to close our eyes…that this was not a sight for us. I pretended to obey and put my hands over my face. But peering through my fingers, I saw ugliness I'd never before encountered. Men and women were covered in blood and wielding knives and axes. They were hacking away at live pigs! Then, after waving around the bloody pieces they had chopped off, they would hand them to their children who would, no doubt, take them home.

"When I heard my father say 'Oh, no!,' I took my hands away from my eyes. All of us looked up at a cart full of living swine – their legs lashed together – tearing down the steep slope of Mount Testaccio. In no time, the rickety wooden vehicle crashed at the bottom of the hill 'freeing' all the animals to their appalling fate. Just as another chopping frenzy was starting, our cart was beyond the gathering. However, we could still hear the people shouting and making merry.

I asked my father why they did this. All he could say was that it was a very old custom, and they probably needed the meat.

She remained silent for a moment to catch her breath, then wiped away her tears with the back of her fingers. Jacoba looked at her husband with a sadness in her eyes that he had never seen. Then she continued: "…and now they will dismember Philip."

Jacoba started sobbing all over again. Even the closeness of her husband could not bring her solace. He wisely let her cry for a few moments more.

Then she spoke between sobs, "Gratien, I think what I fear most is seeing you on one of those tables. Why must there be such violence? What is gained? And I'm of no help really to you or anyone else!"

Gratien was silent for several minutes. "God put us here for some reason. Even though we cannot understand His purpose, we must be brave and trust in Him. I have no answer other than that, my love.

"As for the violence, all we can do is try to bring peace to the moment and the circumstances in which we find ourselves. Marco told me that while you have notable skill with the needle, it was your presence and your touch that brought great comfort today to the wounded. He says you were born to be a healer."

Startled by Gratien's last sentence, Jacoba looked up at him and said, "I felt as if I did nothing to help anyone!"

"Sometimes it takes another to notice strengths we can't see in ourselves," Gratien responded. Then, trying to lighten the moment, he added, "Of course, you were quick to point out to me your other strengths in arithmetic and childbirth."

Jacoba gave him a wan smile. Then he asked if she would return to the "hospital" and "mortuary." She slowly nodded affirmatively, adding, "Only if you promise I will never see ***you*** there…"

"I'll do my best." Gratien hugged her, gave her a kiss and said they both needed to rest because dawn would soon be approaching, and with it would likely come another skirmish.

ꟷ

Nearly every day for the next two moons there was hand-to-hand combat in the street that fronted the Septizonium. Casualties mounted as did the fatalities.

With each day, Jacoba gained greater confidence in her healing skills. She also assisted Felice with postmortem rituals. Although Jacoba could not bring herself to help Felice eviscerate bodies, she soon grew at ease cleansing them with Aqua Vitae and solemnly rubbing them with perfumed oils while praying for the souls of the fallen warriors.

One evening after a particularly grueling day, Jacoba fell asleep earlier than normal. She slept so soundly, she didn't notice her husband had joined her. It wasn't until a dream woke her that Jacoba remembered her promise to Marco to mix a particular potion that he would need first thing the next morning. She shot out of bed, grabbed a small oil lamp, threw a large shawl over her night chemise and hurried down to the workroom to put together the medicine. In a deep sleep himself, Gratien had no idea Jacoba left their bed in the middle of the night nor that she was in danger.

There were guards posted in various locations along the route from her bed chamber to the makeshift medical center. So, Jacoba felt quite safe walking the corridors and stairs. On her way to the pharmacy/mortuary room, she peeked into the little 'hospital,' and was thankful all the patients – if not sleeping – were at least resting comfortably thanks to a special preparation Marco gave them earlier in the evening.

While Jacoba noticed there was no guard at the hospital's doorway, she didn't give it a second thought. "He must be making rounds elsewhere or taking a break," she rationalized to herself as she walked farther down the hall. The corridor seemed more dimly lit than usual since the oil in some lamps hanging from the ceiling had not yet been replenished.

Because the workroom was in the lowest level of the palace, natural light was limited to a small iron grate high up on one of its walls, so oil lanterns mounted on the walls were kept lit day and night.

When Jacoba came through the door of the pharmacy/mortuary, she was glad to see at least one oil lantern on the wall was still burning as brightly as it had been all day. It would provide enough light for her to work. She put down the small lamp she was carrying on the large work table and began to scan the nearby shelves for ingredients needed to make the medicinal potion.

Out of nowhere, a bulky hand came across her mouth, and she noticed the glint of a knife blade nearing her face. "Don't move or make a sound or you *will* be dead." The voice was gravelly and menacing. She could feel the man's body against her back. His breath was foul, and his clothes reeked of body odor which sickened her. But it was his words that hit her in the pit of her stomach. "Now walk quiet-like toward the light and turn yourself around slow so I can see your face." She didn't know what to do except obey.

The force of the assailant's body pushed her forward. She turned around as he commanded. The hand covering her mouth had been removed, and the knife was now at her throat. The man's face was as dirty as his hands. His dark beard and hair were filthy and matted. Rot infested his teeth. "Who are you?" Jacoba asked stridently in an attempt to hide the terror she felt within. "And what do you want? How did you get in here?"

"Ain't you the nosey one… I'm here with my buddies to take us a Frangipane or two. Maybe I'll let you go if you can lead me to one of 'em." Jacoba was now frightened more than ever since she knew it was common practice for some of the less wealthy power-hungry Roman families to hire thugs to kidnap aristocrats. The ransoms – which the wealthy families nearly always paid – were usually sums that were large enough to finance a small army or build numerous war towers.

"What are YOU doing in this place?" he asked as he kept rubbing up against her with the force of his weighty body until he harshly backed her into one end of the large work table. Jacoba felt a sudden, deep pain in her back that seemed to shoot right through to her stomach. In that instant, she knew she may have lost the child who had begun growing within her. She was going to tell Gratien about her pregnancy the previous evening but fell asleep before he came to their bed chamber.

"Were you gonna meet your lover here perhaps? Maybe I'll take his place before you take me to the 'lady of the palace.' What do you say? Are you up for a little ride?" The assailant's right hand held the knife at Jacoba's throat while his left hand lifted his tunic and loosened his braies. Keeping her pinned against the table with his body, he now used the knife in his right hand to snag Jacoba's shawl and roughly pull it from her. Her arms instinctively went up across the front of her body as she blurted out a tearful, "I am with child. Please have mercy, sir."

"'I am with child. Please have mercy, sir.'" He repeated her words in a mocking tone once again bringing the knife to her throat and moving his other hand slowly down Jacoba's chemise from her shoulder to her belly. Jacoba cringed at the feel of his hand through the silk of her chemise. "I think you're no servant girl. Look at your fancy little gown. I'd bet you're one of 'them,'and that's a little

Frangipane in the oven." The attacker now had the knife at her chest and began moving it across her silk chemise as he audibly pondered his alternatives, "Hmm, maybe I should just kill you right now and get two Frangipanes at the same time. That'd be worth something to my employer. Or maybe I should plant my seed in you and let you go so you'd have two at the same time....You and your fancy family wouldn't know which was which, so my little bastard would grow up a noble....Hah, That's pretty clever. Well, anyway, I guess I can plant my seed in you no matter what and then decide your fate." His left hand was now pulling up the lower part of Jacoba's chemise while the knife in his right hand easily sliced through the ribbon fastener at her bodice.

On the verge of fainting, Jacoba glimpsed the blade of a knife coming toward her as she momentarily blacked out and fell backwards on the table. In a matter of seconds, she came to, and the assailant was on top of her with his full weight. His eyes were open wide, his lips were near hers and there was blood dripping down his chin. She began to scream but stopped short when she heard her husband's voice say *"Jacoba, he's dead... I'm here... It will be all right...."* as he pulled the heavy corpse off of her. "Are you okay? Did he hurt you?" Gratien asked in a hushed voice. The blade she saw before fainting wasn't coming at her. It was Gratien's dagger destined for the carotid artery of her attacker. Several of the palace soldiers were now in the room preparing to remove the body.

Jacoba eased herself up to a sitting position on the table and practically collapsed into her husband's outstretched arms. "Don't try standing just yet," Gratien told her as he sat down beside her. He put his arm around her to comfort her as well as physically support her. With tears streaming down her face, Jacoba just stared ahead for several minutes as if in a trance. She couldn't believe what had just happened. She didn't want to believe it. Her hands were trembling. She began rocking back and forth slightly as she looked down at her chemise drenched in the blood. Gratien said softly, "Are you okay?" Jacoba nodded her head up and down slowly. Gratien followed up, "Did he hurt you? Shall I get Marco here to examine you?" Jacoba shook her head back and forth to both questions.

"Gratien, your child. I think he killed your child," Jacoba choked out the words as she sobbed anew.

"Giacomina… both children are safe. Remember…I took them to Trastevere…They are with your parents," Gratien tried hard to make his tone of voice gentle. He was worried that perhaps Jacoba's mind wasn't quite right because of the shock.

"Gratien, I am with … I was with child … I was going to tell you last night that you will again be a father, but I was so tired, I couldn't keep my eyes open. Then I woke up and remembered I had forgotten to make a potion for the healer so I came here to do it…and then that man ….that man… " Jacoba was having trouble finding words to finish the sentence. She paused and turned to look at her husband. "Gratien, you are hurt!!!" she shouted. The sight of blood on her husband's face put a sudden end to the daze caused by her ordeal.

"This is nothing, my dear," Gratien said in a nonchalant way as he put his fingers to the wound and wiped away the blood. "The blade from the man's knife must have caught me on the cheek."

"Would you like me to sew it up? You know I'm getting almost as good at that as Marco!" Jacoba said with a feeble smile. Gratien knew then that she would come out of this all right.

ℵ

The civil unrest in Rome eventually died down. Pope Innocent III was a savvy political leader as well as an inspired spiritual one. Unlike other cities, territories, and individuals that presented the pope with gifts to show their fealty to him, the nobility of Rome demanded payment from the pope in order for him to gain their loyalty. After the Pontiff gave the rich and powerful families even more money than they demanded, life in Rome returned to its more usual chaotic state.

Jacoba and Gratien talked little about the night she was attacked. The Settesoli Frangipani never learned who was behind the kidnapping attempt because the three individuals involved were killed in the act of their treachery.

One of them was a young man who had been recently retained to guard the Septizonium's "hospital." He was the "inside" man who opened an entrance not far from his guard post for the other two kidnappers. He then led one of them via a seldom used stairway to the second floor where the family's bed chambers were located. That was when a long-time guard realized what was happening and stopped the duo. The fracas in the corridor awakened Gratien who panicked when he realized his wife was not beside him. He instantly surmised she must have gone to the hospital or mortuary and ran there faster than he ever thought possible.

The intruder who attacked Jacoba had remained on the lower level to make sure the kidnappers' escape route stayed clear. Gratien was secretly sorry the man died so quickly. He wished there would have been an opportunity to have one of his people torture him…not so much to learn who was behind the plot as to make him suffer for what he did to Jacoba and for killing their unborn child.

Jacoba's miscarriage happened within a day of the attack. Felice suggested to Jacoba that they bury the bloody discharge containing the tiny unborn child under a tree on the Palatine Hill not far from the palace. Together they prayed and cried. And it was never spoken of again by Jacoba or Gratien.

By the end of the following year, Jacoba was once more with child.

Chapter XIV
Flesh and Blood

September, 1205 – Rome

It was late afternoon when Jacoba returned to the Septizonium from her visit to St. Peter's and her brief encounter with Francis. She expected Gratien to return late that evening. She hadn't received word yet as to how the fighting in the Marches went, but she had prayed that her husband would return unharmed and in relatively good spirits.

Sabina had drawn a bath for her ladyship since Jacoba wanted to wash her face and hair as well as clean the dust of the day from her feet and legs. She had already cleansed her teeth and sweetened her breath with a mixture of salt and sage which she rubbed on her teeth and gums using a small cloth made of rough linen.

Since the attempted rape of her in the lower level of the Septizonium, Jacoba no longer bathed in any of the palace's sumptuous pools located there unless Gratien was with her. Instead, a large wooden bathtub had been brought to her bed chamber. To give Jacoba further privacy within the spacious room, Sabina had one of the servants place a screen around the tub, just in case another attendant or family member entered the room. Jacoba was excessively modest around everyone except her husband.

Sabina sat on a small stool on the other side of the screen while Jacoba disrobed and got into the tub. Most of the Frangipane women had their servants wash them. However, Jacoba grew up accustomed to bathing herself, but she always needed help washing her back and rinsing her long hair. So, Sabina would remain on the other side of the screen until Jacoba called for her.

"Do you have all you need, my lady?" Sabina asked, then quickly added, "Oh no! I'm so sorry. I forgot to bring your drying cloths. I'll fetch them immediately."

"You don't have to hurry, Sabina!" Jacoba responded and then closed her eyes, "I'm enjoying just resting here. Oh...and please make sure the perfuming oil has been added to the ewer when you give my hair its final rinse."

Sabina left the chamber to gather what was needed. When she returned, just as she was opening the door to re-enter, she saw Gratien coming toward her down the hall. He put his finger to his lips signaling her to be quiet and not acknowledge his presence. He then whispered, "I'll take those things from you. Thank you, Sabina. You may go."

Jacoba heard the door close and assumed Sabina had returned with the towels. She then said with a bit of a sigh, "I hope you remembered the perfume. I want to smell good for Gratien." There was a pause, then Jacoba added, "I'll close my eyes so you can come rinse my hair now with the perfumed water. And please soap my upper back a bit, you know the place by my shoulder I always have trouble reaching myself."

Gratien peeked around the screen. Since Jacoba's back was to him, he decided to continue his charade a few moments longer. He began pouring the perfumed water over Jacoba's hair. She said, "I think this scent smells so good. I hope Gratien will like it." Jacoba still kept her eyes closed since the perfumed water had washed over her face as well as her hair.

Gratien quietly began soaping Jacoba's back. She gave a little twitch when his hands touched her like something wasn't quite right. Suddenly his hands very tenderly glided down the small of her back to her tailbone. Jacoba's eyes flew open as she barked out, "Sabina, What in the world are you…" She turned quickly to reprimand the impertinent servant but didn't even complete the sentence when she saw it was Gratien.

She stood up, threw her dripping wet arms around him and kissed him. "May I join you, my lady?" He asked with mock politeness. "Of course, my lordship! Your child and I welcome you to our humble nymphaeum," She replied, taking his hands and placing them on her swollen stomach. Gratien smiled and gently stroked her abdomen, then pulled her close and kissed her lovingly on the head. "You make me so happy, Giacomina. I could not live without you."

After they finished bathing and dried off, the couple lay in her bed together and talked. She asked Gratien all kinds of questions about the "little war" in which he had been involved for the past several weeks. He didn't share details of the combat but said that doing what his family did most likely would help save many lives in the future. "There is now an uneasy peace in that area, but at least it is peace," he said.

Jacoba was holding back tears. Gratien's wounds from the previous three years of strife in Rome had barely healed, and now she noticed large bruises on his back and chest as well as his arms and legs. There were also several small and relatively fresh gashes near the bruises. Gratien noticed that she had noticed.

"I know I'm a bit of a mess," Gratien said reflectively as his fingers involuntarily moved up to his cheek and traced a large scar acquired two years ago during the fighting in Rome. "I'm no longer the 'handsome prince' of long ago, but please believe my love for you, Giacomina, is stronger than ever."

"Gratien, why can't we walk away from this life? Why can't we just leave with the children and never come back? I can't bear to see your body and our souls hurting this way," Jacoba said quietly.

"I wish we could, my love…but you know why we can't. The lives of so many other people depend upon us, and the Church needs our protection here in Rome," Gratien responded sadly and then stared in silence at nothing.

Jacoba waited a moment and then leaned over him. She looked into his eyes as one of her fingers grazed the newer, large scar on his cheek and then moved on to the faded scar on his temple. "Gratien, you will always be my 'handsome-prince-who-taught-me-archery,' and I feel the same way now about you as I did on that day…and on our wedding night! Do you remember?"

Of course he remembered, and he smiled. He soon felt the warmth of her lips not only on the scars of his face but also on every other scar that she could find.

After they made love, they fell asleep in each other's arms and barely moved all night. The sun was already up when Jacoba shot out of bed with an "Oh, no! I forgot to tell you, Gratien, that I ran into Francis yesterday when I was visiting St. Peter's. You said you wanted to meet him; so, I invited him to morning Mass at Santa Lucia…and then to break bread with us here afterwards."

She quickly explained the whole scenario of her chance meeting with Francis to Gratien and then added that she was hoping he would take Francis on a tour of the grain mill, vineyard, olive grove and perhaps the wheat and barley fields if there was time. She also told Gratien that Francis said he had something he wanted to discuss with him.

Gratien's head was spinning. He would have preferred just staying in bed all morning with his wife. He asked himself why on earth would she think he wanted to meet Francis. Then he remembered what he told her after they had 'the archery lesson'…when all he wanted to do was kiss her and wasn't thinking clearly. He smiled to himself.

But his happy thoughts quickly passed. Gratien was thankful that Jacoba hadn't told him last night or he would have never fallen asleep. As it was, Gratien's thoughts were screeching around his brain like a murder of agitated crows: '*Was it really by chance that this Francis met Jacoba or did Francis somehow find out that she would be visiting St. Peter's at just that time? Maybe he heard that her husband was out of the city and thought he could lead her astray. Is he now living in Rome so he can become her lover? Does he think I'm a feeble old man? Does he want to fight for her love? I'll break him in half if he thinks he can take her from me. What if she loves him more than she loves me? She wouldn't betray me, would she?...*

Gratien's mental rampage was interrupted when Jacoba said they needed to leave right away because Mass would be starting in 10 minutes. Gratien told her to go ahead. He would be right behind her.

Actually, Gratien intended the delay so that he could observe this Francis character and his wife … and how they interacted without them noticing him. His heart ached every time he envisioned what he expected to see: a tall, ruggedly handsome young man – no scars, of course – dressed in fine clothing sitting inappropriately close to Jacoba and exchanging glances with her throughout the service.

Gratien waited for Mass to start and then lingered in the shadows in the back of the church. He thought to himself, "*Hah! The guy is late...maybe he's not even going to show up!*"

Jacoba was sitting up front on the right side next to two ladies who regularly volunteered at the diaconia with her. The only other person in the church was a rather scraggy little man wearing an old tunic that was patched in several places. He was also seated up front but on the far left next to a pillar, positioned so he could not see the women nor be seen by them. Gratien assumed the man to be a beggar who would be looking for a handout at the church's diaconia after Mass.

There was an empty seat next to Jacoba. Gratien wondered if that's where Francis would sit when he arrived.

Gratien loitered in the back of the church for a few minutes more to see if Francis would show up and seat himself next Jacoba. Then, Jacoba turned around, spotted Gratien and motioned for him to come up and sit next to her. He hesitated a moment and looked around to make sure he himself was truly her intended target. "*I guess I'm it. No Francis today,*" Gratien thought to himself somewhat smugly as he walked down the aisle.

Gratien whispered in Jacoba's ear, "Where's your Francis?" She looked up at him with eyes that more than suggested he needed to be quiet since the service had already begun. "You'll meet him after Mass since you didn't make it here early enough to meet him before it started!" Although her voice was soft, its tone was unexpectedly stern, indicating she was not pleased with Gratien's tardiness. Gratien didn't really care, but he wondered why if Francis had been there he hadn't stayed for the service.

ꟻⲟⲥꟼ

When Mass was finished, Jacoba and Gratien walked to the back of the church. The two women who had been sitting next to them exited the building, but Jacob made no effort to leave the vestibule. "Won't your 'special love' be waiting outside for us?" Gratien asked, sarcastically emphasizing the words "special love."

"Why would he? He's right over there," she said, nodding her head toward the figure kneeling near the pillar. "I guess he wanted to say a few more prayers," she added.

Gratien was speechless and wasn't sure if he should laugh or be frightened. He asked himself how this exquisite, aristocratic woman at his side could have ever been in love with the scrawny vagabond who was now walking toward them. Gratien then remembered Jacoba telling him Francis gave his fine clothes to a beggar at St. Peter's in exchange for the tattered tunic he was now wearing. Gratien wondered if Francis's current outfit was merely a ruse to make him seem less threatening to Gratien while gaining Jacoba's sympathy and concern. Gratien didn't like Francis already. He assumed the man couldn't be trusted.

Jacoba wisely kept their introduction simple, "Gratien, I want you to meet Francis Bernardone, my special friend from Assisi. Francis, this is my husband and the father of my children, Gratien Frangipane." The two men exchanged formal acknowledgments. Then, there was silence. Before the hush got too uncomfortable, Jacoba spoke up, "Let's start walking since the cooks have prepared a meal for us, and I'm sure it is ready by now. We can talk on the way. Francis, we'll introduce you to our children after we eat, and later, Gratien will show you around the property so you two will have time to get to know one another better."

Gratien's eyes were now shooting daggers at his wife. His look was saying he wanted this "vagabond" to go away. Jacoba pretended not to see her husband's expression and began asking Francis about his trip to Rome and how things were going in Assisi. She hoped their guest hadn't noticed her husband's annoyance. Gratien didn't really care and said very little as the trio walked to the Septizonium.

Gratien's training as a knight forced him to be a keen observer of other men's intent. Besides making him a formidable opponent to those who would threaten him, Gratien's intuition and his ability to empathize with others made him an exceptional leader and an uncommonly thoughtful husband. He learned at an early age to "read" the eyes, the facial expressions, and the tiniest movements of anyone he encountered – be they friend, foe, or wife. He sized up situations quickly and responded immediately. In war, his very life depended upon accurate observation and instantaneous action.

Gratien perceived the surprise visit from Francis as a potential 'act of war;' so, he strategized the meal-time seating to give himself the best vantage point to observe 'the enemy.'

As the trio entered one of the smaller dining rooms within the Septizonium, Gratien over-graciously told Francis to '*please take the seat at the head of the table since you are our special guest*. Gratien gave a fleeting scowl Jacoba's way when he said the word "special."

After Francis was seated, Gratien pulled out the chair to Francis's left for Jacoba and then seated himself directly across the table from his wife, to the right of Francis.

Gratien offered grace, and Francis thanked Gratien for his hospitality. The conversation at the table began with affable generalities and moved on in an unexpectedly cordial way from topic to topic. Gratien was able to easily observe both Francis and Jacoba as they interacted, and he was pleasantly bewildered by what he didn't "read" on their faces or see in their actions. There were no inadvertent "gazes filled with desire." There weren't even any sidelong glances between them. Francis's hand never "accidentally" brushed against hers nor did his arm ever touch hers.

Even when the subject turned to Jacoba's summer in Assisi, Gratien never felt like he was being left out of the conversation by either of them. And when Francis learned Gratien had been to the Holy Land, he flooded him with question after question. Francis seemed genuinely interested in getting to know Gratien as a man – and it seemed not just because he was married to Jacoba.

Gratien noticed, too, that Francis didn't attempt to flatter Jacoba with honeyed banter the way other men sometimes tried to do. He detected no guile in Francis's words.

Gratien had to admit to himself that Francis seemed a sincere and likeable guy. He now appreciated how Jacoba could have befriended the man, but fall in love with him? That was still beyond his comprehension. So, after the meal Gratien closely watched Francis as he interacted with the two Frangipane children. Gratien was surprised and a little bit pained that his own offspring took to this odd stranger so quickly. Sometimes it took them more than several minutes to warm to their own father after he'd been away for awhile. Yet, here was this beggar-man sitting on the floor laughing and playing *with my own children* more happily than I. Gratien was annoyed and felt a twinge of envy.

Gratien then began sizing up Francis physically. First, Gratien pictured Francis in more expensive and fashionable attire. Francis was young and probably wore fine clothing well, especially compared with Gratien himself. Francis was much shorter than Gratien. He wasn't even as tall as Jacoba, but he had a presence. Francis's face was gaunt but bore no scars the way Gratien's did. His beard was rather sparse but dark. Francis did have a warm, inviting smile.

Gratien considered Francis's eyes his best asset. They were dark and penetrating. They seemed alert, joyful, and serene at the same time. As a result of looking at his ragged guest in this new light, Gratien better grasped how his wife could have been charmed by him.

Now Gratien couldn't help but wonder whether there might not still be a physical attraction between them. He wanted to understand what this man's intentions were toward his wife. He *needed* to know. So, Gratien asked Jacoba to take the children and told Francis he was ready to show him around some of the family's properties in what had been ancient Rome's Circus Maximus.

☙❧

Gratien and Francis walked in silence to the grain mill which was not far from the Septizonium. Once inside, Gratien rather curtly told Francis about how the mill worked and how they were able to provide grain for not only their own storehouses but had enough to share with the poor who lived nearby. As they neared the door to leave, Francis stopped Gratien to ask if something was bothering him. "I'm sorry, Lord Frangipane, did I say or do something to offend you?" Francis posed the question with earnest concern, adding, "You've been very hospitable to me, and I would like to know if I've wronged you in some way so that I may apologize appropriately."

Gratien realized he himself had been the one behaving rather poorly. He also realized Francis apparently could read people as well as he himself could. "Francis, may I talk frankly with you?"

"I wouldn't want you to speak to me in any other way," Francis responded with sincerity.

"Then I must ask you a question," Gratien said. "What are your intentions with my wife?" Francis gave him a puzzled look, so Gratien continued. "Jacoba once told me that she loved you … she actually thought she would marry you…and she told me you would always be her 'special love.'"

Francis's heart leapt when he heard *'she told me you would always be her love.'* Although Gratien's words ignited a feeling deep within Francis, he wouldn't allow his mind to follow. So, he responded instantaneously with, "We were both children, Gratien."

Now it was Gratien who gave Francis a puzzled look. "I know that this love went somewhat beyond mere childhood, Francis, and that you had tasted her lips more than once when you yourself were about to enter manhood."

"Gratien, be assured we never made love together," Francis replied, quickly adding, "True, her lips were the first I ever kissed, but they were most definitely not the last." He was not lying to Gratien. However, he dared not tell Gratien the *whole* truth of his love for her. When his letters to Jacoba went unanswered, when he was no longer welcomed at the Normanni palace, when he thought Jacoba abandoned him of her own will, he sought both refuge and revenge in wanton activities readily available to rich young men in Assisi.

Young women with loose morals almost always figured into his frequent evenings of carousing. Francis was attracted to any female whose appearance even hinted of some small physical resemblance to Jacoba – similar eye color or perhaps comparable height or maybe hair that fell on a woman's shoulders the way Jacoba's did. Francis searched for another Jacoba in every woman he saw. And when he embraced a woman – which was often – he always pretended she was Jacoba, even if there was no physical resemblance at all.

His amorous encounters always ended the same – in deep disappointment. The lips never tasted like hers. The hair never smelled like hers. The skin never felt like hers. But this was something he would not share with Gratien…or anyone else…particularly Jacoba. It would be too hurtful. This indecent way in which he thought of Jacoba let alone treated women in years past was now something even too hurtful for a repentant Francis himself to ponder.

"Do you still love her, Francis?" Gratien asked with a trace of exasperation in his voice.

Francis didn't give his answer quite as hastily as his previous responses since to say "no" would be an outright lie but to bluntly say "yes" would not be prudent. So, he simply answered Gratien with a question, "Did your wife ever tell you my best friend and I called her 'Brother Jacoba?' Gratien, your wife was, above all, a special friend not only to me but also to Elias and Prassede."

While Francis didn't bring up the blood oath that he, Jacoba and Elias took, he talked generally about their activities when Jacoba lived in Assisi for the summer of her 8th year. He especially focused on their games with other children involving knighthood and chivalry and that the 'special love' that developed between Jacoba and him was just a chivalric term for friendship and mutual esteem.

Francis told Gratien how his feelings now for Jacoba were no different than when she was eight years old….He explained that he would always have a 'courtly love' for her, which would go no further than sacred admiration. "Our love was innocent and pure, and I promise you it will always remain that," Francis said the words convincingly. He continued, "Jacoba is your wife. I have never loved her in the way that you do nor will I ever attempt to love her the way you do, Gratien.

"Please understand that when we kissed, Jacoba was not yet a woman. And while it is true that my body was nearing manhood, my heart, mind and soul were still those of a boy. I didn't grow into true manhood until I went to war," Francis said solemnly.

"You fought?!," Gratien responded in astonishment.

"Assisi's war against Perugia." Francis responded in a rather flat way, adding, "I was in the Battle of Collestrada."

"I heard it was a bloodbath!" Gratien said this in a way that let Francis know he wanted to hear more about it.

"It was worse than anything the ugliest imagination could create. I first realized I was not yet a man when a sword gashed my arm, and I fainted. When I came to, I was face down in the dirt that was turning into mud before my eyes as it mixed with my blood and that of the countless casualties around me.

"While I now consider myself blessed to have survived, at the time I wished I had been run-through like so many of my companions because I soon found myself imprisoned in Perugia. I was there for a year until my ransom could be arranged. In that dark, dank hole that reeked of every revolting odor that one could conceive, I died each day … again and again … for more than 11 moons.

"Many of those imprisoned with me never survived. One or two men would die every few days. Their corpses would lie here and there among us for days, sometimes even a week or longer, until the guards themselves tired of the stench and removed them.

"We never truly knew day from night because our only view of anything except the hard rock walls was a tiny air shaft high above our heads. The air we breathed was filled with the putrid smells of fetid wounds and decaying flesh combined with the stink of our normal bodily functions. There was no way to escape the miasma, and all who survived the imprisonment became grimly ill.

"It was sickening to eat what they passed off as food. It was slop, full of hair and pieces of the rodents that infested our dwellings. The rats running wild in our quarters were nothing like the dormice that are considered delicacies in some Umbrian homes. While the dormice cultivated in Umbrian kitchens feed on grapes and other fresh food, prison rats feed on cadavers and waste. My bile comes up at the thought of what we ate to survive."

Francis went on to explain that in addition to his wound which quickly became infected, he contracted a fever and some type of disease that continued to debilitate him long after he had been ransomed and returned to his home. "What was harder to endure than the aches within my body were the grotesque images in my mind and the abject misery in my heart," Francis added.

He said the only good thing to happen in that dank, dark, desolate "tomb" was that he started to think more about spiritual things.

He did not tell Gratien that before his thoughts turned to God, he would spend hours of his long captivity fantasizing about Jacoba and hoping she would have mercy on him and take him back. During his long imprisonment, Francis had no idea she was already married.

Gratien was silent for a moment. His eyes were downcast. With a slight sigh, Gratien softly, somberly and sincerely said, "Francis, I am sorry. I had no idea. I don't think I could have survived as well as you did."

Gratien gained a new respect for the "vagabond." He told Francis he thought him brave for living through the ordeal of captivity. Gratien admitted to Francis that imprisonment was his own greatest fear. Before every battle, especially when fighting in the Holy Land, Gratien told Francis he prayed God would spare his life…but always added to please "take me" rather than let me be captured.

Then, Gratien said something surprising. "Francis, tell me more about this spiritual awakening that you are having."

The two sat on a bench outside the granary, and Francis told Gratien about what brought him to this point in his life. Francis talked about how while in captivity he met an elderly knight who was far more serene than he himself or any of the other prisoners. The old man never bemoaned his fate or wept about the pain from his injuries. He never complained about anyone or anything.

Francis continued his story, "Initially I thought perhaps the man had some type of head injury no one could see that made him simple in his mind. Yet, his conversation – although limited as was mine and the other prisoners – was not that of a simpleton. One day, I finally approached him to ask why he didn't commiserate with the rest of us on the wretchedness of the prison and hopelessness of our situation.

"He responded to me with a question: *'Young man, do you believe Jesus is God?'* When I nodded 'yes.' Then he asked another question: *'Do you believe what's written about Him in the Bible...that he was an innocent who endured profound pain and a cruel death without complaint for our sake?'* 'Yes, of course I do!' was my response. The old knight then replied, *'Contemplate* ***His*** *extraordinary suffering and agonizing death, and you will have your answer.'*

"It was then my thoughts began to shift direction. It was then I began to realize when wicked things are done to us, we can offer them up to God as a sacrifice. And the joy that our offering to Him will bring to our souls can transcend the pain our body experiences. His words were a revelation to me.

"This is how I began my journey to God, but I'm not there yet. I know in my soul I cannot return to my old life nor can I pursue the kind of life my father wants for me. I'm not who I was. I'm searching to find who I should be…what Gods wants me to do."

As soon as Francis finished speaking, Gratien began asking questions. And the two talked for several hours.

Even more surprising than their lengthy conversation was what followed. Gratien asked Francis to come to the Septizonium again the following day so they could talk some more. “I think Jacoba, too, would like to hear your words, Francis. Although she hides her sorrow well, she and I have seen more personal tragedy during the past couple years than in all the previous years of our lives. I think the words you shared with me today could give her strength and joy and hope.”

Gratien then invited Francis to spend the night in the Frangipane palace. However, Francis declined. He said he already had a place to stay but happily agreed to return to the Septizonium to talk with the couple the next day, following morning Mass.

Francis bid a quick “good evening” to Gratien and asked him to convey the same to Jacoba on his behalf. The sun was setting, and Francis told Gratien he wanted to reach his destination before nightfall. Gratien surmised that destination was probably not an inn or the household of a family friend but more likely a patch of stony, uncomfortable ground somewhere in the disabitato. Gratien never met anyone quite like Francis. Jacoba was right. This man was special.

Chapter XV
Restless Blood
1205 - Assisi

Francis was agitated and confused. He had gone to Rome in his finest clothes to seek out Jacoba and confront her about her marriage. He planned to make her feel deep regret for marrying *a stale old man* when she could have had a wealthy, witty and virile *young* one.

However, when Francis actually stood in front of the massive entrance to the Septizonium, he either lost the courage to face Jacoba or perhaps found the strength to forgive and forget. Whichever his motivation, he decided to go to St. Peter's instead to get better acquainted with "Lady Poverty" as well as atone for his vengeful intentions. He thought it ironic not just that Jacoba *found him*, but that she found him as a miserable beggar dressed in rags and pleading for alms.

Now back in Assisi, Francis fingered the splendid garments he put on as soon as he returned home and began second guessing himself on his impulsive decision to trade clothes with a beggar. *Should I have kept my finery? Maybe I shouldn't have traded my clothes so soon. I could have worn them to the Frangipane palace. How was I to know Jacoba would show up at St. Peter's, find me begging, and invite me to meet her husband?!* Unexpectedly, Francis chuckled to himself about the strange first impression he must have made on the handsome and powerful Roman noble.

"Oh well, the past is the past," he thought, surprising himself that he no longer cared so much about his appearance as he once did. He sensed something major had changed within him and was still evolving, but he wasn't quite sure what to make of it.

He mulled over his transformation that began in 1202 when he was imprisoned in Perugia. After he was ransomed a year later, things just weren't the same when he returned to Assisi. The imprisonment left him feeling physically weak and emotionally depressed. He was sick and sad, and old pursuits no longer held his interest the way they once did.

Back then he began spending hours in Torrione, the ruin of the old Roman tomb at the edge of town, or took long walks in the forests of Mount Subasio. Most of the time, Francis was alone. However, sometimes he would meet his old friend Prassede. They would talk, and without realizing it, Francis would find himself praying with her. He didn't care much about God or religion until his imprisonment. He talked a lot with Prassede about God. Francis found the peculiar woman-hermit to be particularly close to the Lord as well as his own kindest and truest friend. He was most comforted in her presence.

When some of his former reveling buddies had seen Francis from a distance walking in the forest with someone they didn't recognize, they asked about his "companion." The only thing he told them was that it was an old friend who was not from Assisi. Because of his childhood promise to Prassede, Francis never disclosed her name to anyone except Gratien.

He and Prassede would occasionally talk about the summer they first met. He confided he now felt abandoned by Elias who moved with his family to Bologna and betrayed by Jacoba who abruptly stopped seeing him and corresponding with him for no apparent reason. Prassede had no advice for him except to pray and be open to whatever God's wishes may be for him.

As soon as Francis regained his physical strength, he wanted his life to be like it once was, so he began to again participate in local "serenades" with his friends. Francis retained his reputation as a popular and generous reveler, and the other young Assisians welcomed him back to their clique, often proclaiming him "king" of their little bacchanals.

As a result of his renewed physical strength, Francis toyed once more with the idea of becoming a knight. When an extraordinary opportunity arose to pursue that particular aspiration, he took it as a sign from God. A noble from Assisi announced he was seeking young men to accompany him on a military expedition led by Walter of Brienne that would result in honors and riches. Francis signed up.

When informed of his son's plan, Pietro Bernardone gladly paid to outfit Francis with the newest and best equipment. It was more lavish than that of the nobleman leading the group.

Two nights before he was to leave, Francis had an extraordinarily vivid dream about a man who led him into a beautiful palace. The walls of its vast halls were hung with glittering coats of chainmail, shields, swords, spears, and armor. The man in his dream told Francis the building and its treasures were for him and his knights.

The next morning Francis was certain the dream was a foreshadowing of things to come: not only great riches but also a noble title. He was ecstatic and shared the content of his nocturnal vision with some comrades leaving for Apulia with him.

What he wisely kept to himself was his assumption that once knighted, he would marry Jacoba and move to her family's Trastevere palace. Only then, would this prophetic dream be fully realized.

On the first day of its journey south, the Assisian entourage stayed at an inn in the town of Spoletto. After a few cups of wine, the troubadour in Francis surfaced, as it always did when partying with his drinking buddies. Because of his recent vision, Francis began singing happily of his true love who would become his wife. He sang of her wealth, her nobility and her beauty.

Francis's song was interrupted when his words became physically descriptive: *'...tall, graceful, and fair with bewitching green eyes and chestnut hair."* That's when a half dozen knights from Rome reveling on the other side of the room began talking loudly among themselves saying *that bard is describing our liege's young wife!*

One of the soldiers shouted, slurring his words, "Hey, Assisi guy, sounds like you're singing about Master of the Septizonium's bride. If there's another one out there looks like Gratien Frangipane's wife, I want to *meet* her – if you know what I mean." Another intoxicated soldier piped up in a sloppy voice, "We'd all like to *meet* Lady Jacoba! Humph…but she just has eyes for her lordship." Francis stopped singing as soon as he heard the word *Jacoba.*

A third Frangipane knight, equally drunk, staggered over to Francis, began poking a finger into Francis's chest and asked "What's *your* bride's name?"

Francis was dumbstruck momentarily. Without any forethought, he blurted out for the whole room to hear, "My bride is to be Lady Poverty. She is noble, gentle, and beautiful…and I will embrace her from now on."

It was the first thing that came to Francis's mind: *If I can't marry Jacoba, I will be poorer than poor. So, I might as well take poverty itself as my lady.*

Everyone was now laughing heartily and hoisting their cups in a toast to "Lady Poverty."

Feeling sick to his stomach at the thought Jacoba was already married as well as ashamed of making his senseless comment, Francis made a quick exit to his room. But it wasn't soon enough to avoid hearing one of the Frangipane knights say, "That guy is either very drunk or very nuts…or very both."

Francis had another vivid dream that very evening. The same man appeared. Only this time, Francis recognized him. It was the Lord Himself.

"Who do you think can best reward you, the Master or the servant?" the figure asked.

"The Master," answered Francis.

"Then why do you leave the Master for the servant, the rich Lord for the poor man?"

Francis replied, "O Lord, what do You want me to do?"

"Return to your place. You will be told what to do. First, you must interpret your previous vision in a different way. Yes, Francis, you will become noble, but your principality will be of another sort. The 'shining arms and splendid palace' you saw are not what you thought. They are intended for 'knights' much different than those *you* had in mind."

The dream was so real it awakened Francis, and he couldn't fall back to sleep. He spent the whole night thinking about it. He concluded God would be giving him some kind of direction for his life. He was glad about that.

He abruptly gave up his thoughts of knighthood and going to Apulia for glory and riches. Instead, he left his expensive armor and other equipment at the door of a needy knight he met the previous evening whose accoutrements were old and battle-worn. As soon as it was light enough to travel, Francis was on his horse, heading back to Assisi.

Once home, Francis's companions were happy their generous friend was back. They asked him to be king of their revels since that meant he would be expected to treat them all to a magnificent feast. He thought perhaps partying with old friends might do him good, so Francis consented.

It was one of the most opulent banquets the revelers had ever attended. After gorging themselves, the carousers left the building and began loudly "serenading" no one in particular and everyone in general as they drunkenly paraded through Assisi's narrow lanes.

Their "king," however, was not leading them. He was no longer even walking with them. They turned to see where he'd gone and noticed Francis standing motionless several yards behind their unholy procession.

He was staring at nothing in particular with his sham crown in one hand and mock scepter dangling from the other. His companions were amazed and momentarily disturbed. Drunken voices started tossing questions and comments at him: "What's wrong, Francis? You look different Francis! Why didn't you follow us? You're not like you used to be. Are you in love? Are you thinking of getting a wife?"

Francis responded to the last question in a sober voice, "Yes, I am going to wed the noblest, richest and most beautiful bride in the world!" His friends laughed and made hand signals to each other indicating they thought he was crazy. Then, shaking their heads or shrugging their shoulders in disbelief, they continued on their drunken march through Assisi, too inebriated to be concerned any further about their "king."

Francis didn't catch up with them that evening nor did he ever again participate in a "serenade." In that moment he confirmed he was destined to live a different life, although he didn't yet have a clue as to what it might be.

He did know that before he could seriously consider taking any kind of vow to this "bride" called "Poverty," he should get to know "her" better. Francis realized he also needed closure with his previous affair of the heart – his unrequited love for Jacoba. He hadn't heard from her in years. Did she actually marry some old man? Francis decided he could resolve both issues by going to Rome.

But now that he was back from his "quest" in the ancient city, Francis felt more lost than ever. When in Rome, he experienced feelings he'd never had before – not even in prison. While incarcerated, everyone shared similar wretchedness. It made them closer to each other. In Rome, posing as a "poverello," Francis suffered a profound aloneness. In beggar's garb asking for alms, he was most often intentionally overlooked by passers-by the same way they might ignore a piece trash on the street.

In the elegant Frangipane palace, Francis's raggedy appearance made him feel uncomfortably out of place and caused him intense embarrassment. Servants looked with disapproval at him – the vagrant whose very clothing disrespected *everyone* in the noble household. Although warmly welcomed by Jacoba, Francis was initially greeted by her husband with obvious iciness and condescension that Gratien didn't even try to hide.

Francis was now having ambivalent feelings about his trek to Rome since he didn't get the clarification from the Lord that he sought. One thing, however, was made clear: Francis realized he liked giving coins to the poor rather than asking for them. So, he made up his mind he would never again refuse alms to *anyone* begging in the name of God.

Chapter XVI
Papal Blood
1209 - The Lateran Palace, Rome

Bathed in April sunlight, the Hall of Mirrors in the Lateran Palace looked magnificent, but His Holiness didn't notice. Lotario dei Conti di Segni looked only at the floor he paced. He never dreamed being pope would be so taxing. He anticipated stress dealing with temporal problems: the politics of appeasing some rulers while chastising others; negotiating peace and starting wars; generating church revenue then spending it astutely.

Those things didn't worry Pope Innocent III today. It was something much more sinister, perhaps inspired by the devil himself. The Pope's eyes were recently opened to insidious spiritual crises threatening the core of his Church.

Exorbitant sums of money were being exchanged in the buying and selling of holy relics. It didn't matter if they were genuine or fake. Simony was out of control. Too many

Church leaders considered the practice not merely acceptable: it was commendable when benefitting their coffers.

Then, there were the heretics. A new unorthodoxy seemed to pop up every few months. Most died quickly, but some blossomed. Next to Islam, the Albigensian Heresy was the most troublesome. The sect of the Cathari, headquartered in Albi, France, adopted an Eastern belief in two spirits – Good and Evil. The Cathars believed physical and material things were inherently evil, and totally rejecting them was the true path to salvation.

How can these spiritual dualists call themselves Christian when they not only create their own version of God but even dare to deny the doctrine of Redemption? The Pope shook his head as if to rid his mind of the mere thought of such heresy.

What bothered him most was that the Cathars were not only increasing in numbers but were also growing bold and dangerous.

Lotario's blood boiled as he considered the murder of his Papal Legate sent last summer to crush the heresy. Harsher measures were needed in France. Already at war with the Moors in Spain, Lotario didn't relish the prospect of fighting on an additional front.

On top of everything, reports of scandalous activities involving priests, monks and nuns had become pervasive. Even more distressing, their leaders weren't reprimanding them. The higher-ranking clerics feared fingers would be pointed back at them. The Pope surmised if he could get his clergy under control, the number of heresies might diminish.

Reform was needed. Innocent III knew that. But he didn't know what to do. He consulted cardinals, talked with bishops, met with his confessor. No one offered useful ideas to counter the rampant spiritual troubles. He prayed and prayed, but his pleas to the Holy Spirit seemed unanswered.

Innocent III was at wit's end when his ruminations were interrupted. A servant with two *urgent* communiqués approached him as he paced. The young man said messengers waited at the door because their masters required immediate responses. His back to the servant, the Pope rolled his eyes. He stopped and turned toward the young man for an instant to grab the missives, then brusquely resumed pacing as he read the notes.

One was from the Pope's confessor, Giovanni di San Paolo – a Benedictine monk whom he elevated to Cardinal Bishop of the Papal Territory of Sabina five years earlier. He also put Giovanni in charge of handling new religious groups. The message asked Innocent to give a few moments of his time to a young man named Francis leading the *Poor Penitents from Assisi*: *"He walked here with several of his followers. He is known and recommended by Bishop Guido." – Yours in Christ, Giovanni.*

The Pope knew of Bishop Guido's reputation as an orthodox and loyal practitioner of the Faith who wouldn't tolerate heresy within his jurisdiction. Looking over his shoulder toward the servant, he said, "Tell Cardinal Giovanni's man I will see this Francis because I trust his judgment and Guido's, too."

"Wait a moment while I read this other 'important' correspondence." He sighed in exasperation. When he saw the Frangipane crest on the wax seal, his demeanor improved. He smiled as he opened the note and read it.

"Tell Frangipane's man to let Lady Jacoba know I remembered our dinner this evening and look forward to seeing her and Gratien. Thank you, Paolo. You are dismissed."

The Pope continued to pace but took a breather from his troublesome ponderings as he anticipated his evening at the Septizonium. Lotario could relax there because he never felt he had to be on guard as he did in the households of other Roman nobles.

Besides their friendship, the Pope was also grateful for their generosity. The couple forgave a debt he owed them, and they were now considering giving up property rights in Ninfa to help in his efforts to reconstruct the Papal States. In addition, Jacoba used her personal holdings to repay money owed to Lotario's nephews by some of Gratien's relatives.

Lotario recalled his distress when Gratien and Jacoba had been inadvertently drawn into a conflict with members of his own Conti family a few years earlier. He was thankful the two did not hold that against him because he valued their friendship.

Beyond food and conversation, what the Pope liked most about visiting the Septizonium was that Gratien and Jacoba never asked for favors the way everyone else did. In addition, they showed him appropriate respect in front of others but called him Lotario – at his request – when only the three of them were present. The Pope thought even a brief respite from being "Your Holiness" would be relaxing.

Lotario's daydreaming was interrupted when his pacing led him to the end of the long room. As he turned to continue his stroll to nowhere, he saw some "thing" just inside the doorway at the opposite end of the grand hall.

"Who goes there?" The Pope's voice was abnormally loud. He slowed his step. He was in no hurry to approach the unannounced visitor standing with his head lowered. *It appears to be a mere beggar, but maybe he means me harm.*

"If you're here for money, please leave. I have none with me. But you may tell one of my servants I said to give you alms." When the man remained where he stood, still submissively looking at the floor, Innocent walked a bit closer. The Pope could now see his uninvited 'guest' was wearing a dirty, patched tunic cinched at the waist with a piece of fraying rope. Around his neck was a small cross made of twigs hanging from a thin, rough cord. His hair was long and straggly. A sparse beard smudged his face.

Lotario continued eyeing Francis as he wondered how this disgraceful vagrant made it past papal guards and servants as well as the multitude of clergy scurrying about the Lateran. *Someone should have stopped this intruder long before now. This fellow didn't even have the common decency to bathe and dress appropriately for a papal visit. He must be one of those rebellious fanatics roaming about.*

"I'm not here to beg. I'm here to see His Holiness." Francis said with respect and then launched into the "Rule" he had written to guide his followers. At once, the Pope interrupted.

"Well, now you've seen the Pope!" Lotario was annoyed. "And since you look like you belong in a sty, go find some swine and preach your *rule* to *them.*" Innocent abruptly turned away and began walking back to the other end of the room.

Holding the paper from Cardinal Giovanni as well as the one with his Rule, Francis left the great hall as quietly as he entered it. Only when the Pope reached the far side of the room did he turn his head to make sure the strange, grimy man had gone. *These itinerant preachers will be the death of me, and now I have to worry about palace security on top of everything else.*

ꕥ

The Pope arrived at the Septizonium before sunset with two guards, one servant and no pomp. He was greeted with respect and shown to the palace's dining hall. The room's only decorations were exquisite mosaics of mythological sea gods that had been there from the time of the Empire.

Gratien and Jacoba never disappointed when it came to scrumptious food and delightful, stimulating conversation. This evening was no exception. As the meal was winding down, Jacoba hesitantly spoke, "Lotario, do you mind if I ask you a question?"

"Jacoba, I can't believe it." Lotario said smiling broadly and shaking his head. "This is the first time you've ever sought permission to be inquisitive." The Pope looked over at Gratien and said, "Even as a little girl, your wife was always speaking up, asking things." Gratien responded by nodding his head toward Jacoba acknowledging she had the platform.

"Your Holiness…Why did you dismiss Francis today when he walked all the way from Assisi just to talk with you? You sent word to Cardinal Giovanni that you would see him, no? He had the letter from the good Cardinal, but you still wouldn't see him." Jacoba was not pleased, and Lotario could tell.

"I saw no one named Francis today!" The Pope was adamant.

Jacoba was just as unyielding. "Oh yes you did!!! Why did you tell him to preach to pigs?"

"Oh no…" Lotario threw his chin up and looked at the ceiling far above him. He didn't want to face Jacoba or Gratien at the moment. He shook his head back and forth: "It's not possible. The only person I sent away today was a beggar who showed up unannounced. I thought …"

Gratien interrupted the Pope. "*That* would be Francis. I had the same reaction when I first met him."

"Lotario, Francis is a truly holy man, and Your Holiness turned him away in a most ungodly manner!" Jacoba was respectful but forceful. She was one of very few people in Rome or elsewhere who could get away with such a reprimand.

"How *in the world* do *you* know this Francis character? He's not from Rome or even one of your families' territories. And how did you know he was coming to see me?" The Pope was incredulous.

Jacoba and Gratien took turns telling the Pope about Francis—how they met him and how he helped them grow spiritually over the past several years, especially in the aftermath of the Roman violence that personally touched them.

"So, is this 'sacred beggar' of yours here in the Septizonium right now? If so, I will meet him at once.

Jacoba, I'm surprised you didn't have him join us for dinner." The Pope feigned annoyance to cover embarrassment.

"He's not here," Jacoba answered kindly.

Where do *you* think he is, Lotario?," Gratien said with a dash of sarcasm.

Jacoba sensed the Pope's unease and spoke in a reassuring way: "Francis's life is lived according to the Gospel. Although he didn't seek followers, some approached him wanting to join him and emulate his ascetic lifestyle. As the spiritual leader of a growing group of men, Francis wants everything he and his followers do to be within the authority of the Church. That was why he came to see you. He wanted your blessing on the Rule he wrote. He is a very humble man – not exactly like the three of us, Lotario. So, when 'the Pope himself' told Francis to go preach to the swine, that's exactly what he did!"

"No…You are not serious!" The Pope laughed an uncomfortable laugh. He was skeptical and bewildered. He thought: *If only more of the flock were as compliant, I wouldn't have so many difficulties.*

"Where is this Francis now?" The Pope's tone was subdued.

"Who knows…probably somewhere between here and Testaccio still sermonizing I expect." Gratien smiled.

"I'll send some of my servants to look for him tonight and bring him to me so I can apologize for my awful behavior." The Pope sounded sincerely contrite.

"You can send someone tomorrow morning to Trastevere," Jacoba said. "When one of the friars traveling with Francis told us what happened, we arranged for all of them to stay with the Benedictines who live near the river. I'm sure Francis will join his companions when he's finished *sermonizing*. I think you know where the place is. It's not far from the Normanni palace," Jacoba was also now smiling. "Thank you, Lotario. God will bless you for meeting with Francis."

ꕥ

As promised, Innocent saw Francis the next day. Bishop Guido accompanied the 'Poor Penitent' and held out Cardinal Giovanni's letter as the two stood in the imposing doorway of the meeting chamber. High-ranking clergy crowded the spacious room. They, too, were waiting to see the Pope.

Innocent's attitude toward Francis changed dramatically since the previous day. Not only did he take to heart Jacoba's words, but that night he also had a strange, vivid dream. In it, a beggar who looked like Francis supported the heavy weight of a Church on his frail shoulders. *Perhaps it was a sign from God, and this Francis is the answer to my prayers.* Innocent thought about the dream as he motioned to Francis and Guido to enter.

The clerics milling about stopped in their tracks when they noticed the beggar come in. Some of them gasped when Innocent welcomed the unkempt man and 'bumpkin' bishop with a smile. Even more expressed shock when the Pope's hand motioned the unusual duo to approach his throne as if they were old friends.

Francis wore his usual garb – threadbare in some places, patched in others: attire reserved for the poorest of the poor. The coarse woolen tunic made him look slight and gloomy compared to others in the room. Many of the clerics were rotund to begin with, and the additional layers of clothing in high quality fabric and rich hues made them appear even bigger.

Francis walked meekly past the high-ranking clergy. He paid no attention to their murmurs and unkind remarks. However, Innocent did. With the solitary word *silencio,* the Pope commanded the clerics to be quiet and pay heed to his invited guest.

However, before Francis could begin addressing the group, Innocent motioned for him to come closer to the papal throne. So no one else could hear, Innocent whispered, "I'm sorry about yesterday. Forgive me, Francis."

With a twinkle in his eye, Francis whispered back, "Forgive Your Holiness for what? … Pigs are God's creatures, and I think they may be better listeners than some in this room."

The Pope looked Francis in the eye and smiled. He motioned to Francis to move from the platform to the floor. It was followed by a grand flourish toward the audience while loudly saying, "Francis, please speak so *all present* may hear what you have to say."

The troubadour in Francis surfaced the moment he started his story. "I am a sinner!" After capturing everyone's attention, Francis recounted various mystical experiences that changed his life and brought him to God.

He told of his visit to San Damiano, a dilapidated old chapel just outside Assisi's walls where God spoke to him through an ancient crucifix. A few of the Cardinals rolled their eyes, but most sat still, attentively listening.

Looking upwards, Francis said, "A voice told me *'Francis, Go repair my house, which as you can see is falling into ruin.'* I felt I had to obey and went to my father's clothing shop, took some fabric and sold it at the Foligno market – along with my horse – to raise funds to fix the crumbling San Damiano.

"When I brought the coins to the church, the good father refused my gift. He knew the money I 'gave' him wasn't mine to give. I threw the coins at him! He was supposed to thank me, wasn't he?!?

"I wanted to be alone and think; so, I headed to a cave in the hills where I used to play as a child. I was angry and embarrassed but really I wanted to hide because I was afraid of my father.

"I lived as a hermit for a full moon, seldom eating or drinking and never bathing," Francis smiled as he dramatically eyed his dirty arms, clothing and feet then quickly became serious. "I did none of those things because my time was best spent in prayer."

"When I left the grotto, I was filthy and wasted. I hoped my father wouldn't recognize me, but he did. Word travels fast in Assisi. He came to the edge of town where I was sitting with some beggars and dragged me home.

"As I staggered through Assisi's streets behind him, I considered how ironic my situation was. I laughed out loud and must have appeared a crazy man. In these familiar streets where I once 'ruled' as king of the merrymakers, I was now treated as a pariah. People who saw me shouted insults and pelted me with whatever was handy – pebbles, dried dung, trash.

"Once home, my father had me wash and put on 'proper clothing.' He questioned me then got angry when I told him I now answered to God and the Church, not him. He called me names, beat me, tied me up, and locked me in a dark, windowless room. I didn't really mind. It gave me time to think and pray some more. I could not get out of my mind the message from the crucifix: *Francis, repair my house.*

"My mother finally freed me after my father left on a business trip. So, I hurried back to San Damiano and put myself to work. I gathered rocks from fields and begged for other building materials. I began to repair the church's walls. I liked working for God.

"I had nothing. I wanted nothing. I was content. My father was not. The return of his coins from the church wasn't enough for him. He decided to formally disinherit me. Since I was in the service of the Church, this was not a civil matter. So, he took me before our bishop." Francis paused only long enough to acknowledge Bishop Guido who was seated nearby.

"Quite a crowd had gathered to watch the proceedings outside our town's cathedral. Words were exchanged. My genuine joy in being disinherited fueled my father's rage. Finally, I took off my clothes – clothes purchased with Pietro Bernardone's money – looked my father in the eye and said, 'Until now, I called you my father on earth, but from now on I will say only *Our Father who art in Heaven.'* That was that.

"My path to God lay in foregoing all worldly goods, honors and privileges. I have committed myself to the only 'lady' who could bring true joy – 'Lady Poverty.'"

The Pope and the Cardinals had been listening intently without expression until now. Suddenly, some were clearing their throats or fidgeting in their seats. Francis's talk about rejecting material things made them uncomfortable.

Bishop Guido incorrectly thought the clerics were upset at the mention of Francis's nakedness. He rebuked himself for not chiming in to explain that when Francis stripped, it was he himself – the bishop of Assisi – who, out of concern for modesty, gave the young man a cloth to cover himself. By the time the bishop gathered courage to say something, it was too late.

Francis was now talking about his joy in caring for lepers. This admission caused even more discomfort. Some clerics raise their eyebrows while others exchanged looks of disbelief. All, however, remained interested in Francis's narrative.

"I had built myself a little hut very near the Porziuncola chapel so I could pray there often. It was a winter morning when at Mass I heard God speak to *me* through the words of that day's Gospel. He told me disciples of Christ should not possess worldly goods like money or other valuables…nor should they have shoes nor two tunics nor staff nor even bread but should preach the kingdom of God and penance. This was exactly what I wished…what I sought...what I longed to do with all my heart!

"I took off my shoes, laid down my walking stick, and unfastened my leather belt. I never looked back. What I wear today is not meant to offend anyone." Francis was now outstretching his arms to show the Pope the lines of his very simple garment. "This – my only tunic. Its shape reminds me of Christ's cross and his suffering for my sake. And its rough fabric does a good job of telling me I should *crucify* my own flesh, with its vices and sins, to beat off temptations of the devil."

Now smiling, Francis turned slightly toward the Cardinals and added with a glint in his eye, "I don't think my tunic will excite the covetousness of the world, do you?" Some of the Cardinals chuckled while others just stared stoically at the 'Poor Penitent.'

After a dramatic pause, Francis continued his narrative: "I had chosen *my* path. I did not think anyone would notice or care, nor did I anticipate others would join me…but they did. Possessing nothing of worldly value…begging for crumbs of bread to survive…sleeping on the ground…caring for the unclean…These are not what most people seek.

"I was especially surprised when one of the city's wealthiest young men Bernard Quintavalle expressed a desire to join me. After Bernard, more came. There are now 12 of us 'minores' living the Gospel and sharing it with others."

The Pope wondered if the beggar realized the significance of the number he so casually offered. *Twelve – like the 12 Apostles.* It was now obvious to Innocent God had answered his prayers.

ꙮꙮ

Although the way of life Francis presented was modeled on Christ's life, it seemed utterly alien to many members of the Sacred College. The day after hearing Francis speak, some of the Cardinals brought their "concerns" to the Pope. They said Francis's Rule was impractical and unsafe, not to mention the potential for heresy in allowing this *Poor Penitent* movement to move forward.

The Pope had no such misgivings. He invited Francis and his followers to the Lateran the following day and verbally approved Francis's simple Rule for the Friars Minor. They would live Gospel values, committing themselves to poverty, chastity and obedience. The Pope also gave permission for the 'lesser brothers' to preach repentance. Finally, in a special rite, the men from Assisi were given ecclesiastical tonsures, the distinctive haircuts indicating they had been received into a clerical order.

When the business of the day was finished, the Pope walked through the Hall of Mirrors toward his private chambers. Suddenly he stopped, scanned the room and thought how magnificent it looked bathed in the diffused light from the setting April sun. He closed his eyes for a moment and offered a prayer of thanks.

Chapter XVII
Troubled Blood
March, 1212 – Hermitage of Sarteano

The dreams. Each different, yet the same. They'd come more frequently to Francis since his last visit to Rome more than a year before. Since the last time he saw Jacoba.

He'd gone there to pray at the tomb of St. Peter for his upcoming pilgrimage to the Holy Land. As always, when in Rome, Francis stopped at the Septizonium. He'd not only become spiritual advisor to Gratien and Jacoba but also favorite "uncle" to their children.

When he arrived, Francis learned Gratien was away, dealing with business issues.

"He left from Ostia two weeks ago, Francis, and you know how he hates big ships. They make him seasick." Jacoba said. She was in good spirits because her husband's return was imminent.

Always hospitable, she offered Francis his favorite almond cookies, a staple of the Frangipane household. Most Romans called them mustaccioli, but Francis referred to them as *peccata faucium* – Latin for "sins of the throat."

As soon as they learned Francis was in the palace, the Frangipane children gathered around their beggar "uncle" and peppered him with questions. "Where've you been? Did you bring us anything? Are you going to stay with us? Where are you going next?" Jacoba stood a few feet away watching the interaction. She smiled at her children's exuberance and Francis's patience.

A servant slipped into the room, handed a note to Jacoba and quietly left. As Jacoba read the letter, Francis saw the blood drain from her face. He realized she was about to faint. He reached for her, pulled her to himself and held her closely as she sobbed.

Her body trembled as she rested her head on Francis' chest for what seemed to him a long time. He had forgotten how it felt to be so close to a woman that you were aware of her beating heart and could smell the fragrance of her hair.

"He's dead, Francis. Gratien is dead." Jacoba was in a daze as she spoke through tears. Francis quickly tried to collect his thoughts and regain his composure.

"I'm so sorry, Jacoba," Francis offered sincere condolences and reflexively kissed her forehead. Jacoba just kept crying.

The moment her intense sobs subsided and Francis felt she had overcome the initial shock, he led her to the closest chair. She half-sat, half-collapsed into it. He remained standing. The children, now also crying, surrounded their mother. They hugged and kissed her. Hearing the commotion, several servants, including Jacoba's handmaid, rushed into the room. Francis seized the moment to quietly take his leave unobserved.

He wasn't sure if he should return to Rome for Gratien's funeral. He wasn't sure he should ever return.

When visiting the Eternal City, Francis and his friars often relied upon the hospitality of Jacoba and Gratien. Their marriage was strong, and they were good people trying to use their power and riches in ways that were virtuous. He was confident his youthful temptations of the flesh related to Jacoba had been overcome by the grace of God … until that moment when he once again held her in his arms.

ജ൦

The instant Jacoba became a widow, Francis's long-forgotten dreams and longings related to her began to resurface despite his earnest efforts to obliterate them.

In the process of his conversion to life as a poor penitent, Francis had come to love Jacoba in a completely pure way. He believed he had conquered every shred of his past carnal desire of her. Now he wasn't so sure.

Unwelcome and disturbing thoughts darted through his head. He feared perhaps she was the reason he chose not to take priestly vows. Did he think it would now be possible for Jacoba to be with him? Pictures in his mind he dared not envision in the past started popping up willy-nilly.

To make matters worse, Francis couldn't be sure that somewhere deep within him wasn't an unspeakable, involuntary desire for exactly what happened. An unconscious death wish for Gratien was too terrible to contemplate.

Convinced the notions and images now flooding his brain came directly from the devil, Francis immersed himself in prayer and penance to ease his mental torture.

During waking hours, he was able to successfully cut off his thoughts whenever they drifted to fantasies about Jacoba. But asleep, Francis couldn't stop the dreams. Always dreams of lust, they tormented him beyond words.

He tried to escape his uninvited nocturnal temptations by hiding away. The year before, he spent all of Lent alone on an island in the middle of Lake Trasimeno. The solitude helped.

This year, Sarteano seemed perfect. For a short time, he stayed with local monks and helped them care for the sick in a small hospital. Unfortunately, even there it seemed everything he saw reminded him of Jacoba.

So he headed for a hermitage a couple miles above Sarteano. Situated on a small plateau on Mount Cetona, the place consisted of tiny caves hewn out of rock by the Etruscans. The ancient inhabitants used them as tombs more than a thousand years before. Here was nothing and no one to remind him of Jacoba.

Yet the erotic dreams still came. Tonight's were the worst yet. More agitated than ever, Francis took off his clothing. He used the cord that cinched his waist during the day as an instrument of pain, beating himself until welts covered his body.

Even this self-scourging couldn't purge the powerful temptation of the flesh that bothered him this night. Francis was now frantic. He threw open his cell door and staggered barefoot and naked into the freezing night air. He had to do something.

He walked to the garden and threw himself onto a deep pile of snow. His limbs and torso were red and swollen from his beating. He lay there for a moment. Suddenly he jumped up and feverishly gathered handfuls of snow. Packing them into seven lump-like balls, he began to talk loudly to himself: "Behold, this larger one is your wife. These four are your two sons and your two daughters. The other two are your servant and your maid. Hurry and clothe them all, for they are dying of cold. But if caring for them in so many ways troubles you, be even more concerned that you should be serving God alone!"

Francis collapsed into the snow momentarily but quickly picked himself up and calmly returned to his cell. His strange performance left him feeling cleansed of the temptations, and he praised God.

One of the hermits had been praying at the time and saw the entire episode by the light of the moon. When Francis noticed the man had been watching him, he told him to never to tell a soul about it as long as he lived.

Now embarrassed and inconsolable, Francis returned to his cave. There was only one thing he could do. He dropped to the icy ground of the cell. Until dawn, he lay prostrate, praying his upcoming journey to Christ's birthplace would result in his own martyrdom.

ꕥ

Martyrdom, however, was not in God's plan. That summer, Francis never made it beyond the coast of

Dalmatia where his ship went aground. He was forced to return to Italy and decided to preach for several months in the Marches of Ancona – far away from Rome and from Jacoba.

Chapter XVIII
Blood Secret
1212 – Trastevere, Rome, The Normanni Palace

Almost a year to the date she lost Gratien, Jacoba was now sitting at the deathbed of her mother. Not ill for long, Maria dei Normanni knew she would not recover. Her will to live disappeared three years before, when her beloved Vincentius died. Earlier in the day she'd been given last rites and said good-bye to her grandchildren, handmaid and others who had been close to her. The only person she requested remain with her was her daughter.

Jacoba sat silently thinking about her husband's drowning and how cruel it was for God to take him somewhere in the Tyrrhenian Sea in the manner he most dreaded. Even worse, there was no chance for final good-byes. And with no body to hold one last time and no corpse to mourn and entomb, there was no opportunity for closure.

"Jacoba, forgive me," Maria said weakly, her voice further muffled by the pillows under and around her head.

"There is nothing to forgive, mother. You have always been so good to me, and I love you very much," Jacoba said with tearful eyes and a kindly smile. She was holding one of Maria's wrinkled ashen hands in her own. It was oddly warm for someone so close to death.

"Since Gratien's dead, you can now know," Maria said as she lifted her arm with great difficulty and pointed a trembling finger at an ornate bronze coffret on a table across the room. The Normanni noble's voice momentarily grew a bit stronger. "That is yours. I'm sorry, your father and I agreed it best you not have it until we were gone…and your husband was gone, too." Maria, now growing increasingly short of breath, paused after every few words. "The key is…on a hook… under the front edge…of the table. Get…it…now…"

Jacoba initially felt for the key with her fingers but could not locate it. So, she crouched on the floor and looked underneath. Even then, it took her a moment to spot it. "You hid the key well, mother," Jacoba said. Trying to sound lighthearted, she added. "So, this is where you kept your jewels all these years!"

"No, Jacoba." Maria's voice was barely audible. "What's in the box… was never mine…always been yours. Open it…when I'm gone…when you're alone…Don't hate us…Don't hate us…We did this…for you…for love…It was best…" Maria tried to take one more breath but could not.

Jacoba gently closed her mother's eyes and offered a prayer. She then kissed her tenderly several times, inadvertently bathing Maria's face with her tears. Jacoba was crying as much for herself as for her dead mother. The adults she most loved and who loved her were now gone – all of them save one, and he deserted her the day Gratien died – the day she needed him most. Jacoba felt so alone her very soul ached.

ꝏ

It took two full moons until Jacoba felt strong enough to open the mysterious coffret from her mother. She had been curious about its contents from the moment it became hers, but she was also apprehensive. She couldn't imagine what her parents had been hiding from her all these years and why it was something she couldn't have shared with Gratien. She knew whatever was inside was probably not good.

The sun was barely up when Jacoba decided this was the day she would open it. With resolve, she bounded from bed, flipped up her sleeping pillow, and grabbed the key she'd been keeping under it. She walked briskly to her writing table where the small bronze chest sat untouched for the past two months. Jacoba hesitated a moment before inserting the key into the lock. Raising the heavy lid, she stared at what was in the box.

A red silk ribbon tied together more than a dozen pieces of unopened correspondence. Each was dated on the front with *1197, 1198,* or *1199* in Maria Normanni's hand. The instant Jacoba thumbed through the bundle and saw the years, she understood her mother's cryptic deathbed request for absolution.

The first five letters were addressed in Jacoba's own hand to Francis Bernardone. She knew without reading them exactly what they said. Then she saw seven unopened letters addressed to her. The five on top were from Francis. She would open them later because the sixth letter in particular caught her eye. It was addressed in a hand that was neither hers nor Francis's, and her curiosity got the better of her.

The wax seal was equally unfamiliar to her as she broke it open, but the mystery was solved before the second paragraph:

Dearest Jacoba,

I pray all is well with you and your family. We get little news of Rome these days. Life in Assisi is tense right now. The city is on edge due to rumors of rebellion. Perhaps sensing dangerous times ahead, several noble families have already left for Perugia. My father does not want our family involved in an uprising; so, the Bombarones will soon move to Bologna.

When he was offered a position there because of old family ties, he quickly accepted. I'm not sure what will happen to his mattress-making business here in Assisi.

The exciting news for me is I will now be able to study at the university there. I hope to become a teacher. I have had some experience because of instructing Prassede to write. She is a fast learner, and I have trouble keeping up with her. We work on our lessons using sticks on softened ground since she has neither quill nor paper. She is one-of-a-kind. Prays all the time. Seems quite content living the hermit's life.

For shelter, she continues to use several little caves on Subasio, depending upon the weather and the whereabouts of animal predators. Most of the time, I've been meeting her in the grotto where you, Francis and I used to play. I've also met with her two or three times at Torrione, but she doesn't like to go there. She says it's too close to civilization.

Sometimes Francis comes with me, but then we don't have a lesson. Francis takes over. He talks on and on with Prassede and always has so many questions. Why does she pray so much? How come she's not afraid? Doesn't she get tired of wearing the same dreary tunic?

He seems captivated by her way of life but is choosing a much different direction for himself. You probably didn't notice anything when we last visited Rome. I only sensed a change more recently — after he returned from an extended buying trip with his father to the textile markets in France. He is now more like Signor Bernardone. He dresses in fine clothes and helps with the business.

He's also become very popular with Assisi's tripudianti, and it's not just because he regularly picks up the bills for their revels. (You know how generous he is.) He's always been quick with conversation, and his friendly manner draws people to him.

One thing that hasn't changed is his love of song and poetry. He usually plays the role of troubadour at the nightly parties. I joined in the festivities a few times but soon tired of the drunken antics. I guess I'm not much of a reveler. I'd rather read a book.

It's good that I'm leaving Assisi because Francis's circle of friends has grown so large; I'm no longer special to him. It seems the only things he and I now have in common are you and Prassede.

He talks seriously of pursuing knighthood, and his father has agreed to finance the undertaking. So, he most likely won't be staying around Assisi either.

Unfortunately, my move north means I won't see you as often. My father's new position will no longer bring him to Rome, and my studies won't allow me time for travel. However, I expect Francis will continue to find ways to see you on his own.

I think of you often, your stay in Assisi and our many visits to you over the past five years. Even if our paths never cross in the future, you will always hold a special place in my heart. If I were of noble birth or on the path to knighthood, I'd ask for your hand. Alas, I know you've already captured Francis's heart, and I'm sure I would lose the battle were I to fight him for it. Though he never said it, I am convinced you are the reason for his pursuit of knighthood.

Please write to me. And I pray we may continue to be friends in the years to come.

Forever Yours,
Elias

She guessed Elias's letter was written around the time she wrote to him about her betrothal – the letter that never got to him. She mused: *Even Elias thought Francis and I would be wed.*

The final unopened correspondence still lay at the bottom of the box. Noticeably bulkier than the other unread mail, it was indeed addressed to Elias Bombarone, and she knew exactly what it contained.

Jacoba hurriedly broke the wax seal that bore the imprint of her mother's family's crest. A silver ring with a red-orange carnelian stone fell to the table. Before picking it up, Jacoba looked at the wedding ring on the third finger of her left hand while her right hand tenderly toyed with the cross Gratien placed around her neck on the day of their betrothal. Thoughts of her husband, their passionate love and happy marriage filled her, and she smiled.

She paused a moment, then picked up the silver ring that fell out of the letter. After walking to the window to get more light, she began studying the image of Minerva engraved in the little stone. Her gaze shifted to the view outside the window but fixed her eyes on nothing in particular. After several minutes, Jacoba tentatively slipped the silver ring onto the third finger of her right hand.

It was time. The ring was a sign from God. If Francis wouldn't come to her, she would go to him. She needed to know why he deserted her and her children when they most needed his guidance and support. *He didn't even know I had Gratien's fifth child!* Her thoughts were those of exasperation. She was too weary for anger.

Francis's followers who availed themselves of Jacoba's hospitality when in Rome told her Francis was planning a trip to the Holy Land, so she assumed he wasn't in ill health. They assured her Francis would stop at the Septizonium the next time he came to Rome. However, they had no idea when that would be. They said he was very busy because many people – women and men – were joining the Poor Penitents. They made sure she knew Francis was preaching a lot, too.

Their excuses were of no comfort to Jacoba. She slipped the ring from Francis off of her finger and prayed God would somehow permit their paths to cross. He answered her prayers the following spring.

Chapter XIX
Blood Pledge

Late April, 1213 - San Leo Castle, Montefeltro

The Italian countryside was in full bloom as Francis preached his way through the towns and villages of the Romagna. With him were his old friend Elias, who joined the growing brotherhood two years earlier, and Brother Leo.

After spending all of Lent again in solitude, Francis was happy to be on the road. The year before, Lent had been a bleak time. However, with God's help, he overcame his nocturnal temptations related to Jacoba. He was thankful he had not dreamed of her in more than a year. During Lent he focused on prayer and penance. Now his focus was preaching.

Refreshed in spirit, Francis and his compatriots delivered the Gospel with great enthusiasm along a route that would take them back to Assisi.

The sun was coming over the eastern horizon as the three friars took to the road. They were surprised to see the path already bustling with foot traffic, so Elias asked one of the locals why. The man explained there was to be a major celebration at San Leo this very day. He excitedly told the brothers everyone from the countryside had been invited to join in the merrymaking. “You can come too,” he shouted over his shoulder as he hurried past them.

When Francis suggested the trio make a detour to the village, the friars gave him skeptical looks. Francis assured them his intent was not to join in the revels but to share God’s Word with a potentially larger-than-normal audience. Since Elias and Leo knew this would delay their return to Assisi by at least two days, they acquiesced halfheartedly.

After walking miles out of their way, they found themselves craning their necks up at San Leo’s walls. The village was up a steep incline, and Friar Leo’s only comment was an exasperated sigh.

“Come now, Leo, let’s go up to that festival, for with God’s help we will gather some good spiritual fruit.” Francis’s enthusiasm infected neither Leo nor Elias as they trudged upward behind him.

Once in the village, Leo’s face brightened. Expectations were exceeded. One of the parades had just ended, and the crowd was the largest they’d encountered during three weeks on the road. Nobles, peasants, soldiers, merchants – people from all walks of life were milling about the square.

Francis immediately seized the opportunity and climbed up a low wall where he could see his audience and be seen by them.

"Good day, good people," he shouted to get the crowd's attention before launching into a dynamic sermon.

Count Orlando Cattani da Chiusi di Casentino, the wealthiest noble in the region, watched Francis from a luxurious viewing box erected so he and other nobles could comfortably view the day's pageantry. The extensive celebration in connection with the knighting of one of the counts of Montefeltro was financed in part by the Count who hosted nobles and their retinues from as far as Florence and Rome.

The 29-year-old widow of Gratien Frangipane was among his invited guests. Jacoba knew Orlando well since she and Gratien visited his castle in Chiusi several times. The Count was a close friend of her late husband. Both had been squires in France and later fought side-by-side in the Holy Land.

Jacoba's eldest son Jacob was currently a squire himself in Orlando's castle in Tuscany, and it was he who insisted his mother preview what his own investiture would be like.

Elias was the first to notice Jacoba amid the crowd, but she didn't see him. She and everyone else were focused on the animated Francis now telling them *the way to endure the hardships of this life and turn them into joy is to offer them to God.*

"More important than helping us bear the unbearable here on earth is that each trial is taking us a step closer to our new life with God in heaven forever," Francis spoke eloquently from the heart, and his words were well received. Ever the troubadour, he gave poetic accounts of the sufferings and martyrdoms of various apostles, disciples and holy virgins.

“So great is the good I expect from God when I die…that all pain I encounter in this life is pure delight…just as it was with them!” His pauses added to the drama.

Jacoba never heard Francis preach the way he did now. She was sure he was inspired by the Holy Spirit. Even the way the morning sun shone on Francis gave him an angelic aura.

Count Orlando, seated next to Jacoba, was also taking in every word of Francis’s hour-long unrehearsed oration.

“Your son told me you know this remarkable man. Is that correct?” Orlando whispered to Jacoba without taking his eyes off Francis.

He noticed from the corner of his eye that she nodded affirmatively and was just as transfixed as he. During a slight pause in Francis’s address, Orlando turned to her and asked if she would invite Francis to join the celebration in the banquet hall. “Your late husband spoke highly of this man, and I would very much like to talk with him.”

“He may not want to feast with us, Orlando, but I’m sure he would be most pleased to speak with you. And I will gladly introduce you,” Jacoba responded.

As the spontaneous homily was ending, Jacoba gingerly worked her way through the crowd toward Francis. When Elias noticed she was approaching, he nudged Francis to look in her direction. When their eyes met, Jacoba couldn’t tell whether Francis was delighted or troubled by her presence. She had no way to know it was a combination of both.

Francis the man had an impulsive urge to take her in his arms and caress her with his lips. However, Francis the leader of the Poor Penitents would dare not even kiss her hand. *This is either a test from God or a temptation from the devil,* he told himself. In either case, Francis kept notable distance between them and offered only a courteous bow to acknowledge her.

"Francis, it's been too long." Jacoba's voice was sad and sincere. "We need to talk."

Jacoba noticed Francis's eyes abruptly dart to the man who had followed her through the crowd and was now standing conspicuously close to her. Count Orlando was a striking figure. A year younger than her late husband, Orlando was as tall as Gratien and as attractive in a different way. Orlando was less rugged with no visible scars from combat. His long dark hair and impeccably trimmed beard were threaded with grey which made him look especially distinguished. Francis noticed Orlando's garments were tailored to fit perfectly and made of the finest fabric the cloth merchant's son had ever seen. He thought Jacoba and Orlando made an exceptionally magnificent couple.

"Francis, I would like to introduce you to a close friend of mine and one of *your* admirers. Count Orlando of Cattani, may I present Francis Bernardone of Assisi, founder and leader of the Poor Penitents." Jacoba's tone was formal.

Francis bowed respectfully to the noble.

"Please, Father Francis. I should be the one bowing to you for your stirring words. I have heard of your good works and your miracles and your privations and …

Francis interrupted the noble. "Signor, I'm not worthy of your deference for I'm not a priest but merely a lowly, unlearned beggar. And the words I speak that you so esteem are not of my own doing. They are a gift to you from Our Lord."

"You are too humble, sir. I know of your stay last year at Sarteano. That area is part of my holdings. I heard you spent all Lent there in a hut made of branches. I've been told it was no better than an animal's den. I also know of your care for lepers and how you denounce your own body and all material things. I'm now the beggar for I must plead with you to dine with us and speak to me about the salvation of my soul. Will you join me at table now?"

"I'm happy to talk with you, but please go to your friends and eat with them since they expect you to be part of the celebration. After the feast, we will talk together as much as you wish."

Francis's thoughtfulness impressed the Count nearly as much as his sermon. "At sunset, please come to the palazzo where we are staying." Orlando pointed to a large building which could be seen from the square. "We shall speak then. You and the brothers must plan to spend the night since I have much to discuss with you. Thank you, Francis."

Without waiting for a response from Francis, Orlando made a slight bow to him then turned to Jacoba.

"I think your son is expecting us." He offered Jacoba his arm, and they headed toward the banquet hall.

ꕥ

Jacoba returned to the palazzo shortly before sunset. Francis was sitting on a bench in the garden and looked surprised to see her instead of the Count.

"Orlando will be here in an hour. He apologizes and hopes you will understand. He had some formalities to deal with." Jacoba sat down next to Francis and looked around. "Where are Elias and Leo?"

"They were exhausted. And when I told them we would accept the Count's hospitable offer and stay the night, they seized the opportunity to rest in real beds before I changed my mind. I prefer sleeping on the ground or a floor, but they aren't as inclined." Francis smiled.

He and Jacoba sat in awkward silence for a few moments until she spoke.

"I've missed you, Francis." She looked at him, but his eyes were downcast as his fingers played with a blade of grass he had just picked. She went on, "I have felt so lonely since losing Gratien. It's not easy to be a mother, run an enormous household and manage the affairs of our family's properties." Jacoba heaved a sigh. "I don't like my solitary life."

The two were silent for a few moments.

"Enough time has passed so you could take a husband," Francis got out the words in an unusually halting way. "Is there someone you have in mind?"

"There is." She said, then more silence.

Francis looked up and swallowed hard. "Does he love you?"

"I believe he does." Now Jacoba's eyes were downcast and she bit her lower lip.

"Then, there's no problem, is there? Francis snapped as he looked at her.

"There's a huge problem, Francis." She hesitated as if trying to bolster the courage to continue. She took a deep breath and looked Francis directly in the eye. "He's already committed to another."

"You mean Count Orlando is betrothed to someone else? How could he do this to you?" Francis's tone was even more irate.

Jacoba smiled through the tears forming in her eyes. "Count Orlando and I are good friends. That's all. No, Francis, the man I love and the only man I would ever wed has a more solemn obligation than marriage."

"No! It can't be. You and a priest are in love?!"

Jacoba laughed to herself. "Of course not!"

"I don't understand, Jacoba." Francis shook his head.

"Francis, I love *you*!" A tear trickled down her right cheek. She smiled as she wiped it away. "You've known that for a long time, haven't you?

Francis threw his head back and looked up at the darkening sky. He had just heard the words for so many years he had longed to hear from the woman he loved. *Why did they have to come too late? Why didn't she tell him before her betrothal? Why did she never respond to his letters?* Francis the magnificent preacher and saintly troubadour was at a loss for what to say – more important – for what to do. Jacoba filled the silence:

"Is that why you so totally abandoned me when Gratien died? . . . Francis, I'm sorry. I shouldn't have said anything. It just came out." Jacoba could no longer hold back her tears. She sniffled and went on. "I hope it wasn't a sin for me to tell you. I'll just give you what I came here to give you, and I'll take my leave." Jacoba tried to regain her composure.

"I found this among my mother's things when she died." Jacoba bent over and slightly lifted the bottom of her gown. She pulled the silver ring with the carnelian stone from the hem of her chemise and held it in front of Francis.

"It belongs to you. It was in a locked strong box in my mother's bed chamber with lots of unopened letters. I tried to return it to you a long time ago when I learned of my betrothal, but my parents intercepted all my correspondence. Your letters to me, too. I never knew until six moons ago that you made three trips to Rome to try to see me back then. When I hadn't heard from you, I assumed you never really loved me." Jacoba had regained her self-control.

"Here. It is *your* ring." Jacoba extended her hand, and Francis took it from her palm. He glanced briefly at the ring and then looked at Jacoba. He hadn't thought about the ring in years.

"How did you know we would see each other here … today?" Francis tone expressed his bewilderment.

"I didn't. Since I found the ring, I've been carrying it with me. I had special pockets sewn into the hems of all my chemises so I could always keep it near. I trusted our paths would cross sometime. Having it with me gave me great comfort just as this cross from Gratien does." She fingered the gem-laden necklace that was always around her neck.

"Francis, I know you have pledged your life to God. I would never dream of trying to lure you away from Him, especially after watching you preach today, but I want you back in my life. I need you. I have no husband, no parents, no brothers or sisters. And since I am unwilling to partake in the intrigues of the Frangipane Family, they want no part of me. I am totally alone.

"I'm sorry. There I go again, saying things I shouldn't say." Jacoba paused. She started to stand up as she added, "God be with you, Francis. Good-bye."

He grabbed her hand and pulled her back, "Wait, Jacoba. Please sit with me for a few moments more."

They sat next to each other in silence, their eyes looking at everything around the garden except each other. After the quiet interlude, Francis turned to Jacoba.

"Give me your hand," he said tenderly. As she began lifting her left hand which still bore Gratien's ring he said, "The other hand." She put her right hand in his, and he gently kissed it.

"I think you are the only person who truly understands me, perhaps better than I understand myself. I have changed from the youth that you knew, but I never stopped loving you . . . and I never will." Francis's voice was strong, but water pooled in his eyes as he continued.

"While our physical union is not possible now or ever, I see no reason why our souls may not be joined, united in our love of God." Francis slipped the silver ring on the third finger of her right hand. "I promise I will be there for you, Jacoba, in spirit. You will be in my prayers always, and I also promise to be a spiritual father to your children as well."

Jacoba was just about to say something when Count Orlando and a small entourage noisily entered the garden.

"Ah, there you are, Francis, Lady Jacoba. I'm sorry for my lateness." After dismissing his retinue, the Count turned toward Jacoba. "Your son requests your immediate presence in our library. I told him about our small collection, and he said you would enjoy seeing it. Francis, let us retire to the red room where we may talk in private.

As the little group began to go its separate ways, Jacoba's and Francis's eyes met. In his eyes she saw joy. In hers, he saw peace. Although they saw each other many times after this day, they never spoke of their bond. They had no need to.

ꕥ

Francis and the Count talked long into the night. Orlando was so overwhelmed with gratitude for the Poverello's advice that he wanted to shower Francis with riches yet knew the Poverello would never accept gold or jewels.

"You have shown me the way to salvation, and my soul needs to give you *something* in return. Will you accept a gift of land?

Francis answered with a kindly smile and no words.

"That's right. You have no possessions and want to own nothing." The count grew silent as he stroked his beard and looked at the floor. All of a sudden, Orlando looked up with a grin on his face.

"There is another way, Brother Francis. There is a mountain I own not far from my castle in Tuscany. It is isolated, wild and well suited for doing penance and praying in solitude. It is called Mount La Verna. If it should please you and your companions, I will sign a document so you may have use of this mountain in perpetuity. Will you accept my offer?"

Francis looked up with an equally broad smile and responded. “Praise God who provides for His little sheep and thank *you*, Count Orlando. I very gladly accept your charitable offer.”

ഌ൫

Francis and his two companions were on the road before dawn. Several days later Count Orlando returned to his castle in Chiusi, Tuscany. In early May, as promised, he legally gave use of the mountain to the brothers forever. He also sent 50 armed men to escort a small band of friars as they explored it to find a place suitable for prayer and contemplation. The soldiers not only protected the brothers from wild animals but also cut down branches with their swords so they could build a hut on a small plateau.

Eleven years later on this mountain Francis would receive the stigmata.

Chapter XX
Blood on Her Hands

November 1213 – Marino

The gloom of the late November sky matched the dimness of Jacoba's heart as her mind replayed events of the previous day: The anger of the crowd. The pleas of the child. The image of the sword slicing through flesh and bone. The severed hand on the ground. The blood spilling from the boy's arm. The red rivulet taking shape on the snowy soil.

She couldn't rid herself of the images. It was her decision to sever the child's hand. Since Gratien's death she was in charge of everything related to Marino, and she hated that. She especially detested being responsible for administering justice.

A panel of Jacoba's subjects was responsible for judging innocence or guilt in criminal matters, but it was she who determined penalties. Until yesterday, her sentences involved only fines not corporal punishment.

Over and over she told herself it had to be done. *The people of Marino sought revenge. The boy sought mercy. I gave them justice.* Jacoba tried to convince herself the punishment was fair, perhaps even compassionate. After all, the boy's victims demanded he be executed, and Jacoba took only his left hand.

The boy didn't scream. He didn't cry. He just stared at his bloody, handless arm with a look of amazement and disbelief before fainting.

Standing a few yards from the child, she recalled wanting to vomit, to run from the scene. She couldn't do either because she was the leader of the Settesoli Frangipane, the Lady of the Castello di Marino. She didn't wield the sword, but she alone bore responsibility for the action.

Jacoba was no stranger to the repugnant. Her earliest and most vivid childhood memory was the frenzied mob covered in blood joyfully slaughtering pigs on Monte Testaccio. Not long after that, she watched the pet leopard of Cencius Frangipane kill one of his servants.

More than once as a young girl, Jacoba caught sight of severed heads impaled on a pikes at Rome's gate. She was always matter-of-factly informed by one of her elders that the heads belonged to criminals or adversaries of whatever family ruled Rome at the moment.

Once Jacoba moved into the Septizonium, she became personally acquainted with violence and its results. Her first day there, she wandered into a room in the lowest level of the palace that was furnished with various implements of torture. Gratien's father explained that while it had been used frequently by his family in the past, he himself used it less than a dozen times. He said that just seeing a demonstration of the cruel implements was usually enough to frighten captives into providing information. He added that he was aware of only three people who were tortured to death in the room.

Various branches of Gratien's extended family were always involved in fighting somewhere in the eternal city, and the injured often sought medical help at the Septizonium. Since Jacoba had experience assisting the palace's physicians, she was usually the person asked to help when one of "the family" showed up with an injury. She saw everything from an arrow through a neck to an almost-severed leg attached by a few ligaments to a gash so large it exposed the man's rib cage. Nearly all of these major wounds resulted in death after much suffering.

Even more distressing was Jacoba's personal blood-spattered encounter with brutality when an enemy of the Frangipani held a knife to her, tried to rape her, and was responsible for the death of her unborn child. At the time, she felt no mercy toward her attacker. She was thankful – maybe even glad – Gratien killed him.

Jacoba knew her late husband had killed more than a few men during his lifetime, but she never dwelled on it. Like her own father, Gratien was a knight and noble. Gratien as well as her father were no murderers. They only took lives to safeguard the people who depended on them as well as defend the Church. Jacoba was aware executions took place in Marino but never witnessed them.

Like every other Roman, Jacoba had also grown accustomed to the sight of people with missing limbs or appendages. She admired knights who lost them in battle and pitied beggars born without them or elders who surrendered them to disease. Until yesterday she felt a self-righteous indifference for criminals who lost appendages as punishment for their crimes.

She had no aversion to the dispensing of corporal punishment until yesterday when she herself had to do it... to sever the hand of a mere child.

The boy was 11 or 12 years old. No one knew for sure – not even the boy himself. Exactly where he lived or with whom he lived was up for debate. No one claimed him. Over the span of a few years, people would occasionally see the boy but gave him no thought until they started linking him to the disappearance of things beyond a bit of produce or a crust of bread.

Boyhood mischief turned into petty theft that quickly evolved into larceny. The youth took a goat from a farmer, an iron cauldron from an inn-keeper's kitchen and a sword from the blacksmith who was repairing it for a knight.

Two elderly sisters swore he snuck into their dwelling one night and took a valuable silver coin inherited from their father. The boy thought they were asleep, but he was wrong.

"We watched him do it, but we were too scared to scream or say anything at all," one of them explained at the trial.

"We just lay there as still as corpses until he left," the other added in a shaky voice.

More than a dozen other townspeople implicated the boy in thefts ranging from a plow to a small holy relic taken from a visiting priest. Items important to the livelihoods of townspeople and country folk were disappearing left and right. Every finger pointed at the boy.

Most recently, he had begun to set fires here and there to distract people while he did his pilfering. Citizens of Marino and the surrounding countryside were on edge as well as enraged.

When two knights on horseback saw the boy poaching in a Frangipane forest, they grabbed him and hauled him along with the animal carcasses to the Marino palace. He sat in the castle's dungeon for 15 days awaiting trial as well as the arrival of Jacoba who would determine his punishment.

Once Jacoba's entourage passed through Marino's gate, two dozen people surrounded the group. Jacoba was on horseback as were the six Frangipane guards who flanked her. The crowd didn't give them time to dismount before loudly voicing their ideas on suitable punishment for the young criminal.

"Hang him! He thieved from us, and he's not even sorry!"

"He put our lives and our livelihoods in danger!"

"Hanging's too good for him! I say he should be put on the breaking wheel!"

"Kill him. It's the only thing that'll stop him!"

The number and vehemence of the boy's victims shocked and disturbed Jacoba.

"That boy's just plain no good, and no one wants him around," said the blacksmith. The shaky voice of an elderly woman added, “Fining him won’t do any good. He’d just have to steal even more from everybody to pay it off!”

Her head held high and looking straight ahead, Jacoba said loudly and calmly, “I will consider everything and determine a fitting punishment.” She paused for a few seconds, then gently spurred her horse. “Make way, we need to get through!”

Once settled in the palace, Jacoba summoned her overseer for a report on details of the situation. The advisor dispassionately relayed the extent of the boy’s crimes and the number of victims. Halfway through the discourse, Jacoba got up and began pacing.

“I don’t understand how a boy could have caused such a disturbance and stolen so many things. Are you sure he acted alone?”

“No one else has ever been seen with him. Some have tried unsuccessfully to follow him to his *lair*, but he has proven to be cunning and quick.” The overseer scratched his head, then added, “He steals, then disappears without a trace.”

Jacoba stopped walking and faced the man. “I will not execute the boy.”

The overseer responded quickly, “My ladyship, we look to you to safeguard us. The people will say you haven’t met your responsibility for protecting them if you do not deal with this criminal – young or not – in a most severe way. A hanging every few years helps keep the peace here. Your husband knew that.”

“I’m not my husband.” Jacoba glared at the overseer for his impertinence, then continued.

“Can the child return any of the property he has stolen?”

"No one knows what he did with it. We think he may have sold the goods in Rome or somewhere along the coast. Perhaps he's working with Gypsies. We know absolutely nothing about him, and he refuses to speak. We have not yet tried torture but we ..."

Jacoba held up her hand to stop the overseer mid-thought. "I've seen great cruelty in the name of justice in Rome, and it has never yielded good fruit. This boy has shed no one's blood. He has molested no one. Why are the people so incensed?"

"The youth shows no remorse, and his path of crime has increased. They are frightened of what he may do in the future. And you should be wary, too. If he is not dealt with most severely now – after being caught red-handed taking what rightfully belongs to your ladyship – others may follow his lead and also help themselves to what is yours – not theirs."

"I understand." Jacoba paused and stared straight ahead at nothing in particular. "But to ask me to take his life? I can't. I won't."

"Then you will have rebellion, and more than one life is bound to be lost. Can you live with that, my Lady?"

"Will anything satisfy the people short of killing the child?" Jacoba rubbed her forehead with both hands and closed her eyes as if these actions would somehow ease the burden of making her decision.

"Cutting off his hands may appease some of his victims and almost guarantee he wouldn't be thieving anymore." The overseer was pensive. "But that may not be enough for others who've been wronged. Honestly, my lady, I've never seen such anger from so many."

"Both hands…That seems very cruel. How could he survive? The boy apparently has no family, and who knows where or how he lives." Jacoba paused for several seconds before speaking again.

"What if we remove only one hand?" Jacoba didn't wait for the overseer to respond before adding, "I think that is what we should do."

The overseer heaved a sigh.

"I think it is too small a penalty for his extensive crimes, my Lady…but since that is your decision, I will make preparations. It will be done tomorrow at midday."

The overseer bowed and excused himself.

Jacoba informed one of her guards that he would chop off the youth's hand.

"Make sure your blade is its sharpest. I want the cut to be swift and clean. There's no reason for the youth to unduly suffer."

She made arrangements with Marino's priest to be present not only for the child's sake but to calm the crowd with the words of the Lord if the punishment itself didn't satisfy them. Should the reverend's words not do the trick, Jacoba made sure her Roman guards as well as Marino's knights would also be present in full force.

Jacoba also had a guard summon one of the boy's victims – the blacksmith – to the palace where the overseer informed him he would be cauterizing the boy's bloody stump.

"Why should I do that for such a no-good thief?!" was the smithy's initial response.

"Because God wants you to…Lady Jacoba wants you to…and 'they' want you to." The overseer rolled his eyes and tilted his head toward the four muscular guards standing to the right of the blacksmith. "You *will* do it, and you will do it correctly or you may find yourself facing consequences similar to the boy's. Do I have to call Father Gilberto here to talk to you about mercy and loving your enemies?"

The blacksmith grumbled to himself and then said, "Okay. I'll do what I can."

Once satisfied the details had been arranged, Jacoba retired to her bed chamber where she prayed much of the night.

ꙮ

A large crowd gathered early to watch the boy receive his "just desserts." There were people from the countryside as well as those who lived within the castle's walls. Onlookers included a multitude of curiosity seekers hungry to see bloodletting as well as those who had been wronged and wanted to witness justice.

After his lengthy stay in the palace dungeon, the youth emerged looking pale, dirty and emaciated. He appeared to be neither defiant nor penitent. He was silent and seemed apathetic. Surprisingly, the crowd was still. A few people muttered in hushed tones as they craned their necks to see the spectacle.

It took less than 10 minutes for justice to be administered. The guard severed the hand, and the blacksmith did as he'd been told. After fainting, the boy came to the moment the searing iron rod touched his bloody stump. The youth's screams were ear-splitting until he once again blacked out. Two of Jacoba's guards carried the boy to the priest's house where he would recover.

The people of Marino seemed placated though not totally pleased by Jacoba's punishment. The group dispersed in silence except for a few people in back whose view of the proceedings had been obstructed. They now moved forward to look at the blood on the snowy ground and the severed hand that still lay on it.

Jacoba returned in silence to her bed chamber in the palace. Once alone, she let the tears she'd been holding back trickle down her cheeks. *What have I done? I spared the boy's life yet I feel as if I have taken it just the same. He may stop thieving, but he's now destined to beg ... if he even survives the amputation.*

Exhausted from crying, she lay on her bed thinking of what Gratien would have done. While the overseer was confident her late husband would have opted for the most severe punishment for the young criminal, she wasn't so sure. In the past, Gratien let justice overrule mercy. However, when he began spending time with Francis, Jacoba noticed gradual changes in him. She realized how much she, too, had changed because of Francis's influence. In private, Jacoba and Gratien had begun to shun many of the trappings of their aristocratic lifestyle. However, they couldn't as easily cast off their responsibilities to their vassals nor could they discard the social and political expectations of their position.

Most all, Jacoba was well aware of her duties to her children, of the properties held in her trust for them. She began to dwell on the sadness the families holdings have caused. What had started as a small disagreement between

Pope Innocent and herself about custody of the thriving community of Ninfa had evolved into a legal dispute. She refused to acknowledge Innocent's continuous claims to the town which she was holding in trust for her eldest son. When the Pope formalized the claims, Jacoba began legal action in Rome against him. *I never thought I could do anything like that. I didn't want to, but I had to for Jacob's sake. I wouldn't be a good parent if I'd done otherwise.*

The more she thought about it, the more Jacoba longed for a life like Francis's. *Wouldn't it be wonderful to get away from all this? ...to be like Francis and live simply ...to own nothing... to be no one...or at least someone who doesn't have to be guarded every moment of every day?* Jacoba realized she no longer wanted to be the leader of Marino or the Lady of the Septizonium. She wanted to live like Francis and his followers, yet she knew she could not abandon the many people whose very lives depended upon her leadership.

What advice would Gratien give her? What counsel would her father and mother provide? She could no longer ask them. But she could seek Francis's advice.

She wiped the tears from her face, got off her bed and headed to her writing table.

A Letter from Jacoba

To Francis

1213

My Dearest Francis,

I write to you with a heavy heart and restless soul. I'm staring at the ring you placed on my finger in the garden at San Leo and hoping you recall the promise you made to me then. I pray you counsel me now in the faith-filled way you did when Gratien was at my side.

I am so unhappy. I am at a low point in my life. I will not burden you with the cause of my misery, but I feel I can no longer bear the weight of my responsibilities alone. My shoulders are just not strong enough.

I want my life to be more like yours...and the brothers...and Clare's. You and the other Poor Penitents have no spouses and neither do I. You have relinquished family and property to devote yourselves to God's work. While I have no parents or siblings, I have other overwhelming obligations impossible to renounce. I cannot abandon my children or forsake their future offspring. Nor am I able to turn my back on the hundreds of souls in Rome, Marino and elsewhere who are the vassals of the Settesoli Branch of the Frangipane Family. Their very lives depend upon my leadership.

Once my children come of age and assume the solemn responsibilities that accompany our Frangipane name, I will perhaps join Clare and her consecrated women in community. What do I do until then, Francis? Is there any way to escape the slavery of my titled existence? I feel so alone.

You've seen the world I live in. I beg you to advise me as to how I may pursue a holy life within such ungodly circumstances. I await your guidance.

Forever Yours,
Brother Jacoba

A Letter from Francis
To Jacoba
1214

My Dearest Brother Jacoba,

If I could come to you right now, I would. Unfortunately, I must remain in Assisi. The brothers have gathered from near and far for our chapter meeting which begins tomorrow at sunrise. I am obliged to be here to pray with them and provide guidance.

When I received your letter, I prayed to the Holy Ghost and fasted for two days before dipping my quill into the inkhorn. Our conversation in the garden at San Leo and the promise I made to you are foremost in my mind as I write this.

Would it surprise you if I advise you to take a husband? Would it shock you even more if I suggest who this mate should be? The riches of his kingdom are matchless. His power is far greater than any ruler or the pope himself. I know he already loves you unconditionally.

It might surprise you, but I believe you've already made his acquaintance. In any case, it will be up to you to approach him. Your marriage would be passionate but not carnal. If you haven't already figured out who I'm suggesting you wed, I will tell you. I'm advising you to pursue a mystical marriage...with Jesus.

If you Love the Lord with all your heart, soul, mind and strength...If you love your neighbor as yourself...If you hate your body with its vice and sins...If you receive the Body and Blood of our Lord Jesus Christ...and if you produce worthy fruits of penance...the Spirit of the Lord will rest upon you and make its home within you.

We are spouses when the faithful soul is joined by the Holy Spirit to our Lord Jesus. We are brothers and sisters to Him when we do the will of the Father in heaven. We are mothers when we carry Him in our heart and body through a divine love and a pure and sincere conscience. We give birth to Him through a holy activity which must shine as an example before others. In other words, when we do God's work, we are not only His children but we become a spouse, sister and mother.

What I have written here I learned from the Gospel. I have also gleaned much from my meetings with our old friend Prassede. I have consulted her numerous times over the years, and her counsel has always been helpful – prickly when my soul needed prodding and comforting when it needed solace.

These past several years as I've preached in cities, the countryside and far beyond, I've encountered numerous people who expressed sentiments similar to yours. Although most don't hold noble titles, they are people of means obligated to others in solemn ways. Like you, if they neglected their worldly responsibilities, those who depend upon them would suffer greatly.

Someday, I hope to formulate a rule to help guide these faithful souls on their quest for holiness in the secular world. When I write something, I will see that a copy is made for you. However, now I must get back to shepherding my growing band of Poor Penitents. I need to make sure they have not strayed from our growing flock.

I beg you not to dwell on my humble efforts at giving you counsel. Instead, look to the Gospels themselves for the best advice on living a holy life no matter what your circumstances. They are the words of life and salvation – whoever reads and follows them will find life and draw from the Lord salvation.

I shall be in Rome in the coming year for a special meeting at the Lateran. It has been called by the Pope himself, and many clergy will attend. I hope I may be able to spend some time with you then.

Forever Yours in Our
Shared Love of Christ,
Francis

Chapter XXI
In Their Blood
Early Autumn, 1215 – Rome, The Septizonium

"Lady Jacoba. Lady Jacoba." The muffled summons was followed by gentle raps on the door of the noblewoman's bed chamber. Deep in slumber, Jacoba unconsciously incorporated the disembodied voice into her dream.

"My ladyship, I'm sorry to awaken you, but you are needed right now." The vocalization was more forceful as were the knocks at the door. Jacoba now recognized the voice as belonging to one of her handmaids. The noble opened her eyes and sat at the edge of the bed a few seconds before walking to the door. She opened it a crack.

"What is it, Priscilla? What can't wait until morning?" Jacoba sounded displeased.

"It's the holy man Francis, my ladyship. Two of his brothers have brought him here. They're afraid he's dying. The guards came to me and told me to let you know right away. I didn't want to bother you, but I didn't know what to do. I'm so sorry." The young servant was nervous and apologetic.

"You did the right thing. I'm just not quite awake yet." Jacoba gave the girl a sleepy smile before continuing. "Where is he?"

"At the main portico, my lady."

"Tell the guards to bring him and whoever is with him to Gratien's bed chamber." Jacoba nodded toward the room next to hers. "Have them put Francis in the bed, and bring some mats and linens so the others can rest on floor. I'll join everyone as soon as I dress.

"Oh, and wake up Sabina and tell her to bring a pitcher of fresh water and some clean cloths to Gratien's room. Thank you, Priscilla." Jacoba waved her right hand to dismiss the servant.

As Priscilla hurried down the corridor, Jacoba walked slowly toward a chair in her bedroom. She rubbed her temples in an effort to massage away sleepiness. She didn't wait for Sabina to dress her. Instead she threw on the gown that had been laid out for her the previous evening. She splashed some water on her face, trying to avoid wetting her nightcap which she intentionally continued to wear not for warmth but to keep her long hair out of her way.

More awake now, Jacoba caught herself imagining frightful scenarios for her beloved friend. She reined in the negative thoughts by kneeling in front of an image of the Virgin Mary and praying. The small mosaic on her wall was a cherished gift from her parents. As she murmured amen, she heard a hubbub in the hallway. Francis had arrived.

With him were the two Poor Penitents who brought him to the palace on an improvised litter. One appeared to be about 14 years old. The other looked no older than 20. Both were beside themselves with worry and alternated recounting what happened.

"He collapsed just outside the city walls. He told us he needed to rest a few minutes, so we sat down," said the younger of the two.

"Then he started breathing really fast and got dizzy when he tried to stand. I hope you don't mind that we brought him here. He had mentioned your name earlier during our journey and said you were a kind woman who was good to the brothers." The older friar barely finished his last sentence before the younger one spoke again.

"We were initially headed to St. Biagio's, but just before he collapsed Francis told us he wanted to come here instead. Is he going to die?"

The two were speaking so quickly, Jacoba interrupted.

"It's good that you brought Francis here. Now, slow down and tell me all you can about how he came to be in this wretched state."

"The past day he wasn't himself. He seemed confused. He wanted to rest a lot. We decided to make the litter so we could pull him. He seemed too weak to walk. When we tried to put him on it, he barked at us and said he'd get to Rome on his own."

"He was argumentative, not like himself at all."

"Then he collapsed. We put him on the litter and brought him here."

Jacoba walked over to the bed and looked at her motionless friend. Francis's eyes were closed. His breathing was shallow and rapid. She put her hand on his forehead. He was warm, but she didn't detect fever.

She laid her head on his chest so she could hear his heartbeat. It was something she learned from the healers Marco and Matteo. Even listening through his coarse tunic she could tell it was beating much faster than it should.

She scrutinized his face. It seemed more gaunt than when she last saw him, and his eyes looked sunken.

"How long has it been since he ate or drank anything?"

The two brothers looked at each other and shrugged their shoulders.

"You mean you walked from Assisi, and he had nothing at all to eat or drink the past few days?" Jacoba shook her head and went back to examining her patient.

"What about relieving himself? Did you notice him stopping more than usual? She kept her eyes on her patient.

"No." The older brother cleared his throat and tilted his head toward the younger one as he added, "We both had more roadside stops than Brother Francis."

Jacoba reached down, took Francis's hand, and gently pinched the skin on the back of it between her thumb and forefinger. When she released her fingers, the fold of skin she created was extremely slow to return to normal. She was still looking at Francis when she began to dispense orders.

She glanced toward the Poor Penitents. "You two come here and prop him up a little more. Use the pillow over there." Jacoba pointed to a cushion sitting on a side chair. "We need to get some liquid into him as soon as possible. Do whatever Sabina asks of you.

"Sabina, get Francis to take some water. Wet a cloth and put it to his lips. Let it drip into his mouth until he is able to sip from the cup. Keep getting the liquid into him even if it's just a drop at a time.

"Priscilla, you come with me."

The two headed to the palace's kitchen where Jacoba prepared a solution of fresh water, a dozen pinches of salt and a couple drops of honey.

"I know it's not part of your job, Priscilla, but fill a kettle with fresh water and start it boiling. Then, go wake one of the cooks and ask her to prepare bone broth as quickly as possible. Tell her I need it for healing, and she will know what herbs to add. Bring the broth to me the moment it is ready. Make sure there is enough for Francis's cohorts, too. And bring some bread for them. If Francis hasn't eaten, they probably haven't either."

Jacoba headed back to the sickroom. The moment she walked through the door, she was met by the young brother.

"Is Francis going to die?"

"That's entirely up to God, of course, but we have to do our best and perhaps God will be merciful." She was matter-of-fact in her response. There was no time for speculation or philosophizing.

"Have you been able to get any water into him, Sabina?"

"A few drops, my lady. He hasn't taken the cup yet."

"Let's try to give him some of this." Jacoba poured her simple concoction into the cup. Sabina got out of the way so Jacoba could sit on the edge of the bed. She slipped her right hand under Francis's head to lift it while her left hand brought the cup of 'healing water' to his lips.

"Please drink this, Francis," she whispered. "Can you do this for your Brother Jacoba?"

She didn't think anyone else in the room heard her, but the Poor Penitents did and looked at each other in bewilderment. She noticed their raised eyebrows.

"Sabina, please take these young men to the kitchen for bread and broth. They must be hungry, and we don't want them to suffer what ails Francis. When they've finished eating, escort them to one of our guest rooms where they can get much-needed sleep. I will stay here with Brother Francis."

ꙮ

Jacoba spent the morning at Francis's bedside giving him tiny sips of her therapeutic water mixture. She also daubed his face with a soft, moist cloth. By early afternoon Francis had opened his eyes and was drinking bone broth. By late afternoon, he was eating small pieces of bread she dunked in the broth.

When Jacoba had turned her back for a moment, Francis tried unsuccessfully to sit up. He fell back on his pillow. Jacoba glared at him.

"Have you learned your lesson yet, Brother Francis? Maybe this is God's way of reminding you there's a time and a place for fasting. Going without water or broth and having no food on a long journey is not virtuous. It's irresponsible. Even John the Baptist ate locusts when he fasted in the desert. You are human like the rest of us, and you shouldn't keep treating your body the way you do, especially after your sickness last year in Spain." Jacoba realized her lecture was going on deaf ears when she noticed Francis using morsels of his bread to entice a small bird on the windowsill to land on his hand.

All she could do was smile and shake her head. "You frightened your young friars, and you scared me too."

"Are Brothers Giovanni and Electus all right?" Francis gave her a mischievous smile.

"They're getting some well-earned sleep after spending the night lugging you through the streets of Rome." Jacoba tried to sound furious but couldn't pull it off.

"I'm sorry for all the trouble I've caused." He sounded sincere. "It was important for me to fast as well as pray in preparation for attending the Pope's important meeting. I offered it up so the Paraclete would be in our midst and guide us."

"Francis, I think the Holy Spirit will be at Innocent's General Council no matter what. But if you had gone without drink a few more hours, ***you*** most likely would ***not*** be going to the gathering. You would have died. You are not yet fully healed from what has been afflicting you for many months. You have to take better care of yourself."

Francis didn't say anything in response. He just smiled.

Jacoba didn't tell him she sensed something more may be happening with his health beyond dehydration. Even if she could have identified the onset of a specific disease and told him, she figured it wouldn't have done any good. Francis was Francis. He was totally focused on his immortal soul. He had no regard for his earthly body unless it was being used to serve God by proclaiming the Gospel, caring for lepers or helping the poor.

She knew Francis would be appearing at her door in the future. It wasn't an altogether disagreeable thought. She liked being in his presence and caring for him.

Chapter XXII
Blood of the Faithful

Late Autumn, 1215 – Rome, The Lateran Palace

"And I quote now from the prophet Ezekiel: *'Go through the city of Jerusalem and put a Tau on the foreheads of those who grieve and lament over all the detestable things that are done in it.'* Is that not a message for us today?" Pope Innocent shouted in an effort to reach not only the prelates crowding his palace's immense hall but also the throngs gathered just beyond its doors. People were everywhere. It was the third day of the Fourth Lateran Council. His Holiness had just finished making a point about the way Saracens were disrespecting Christian sites in the Holy Land.

The biblical quotation segued into Innocent's next theme: reforming the morals of his flock, especially those of the clergy.

Listening intently was Francis. Thanks to the care he received from "Brother" Jacoba, Francis recovered from his dehydration in time to participate in the general session.

"Look at the Tau. Does it not have the same form as the very cross on which Christ Jesus was crucified? Ezekiel is warning us only those marked with this sign will receive God's mercy. St. Paul later reminds us we must 'crucify' ourselves. We must mortify our desires of the flesh and conform our lives to that of our Savior." The Pope continued speaking for more than two hours.

The 400 bishops, 900 abbots and priors, 70 patriarchs, and countless lay people including envoys of kings and princes showed varying degrees of interest in the papal discourse. Some leaned forward in their seats, elbows on knees, heads propped on hands, absorbed in the long homily. Others slumped back, eyes glazed over. Francis sat on the floor in the back of the great hall. Although he couldn't see the Pope, Francis hung on the pontiff's every word.

Since the start of his papacy, Innocent III had been troubled by problems afflicting his Church. In April of 1213, he formally called the Council to sort out major issues and formulate effective solutions.

The religious and secular leaders attending the current monumental gathering approved more than 70 Canons that had been developed during the two-and-a-half year interim. These decrees laid out rules and procedures for reforming problems ranging from heretical movements to scandalous clerics to conducting crusades.

Francis expected to be enlightened by the regulations that applied to his growing brotherhood, and he wasn't disappointed. What he didn't expect was to adopt a "coat of arms" for himself as a result of today's papal discourse. Innocent unintentionally planted the seed of an idea for an emblem to distinguish Francis and his Poor Penitents.

Francis wasn't exactly sure of what a "Tau" looked like; so, he crept along the floor to the bench where the Bishop of Assisi sat.

"Bishop Guido." Francis spoke so softly, the cleric didn't hear him. He tugged at the bishop's sleeve.

"What is this symbol the Pope is talking about – the Tau?"

The bishop leaned down and whispered to Francis while keeping his eyes on the center of the room where the Pope was speaking.

"Ah yes. The Pope loves the Tau. He used it as his signature when he announced this gathering. It's St. Anthony's cross. You know, the symbol the Antonines wear. I think it's Greek. Looks like a 'T.'" Guido spoke quickly as well as softly. Then he abruptly sat up straight indicating to Francis their conversation was over for now.

As Francis crept back to his place, he thought about the Antonines. *"Yes, of course. It was a thick 'T.'"* He recalled seeing the blue letter stitched to the front of Brother Thiebaut's black habit. The old French monk was the last of three Hospitallers of St. Anthony who helped care for lepers at San Lazzaro in Arce, just outside Assisi. The monks came to the area decades earlier when there was an outbreak of "Holy Fire." It was called that because its victims suffered greatly, feeling as if they were being burned alive.

The band of Hospitallers stayed to continue ministering to Assisi's lepers since their symptoms were often similar to the disease that eventually came to be known as "St. Anthony's Fire." In their early stages, both diseases caused gastric disturbances, vertigo, sleepiness, nosebleeds, scaly skin, and boils. Victims also felt as if ants were creeping over their skin. In later stages they would lose fingers, toes and other appendages as each disease took its toll on the body. Both diseases were widely feared and always fatal.

It was at San Lazzaro that Francis began caring for lepers. It was there the men who joined him began their ministries, too.

"What could be more appropriate for my Poor Penitents than this symbol already connected to noble monks and, more important, associated with our Savior's cross?" Francis smiled and mumbled to himself as the gathering dispersed and he headed to the church adjacent to the palace.

It was almost dusk, yet a faint aroma of incense from the morning Mass lingered in the magnificent basilica. The only people in its cavernous nave were a handful of pilgrims and a few religious who, like Francis, came from the meeting at the palace.

Francis sought a shadowed niche far from the others and prostrated himself on the marble floor. He prayed. The seconds turned into minutes. The minutes became an hour, then two. When he finally picked himself up from the cold stone floor, Francis stood gazing at the altar.

"Thank you, Lord, for everything." His words were noticeably louder than a whisper, but there was no one around to hear. Francis believed it was Divine Providence that put the Tau in front of him this day. He felt he had no choice but to use it as the emblem of his Poor Penitents.

Since the Antonines were already stitching it on their habits, he saw no problem with adopting the symbol for himself and his brothers. Francis would, of course, let the Pope know what he was doing the next time they met. "How could the Pope *not* approve my use of our Savior's cross?" he muttered. "His Holiness himself used it!" Francis smiled as he continued mumbling to himself.

ᘓᘐ

The Great Council, as it came to be known, ended several weeks later. As a result of its many clarifications as well as new rules and regulations, the lives of innumerable Catholics would change.

For Jacoba dei Settesoli, it was not the canons or decrees of the Fourth Lateran Council that would have a significant effect on her. It was the assembly's confirmation of the elevation of Frederick II to the German throne.

ᘓᘐ

Francis used the Tau as often as possible – carving it on tree trunks, scraping it on stone, scratching it into hard-packed earthen paths. The ancient symbol became his personal signature, but he never had the opportunity to talk with Innocent about it. Within months after concluding the Great Council, the pontiff died suddenly in Perugia.

Chapter XXIII
Blood Loss
1217 – Ancona

Jacoba gazed at the Adriatic Sea. The morning sun glinted on its waves like distant stars in a liquid sky. The salty breeze was warm and welcoming. The noblewoman didn't notice. She saw nothing, felt nothing. Her senses were numb. Her son Jacob was dead.

She wanted to blame Pope Innocent for ordering the Fifth Crusade as well as Emperor Frederick for ignoring his vow to lead it. She knew it wasn't their fault. She would have held them responsible if her newly knighted Jacob died in battle, not from an illness. He never left the port of Ancona.

Less than one moon ago she received word Jacob had taken ill before his scheduled departure for Acre with other knights going to the Holy Land. The letter said Jacob was in the care of a local family and expected to make a complete recovery. Jacoba didn't know the letter had been written six months earlier and accidentally dispatched to Florence. It was a miracle she received the letter at all.

Jacoba immediately made plans to bring her son home to finish recuperating. The long journey to Ancona required weeks of preparation including settling business and family affairs in Marino as well as Rome. Jacoba was in the midst of tying up loose ends when a second communiqué arrived. It was in Jacob's own hand. It said he had fully recovered and had wed the young woman who *"so tenderly cared for me and brought me back to life*." He explained she was a commoner, the daughter of an honest merchant, *"but Moreta is noble of heart, and I could love no other*."

"She was probably beautiful, too." Jacoba thought to herself. *"And the first female besides me and his sisters to show Jacob any attention."*

Jacoba was thankful for the news of her son's rapid recovery but ambivalent about the 17-year-old's sudden marriage. She and her large entourage left Rome shortly before sunrise within three days of receiving Jacob's letter.

As the assemblage was making its way across Italy and unbeknownst to Jacoba, her son had contracted the bloody flux. By the time the group arrived in Ancona, Jacob was dead.

Jacoba's first thought was to see her son's body, to hold him. Unfortunately, as his 16-year-old widow Moreta explained, he had been buried several days earlier because of the heat. "We thought you would come, but we didn't know when you would arrive. I will take you to his grave. The place is not far from here."

Jacoba and Moreta walked together in silence. Two Frangipane guards walked a few paces behind them. The rest of Jacoba's entourage went in the opposite direction to set up a temporary household in the palazzo of a Frangipane ally.

Jacoba had been planning to have a woman-to-woman talk with her son's young widow. She wanted to determine whether Moreta truly loved Jacob or merely wished to improve her family's social status.

The young woman's red, swollen eyes provided the answer before Jacoba could ask the question.

"We did our best. I sat beside Jacob's body for two nights praying the Psalter. He had a Christian burial." Moreta pointed to a simple grave in the cemetery of a small church not far from the newlyweds' modest stone house.

Jacoba didn't weep. She didn't moan. She made no sound. The intensity of her grief robbed her of the ability to express emotion. She was in shock.

As solemn as Jacoba, Moreta spoke softly. "He suffered little. It was very fast. We were wed for only three moons yet…" She paused. "…I believe I am with child."

Jacoba expressed no surprise and replied flatly. "You are a Frangipane now, and I invite you to return to Rome with me. We will provide for you and for Jacob's child."

"You are very kind, but I cannot leave Ancona." Tears began streaming down Moreta's face. "In addition to killing my husband, the bloody flux took my mother and brother at the same time." She nodded toward two other fresh graves not far from Jacob's. "So, you see my father now has only me..." She paused, looked down and lightly rubbed her abdomen as she continued, "…and his grandchild." Moreta's tears progressed into uncontrollable sobbing.

Jacoba herself began to bawl and instinctively wrapped her arms around her daughter-in-law. The two clung to each other, their tears uniting them in immeasurable grief.

"If there is anything I can do for you and your father, Moreta, please tell me. If you like, I can return with a good midwife when your time comes. If it's gold coin you need…"

Moreta interrupted, "Jacob told me you were a kind woman. He loved you very much. He also told me you were widowed at a young age and had four other children besides him to care for. When I asked him how you managed, he laughed and said you prayed a lot.

"So, I would ask you to pray not only for Jacob's soul but for me, too, and for our child – your grandchild. I need no money. We live simply, and my father has means enough to care for me and the baby.

"Ancona has several good midwives, too. But there is one more thing I would ask of you…" Moreta hesitated. "I loved your son not because he was a knight but despite his knighthood. He was the only 'fighting man' I've ever met who cherished benevolence as well as bravery. He was kind and humble, and I want our child – be it a boy or girl – to grow up to be a good person like him. If something happens to me, will you take in my baby? I love my father, but I fear he is too old and weary to raise a child."

"Of course I would care for your child if something happens to you, God forbid. But are you sure you wouldn't like to come back to Rome with me now? You and your father could live in my household, or we could easily find a separate place nearby for you and your father.

"I'm sorry. I visited Rome once and did not like it there. Its towers were many, and I found the city dark and frightening. I like being near the sea. I like seeing green land and sunshine. And I know my father would never leave Ancona. But maybe someday after my father passes and my child is older we will come to Rome."

"I don't think I can wait that long to see my grandchild, Moreta. I will make plans to return to Ancona sooner. Can you send word when the baby is born? Are you able to write?"

"I can read, but I write very little. My father knows how to write but seldom does. I'm sure I can ask our priest to get word to you after I have the baby."

ꟷ

Jacoba, her servants and guards remained in Ancona for a full moon. In addition to getting to know her daughter-in-law and Moreta's father, Jacoba made sure Moreta's home was well stocked. She had a cradle carved in anticipation of the baby and ordered new bedding for both Moreta and her father. Jacoba also left gold coin so Moreta could hire a wet nurse if she needed to.

While she was there, the Roman noble also spent time at Ancona's harbor. In total the various branches of the Frangipane Family owned a fleet of 12 merchant ships. Two of them were based in Ancona and were specifically part of the Settesoli holdings. Jacoba had learned what she could about the crafts and their destinations by spending time on them with her late husband. She boarded the one in port at the moment and asked many questions. The experience was enlightening but bittersweet. She couldn't help but think of Gratien and how much she loved him, how much she missed him as well as their son Jacob.

ঌ৩

With the help of a local midwife, Moreta gave birth to a boy six moons after Jacoba left Ancona. She named him Angelo. He was small but fully developed and seemed healthy. Jacoba made a trip to Ancona in 1218. It gave her great comfort to hold Jacob's child. She promised Moreta she would return late the following spring and every year thereafter.

Chapter XXIV
Spitting Blood
1218 – Rome, The Septizonium

"Why did he have to do *that*? He had the whole thing memorized in Latin." Cardinal Ugolino of Ostia, the newly appointed Dean of the Sacred College of Cardinals, was distraught and venting to Lady Jacoba when she interrupted.

"Francis is Francis. Do you think because you've offered to be his protector you have some kind of hold over him?" She was smiling and shaking her head. "I wish I could have been there to hear him." She paused then added, "And to see *your* face as he tossed aside the speech you spent two days writing for him."

"You would have been disappointed. I only rolled my eyes."

Ugolino di Conti had become a frequent visitor at the Septizonium after his uncle Pope Innocent III appointed him Cardinal-Deacon of Rome's Sant'Eustachio Church and introduced him to Jacoba and Gratien shortly after they married.

Ugolino saw less of the couple after being promoted to Cardinal Bishop of Ostia in 1206 but kept in touch. Like his late uncle, Ugolino found respite in the home of the Settesoli Frangipani. He could relax knowing he was among friends who were neither plotting nor scheming some intrigue against him or the Church.

It was from Jacoba and Gratien as well as Pope Innocent that Ugolino learned of the saintliness of Francis. Even before meeting the holy man, Ugolino wanted to protect him and his growing order from machinations designed to alter or destroy them.

The year before being appointed Dean of the Sacred College, Ugolino was in Florence conducting business for the Holy See. It was there he met Francis in person.

The "Poverello" was on his way to France when he stopped in Florence. It was Francis's custom to present himself to the bishop of whatever city he was entering before he started to preach. Francis respected all clergy because they were Christ's representatives. Those who truly modeled the Savior held a special place in his heart. Because Francis knew of Cardinal Ugolino's genuine piety from conversations with Jacoba, he was exceptionally reverent as he introduced himself.

Ugolino in turn had an affinity for the sincerely religious who espoused poverty. Recognizing holiness in Francis, the cardinal requested Francis's prayers and offered Francis his protection in all things.

The prelate then did something unexpected. Ugolino cautioned Francis not to finish his journey to France but to remain in Italy to closely watch over those in his care. The good cardinal knew a number of church leaders did not want mendicant groups like Francis's followers to get a foothold in the Church.

Looking back, Ugolino thought perhaps that was why he had so carefully scripted what Francis was to say to the Sacred College. Jacoba interrupted his musing.

"You say he not only gave an entirely different homily, but he also delivered it in an informal manner. Francis is fearless, isn't he?" Jacoba was engaged and didn't want to drop the conversation.

"Not only was his language casual. Francis moved about as he spoke, almost as if his feet were on fire."

"What about His Holiness? How did he react to all this?"

"Cencio was…I mean Pope Honorius…is always calm. Not only was he unflustered when Francis set aside the prepared text and began moving about; he sat there absorbing Francis's every word."

"And the members of the Holy College?"

"As expected, the Cardinals were initially shocked. When they realized he wasn't speaking in Latin, their own tongues started wagging." Cardinal Ugolino sat back in his chair and cracked a wry smile. "As Francis went on, the murmuring stopped. It was replaced by dour facial expressions on everyone there – including me – except the Pope himself. Actually, I now realize our initial reaction to Francis's scolding must have been rather priceless."

"He chastised the Cardinals?" Jacoba raised an eyebrow.

"He admonished all of us as only Francis could do. He told us the bad example of the clergy was a scandal for the Church. Said there was too much arrogance and self-importance among the hierarchy specifically."

Jacoba rolled her eyes in response.

"Yet, he did it in such a way, with such genuine zeal. It was like he was possessed by..." Ugolino paused for a moment to find the right words. "...with the Holy Spirit." Cardinal Ugolino took a deep breath and exhaled with a sigh before continuing.

"Jacoba, the more I talk to you about this, the more I'm coming to realize Francis must have been *divinely* inspired today. His passionate words. His genuine fervor. It's something our Sacred College doesn't experience very often."

As Ugolino went on, Jacoba's expression changed to a look of intense interest.

"He's not wrong, you know, about reprimanding the clergy." Ugolino's tone was serious. "The Pope already made clear besides reclaiming the Holy Land, he wants to spiritually reform the Church. It's going to be a challenge.

"I have to admit that when Francis set aside our written speech, I prayed to God he wouldn't say or do anything to disgrace me. The cardinals know I've taken him under my wing.

"I was afraid my peers would hate his rustic bluntness. But the more I think about it now, the more I'm convinced his profound simplicity was exactly what *we* needed. Some of my colleagues scoffed at his style, but I believe none could find fault with his message. It will be interesting to see what comes of all this."

Just as Jacoba was about to ask another question, a servant entered to tell them their supper was ready. Since the Cardinal stopped in unexpectedly, the two dined on a simple meal of hearty lentil soup and grain bread. The servant also set out small platters with cheese, grapes and Jacoba's signature almond treats which Ugolino liked as much as Francis did.

The Cardinal was at least three decades older than Jacoba but, like her late husband, had the vitality of a younger man. Ugolino reminded Jacoba of Gratien in many ways except appearance. Ugolino was not as tall as her late husband nor did he have a knight's physique. He wore a long beard that matched his grey hair. The skin on his face not hidden by his beard was wrinkled as were his soft, pale hands. The Cardinal's energy came from his intellect and spirit and was expressed in his sparkling eyes and quick wit. He was articulate when speaking and attentive while listening. Like Gratien, his kindness was often tempered by his sense of justice.

"Jacoba, I have to be honest with you. My visit is not so casual." The prelate looked down at the knife with which he was now fidgeting. "The Pope has a favor to ask of you." He was still looking down and toying with the eating implement.

"Well, what is it, Ugolino? Neither you nor Honorius nor Innocent has ever been bashful about making requests in the past? Please do come out with it."

Ugolino put down the knife and looked Jacoba in the eye. "The Pope needs additional help for the new Crusade."

"You mean the one Innocent ordered many moons before he was taken from us so unexpectedly? The crusade that indirectly took my own son's life last year?" Jacoba paused momentarily, and Ugolino noticed a wave of sadness cross her face. Besides grieving for her son, Ugolino remembered how highly Jacoba thought of Innocent. He knew she remained troubled by circumstances surrounding the late pope's death in Perugia. He was also aware Jacoba suspected foul play and considered it possible some of her husband's relatives may have been involved.

She and Gratien were never close to other branches of the Frangipane Family. After Gratien's death, the rift with the family grew into a chasm. Jacoba refused to be part of Frangipani intrigues nor would she permit her children to be influenced by their greedy relatives.

She had been reconciled with Innocent a few days before his death when she told him she planned to drop her claim to Ninfa. But it was to his successor, Pope Honorius, that she formally surrendered her rights to the town.

Although Ugolino saw and understood Jacoba's angst, he decided not to acknowledge it and brought the conversation back to his current mission. "You know as well as I that Honorius believes there is only one person who can win back the Holy Land – Emperor Frederick. You recall Innocent believed it too. Some call Frederick *stupor mundi* – the astonishment of the world."

"I know. I know. When Frederick was put under Innocent's guardianship, he was already king of Sicily, and he was just three years old." Jacoba realized her delivery was sarcastic and reined in her tone before continuing. "Lotario – I mean Innocent – used to talk about the little emperor's intelligence. And now, since our current Holy

Father used to be Frederick's tutor, I would expect a special bond exists between them."

Jacoba paused. She seemed perplexed. "I thought Frederick like a lot of other noblemen had taken the Crusader's Vow three years ago, just before Innocent's Great Council. I'm well aware Innocent was counting on Frederick's leadership of the Fifth Crusade. Thinking Frederick would head the effort was one of the reasons I supported Jacob's decision to go to the Holy Land. I should have demanded he remain here in Italy." Jacoba looked at the floor and shook her head. Besides grieving Jacob's untimely death, she was now unconsciously assuming blame for it. Ugolino did not have to feign his disgust with the emperor's lack of action when he responded to Jacoba.

"Frederick had actually taken the vow *six* years ago when he became king of Germany. That was a key reason the Lateran Council endorsed his elevation to the throne. Now, I'm not so sure the man will ever meet his obligation." Ugolino's own frustration was apparent in his voice. "I'm sorry. I shouldn't speak that way, but I am telling you nothing I haven't told Honorius. I don't trust Frederick in matters of the Church. I don't trust Frederick in matters of politics. I don't trust Frederick at all, but I will do what I can to further the Fifth Crusade. You have always generously supported the Church and its holy efforts. I hope you will once again help."

"I thought the funding had been taken care of. Didn't Innocent require you and the other cardinals to give a tenth of your income for the past three years to specifically fund the war?"

"He did, and other clergy were also obliged to give sizeable sums. I'm not seeking gold from you, Jacoba. His Holiness and I want access to merchant ships."

"For what purpose?"

"They would not be used in battle. We need to transport more forces to fight in the Holy Land – specifically Damietta. Although Frederick did not travel to Egypt last year with the Crusaders, he said he plans to join them. Until he does, the Duke of Bavaria is in command and will soon require more men to hold Damietta."

"I can spare only one ship. It will leave from Ancona late next spring. Will that be soon enough?"

"That would be perfect."

Jacoba didn't hesitate when she said, "I do have one condition."

"And that would be?" The prelate now raised an eyebrow and cocked his head.

"You must also transport our friend Francis and some of his brothers."

"To the battle zone? Does he want to be a martyr?"

"Perhaps. You know as well as I that Francis is consumed with spreading the Gospel. He's been sending his Friars Minor far and wide. It has always been his personal dream to convert Muslims. Are you aware he's already tried to go to the Holy Land at least twice? Storms and rough seas ended his first effort. Sickness, his second. He may have made additional attempts I'm not aware of. So, my condition is that Francis and some the brothers are on the ship. Do you promise?

"Of course." Ugolino nodded with enthusiasm.

"I will be there to make sure you do."

Chapter XXV
Blood Moon
Spring, 1220 - The Adriatic Sea

"Well, he didn't get his wish." Elias Bombarone muttered to himself as his eyes took in everything and nothing at the same time. There was nowhere to focus his gaze – just a vast expanse of water. He tried to distract himself from his unreasonable fear of the sea by speculating about the man who had changed so much since they were young friends in Assisi.

Elias didn't realize his mumbling reached the ears of another until he heard Jacoba's voice.

"What do you mean?" She was also on the ship's deck with a gaze not unlike Elias's. Her thoughts, however, were much different. She didn't fear the sea. She hated it. It took her beloved Gratien and gave back to her disquieting uncertainty. She didn't know whether "the deep" itself killed her husband or whether the waters merely abetted a human act of murder.

The Settesoli branch of the Frangipane Family was no more. A fracture between Jacoba and Cencio Frangipane's clan widened after her husband's death. Two of Cencio's sons –Gratien's Colosseum cousins – were on the ship with him when he was washed overboard by a "sudden storm." The ship's captain and nearly all of its crew were also "lost" in the same tempest. The only survivors were Gratien's two cousins and four "crew members" whom Jacoba later learned served as Colosseum palace guards when not at sea. She tried not to think badly of Gratien's relatives. She tried not to think of them at all. But the sea itself churned up disturbing memories.

The various branches of the Frangipani were initially not troubled by Jacoba's familial ties to Pope Innocent. All of them had been supportive of the "Conti Pope" at first. However, after members of the Holy Father's family built an imposing war tower within view of their palace, the Colosseum Frangipani became more than irate. They were enraged.

A deep hatred evolved for anything or anyone with ties to the Conti Family including Jacoba. While her powerful husband was alive, Jacoba was treated civilly though never warmly by Gratien's Colosseum kin. After Gratien's death, she became a familial outcast.

The split between the branches of the Frangipani grew to a bottomless chasm when Jacoba's friend and distant relative Ugolino di Conti played a key role in selecting a new pope after the sudden death of Innocent III. The Frangipani didn't object to Cencio Savelli becoming pope.

However, Ugolino's overwhelming involvement in the selection process of the old man infuriated them beyond words.

With no Settesoli male "of age" to wield power against them, the Colosseum Frangipani contemplated taking over the Septizonium and Jacoba's other holdings. The only reason they didn't make their move immediately was strategic and involved Jacoba herself.

The "Settesoli Woman," as they called her, had many able knights and guards willing to lay down their lives for her and her children. Jacoba also had strong and powerful Normanni Family allies in nearby Trastevere who could rally to her side. In addition, unlike other nobles continually vying with the Frangipani for control of Rome, Jacoba posed no threat. Managing Gratien's holdings and doing charitable works meant she had little time to plot against anyone nor would she even think to do so.

Jacoba's sole focus these days was on furthering Francis's mendicant movement, not increasing her own power or fortune. At the same time, the Colosseum clan was confident as soon as their attention was no longer occupied by current adversaries, they could with a little effort and a lot of scheming make the Septizonium their own … or completely destroy it.

"Oh…Jacoba. I'm sorry I didn't know you were there. I thought you were still below tending to Francis." Elias turned to her. He appreciated the visual distraction from his current obsession with the frightful Adriatic. "I was just pondering aloud about him."

"Which of his wishes were you reflecting on – the one where he converts Melek-el-Kamel from Islam to

Christianity or the one where he is martyred by the sultan?" Jacoba's reply was accompanied by a slightly wry smile.

Elias offered a wan smirk in return, then responded in a somber tone. "I'm truly glad his latter wish was not fulfilled."

"So am I, Elias, except..." There was hesitation in her voice as if the words were problematical to say. "Although he shed no blood there, that sojourn to Damietta may yet cost him his life."

Elias whispered, "I know. Although I'm not a superstitious man, the moon last night with its reddish color cannot be a good omen."

Both were well aware Francis was developing into a physical wreck. His body had been weakened from fever and malnutrition. His eyes were paining him and looked redder than ever.

"It was Divine Providence that brought you to Acre two moons ago, Jacoba. If ever Francis needed friends – especially us – it was after his trip to Egypt. He came to me drained in body and spirit. I've never seen him so low. The travel in itself was punishing. He tries to hide his physical issues, but..."

Jacoba broke in. "I know. I've tended to him frequently in Rome, but it was only because the friars traveling with him insisted he seek help. And the eye problems are new. He shows no concern for himself at all. He cares only for God and the souls and bodies of others. He also needs to pay *some* attention to the body God gave *him*." Jacoba sounded like a scolding mother. "Elias, I'm sorry I interrupted."

"Jacoba, I think you know this time things went beyond the physical. Seeing the carnage inflicted by the Moors and the Crusaders combined with the licentiousness among the Christian troops did something to his mind and heart. You know how he can get. I don't want to call it despair, but it was close. Let's say it was profound disappointment. Maybe he was also miserable because he wasn't martyred." Elias looked at Jacoba, sighed, then continued.

"When he commissioned some of us Poor Penitents to 'spread the word' in foreign lands, I wondered if he thought he was favoring us by sending us to possible death. When we got word four moons ago that some of our brothers had been martyred in Morocco, Francis went on and on about how we should be happy for them because they were assured places in heaven. He was doing his best to be joyful, yet I sensed he was trying to disguise grief or something else."

Jacoba interrupted again with a statement that came out as a question. "Perhaps he felt some guilt about sending the brothers to Morocco?"

"Who knows. Maybe he unconsciously envied our dead brothers because of his own longing to be a martyr. He surely didn't have any qualms about sending Peter and me to the Levantine Coast a few years ago with his first wave of missionaries. Granted, Acre has been under Christian control for years, but the tension between us and the Muslims here is palpable. I must not be a very good friar because I don't find the prospect of martyrdom as appealing as Francis does.

"When we first arrived three years ago and tried to help the sick or attempted to preach, we would be pelted with stones by the Muslim Mamluks. However, we started to make slight inroads once I donned this." Elias pointed to the skullcap he was wearing.

The head covering was very much like the one he wore as a scholar at the University of Bologna. Jacoba was planning to ask Elias about it, but the right opportunity hadn't presented itself. She knew some monks used skullcaps to cover their tonsures, but she found it odd for one of Francis's Poor Penitents to wear one. Elias read her face and immediately began explaining.

"Muslim men wear something similar to emulate the founder of their religion. Of course, I didn't want anyone to think I was honoring Muhammad, but I did want to let people know I was a religious person. So, I had a skullcap made that looks a little different than their caps."

"And Francis gave you permission to wear it?" Jacoba was stunned.

"Of course not. I didn't ask him. You of all people know if I would have asked, Francis would have told me 'no.'"

"Didn't he say anything about it when he first arrived in Acre?"

"He didn't have to. His eyes said it all. So I instantly told him how it made me less threatening to Muslims and Christians, too, because they could see I was religious which they couldn't detect from my otherwise ragged appearance. Since I was no longer perceived as a potential menace, I was allowed to 'preach the Gospel' by caring for the poor and sick. After my explanation Francis appeared to be more comfortable with what I did." Then Elias lightened his tone and winked at Jacoba as he added, "Besides, it's not like I'm wearing it to keep my head warm. Summers in Acre are almost as bad as they are in Rome!"

Jacoba smiled and gave him a teasing glance. "And of course the reason you're still wearing the cap – despite our being at sea with not a Muslim in sight – has nothing to do with a tinge of pride in your academic accomplishments?"

Elias smiled at her and turned to face the sea which at the moment seemed less dreadful than Jacoba's banter. He rubbed his chin as he considered what she just said. After a long moment, he faced her, smiled and shook his head. "Brother Jacoba, you frighten me almost as much as the sea. I think sometimes you know me better than I know myself. If Francis were not unwell when he first saw me, he probably would have made the same remark." Just as his hand moved toward his head to remove the cap, Jacoba stopped him.

"I think you should keep wearing it, Elias." Her voice took on a serious note. "I shouldn't have said what I said. It was not my place, and I'm sorry. If Francis truly didn't approve of your cap, he would have told you no matter what his state of being.

"You are one of the most learned men in the order. And as the order continues to grow and spread its good works to other lands, it will be in need of more men like you. He will someday need to entrust control of the order to others. I'm not sure Francis realizes that yet. Perhaps he never will.

"He is, after all, just following Christ's words about becoming more like little children in order to enter heaven. I'm not sure there's anyone on earth right now who is as holy as our 'blood brother.' I try, but I cannot leave the world behind the way he or Prassede or even you can…" Jacoba's voice trailed off in a sad way.

"Don't be so hard on yourself. You are the 'brother' who makes it possible for the rest of us to do what we do. Let's face it, Francis left things of *this world* behind long ago." Elias took a breath. "And I admire him for it." Another pause. "But he doesn't understand how difficult it can be for the rest of us 'mere mortals' to even get close to his level of near-perfect austerity. And since he refuses to be part of this world and doesn't permit any of us to do anything beyond praying, preaching and begging, you are our only intermediary with it.

"That's what I was getting around to tell you. What you do to help us lesser brothers and Francis is essential. Unfortunately, I'm afraid he has no idea of the many things you do for him and all of us."

"And I want to keep it that way!" Jacoba cast her eyes downward, embarrassed by Elias's praise. He noticed her discomfiture but continued anyway.

"The day you arrived in Acre, Brother Peter and I couldn't believe our eyes when we saw you on the dock. We'd gone there to see if we could get passage back to Italy for Francis, Illuminato and ourselves. We'd heard a merchant vessel arrived but never dreamed you would be on it."

Jacoba interrupted, "I was equally surprised to see you and Peter. I knew you were somewhere here, but being at the same place at the same time was truly Divine Intervention. I hadn't really planned this trip, and I don't think I told you or anyone else about why I came to Acre." Elias gave her a quizzical look.

"I've sold the Settesoli vessels in the Adriatic." Jacoba's eyes were now moist with tears as she choked out, "Without Gratien…and since Jacob's death, there was no longer any reason to keep this part of our family's business going."

After regaining her composure, she continued. "The buyer made the purchase of our ships contingent on me accompanying him to Acre on his first voyage to personally introduce him to the traders with whom Gratien and I built relationships over many years. I was a bit hesitant until I realized this would probably be my last opportunity to see the places I had once visited with Gratien. I never really made a formal pilgrimage and thought it was time to come here and pray. So, having you, Francis and the other two brothers accompany me and my little entourage was not at all self-sacrificing."

"Except you did a lot more than let us tag along, Jacoba." Elias smiled affectionately as he spoke. "You helped Francis get better – at least for awhile. Believe me, before you arrived here and nursed him back to a much-improved state of wellbeing, he was barely able to walk. He didn't want to eat. He hardly slept. He wouldn't listen to Peter or me or the other brothers even though we thought we were asking him to do things that would help him heal."

"That's the key, Elias. When it comes to getting Francis to do something good for himself, you have to *tell* him to do it. Never just ask." Jacoba shook her head and smiled.

"When Peter and I brought you to our little dwelling on the edge of town to see Francis, I noticed a change in him as soon as he saw you. It was as if you carried hope with you, and he knew you would share it with him.

"I also sensed you could tell something was wrong the moment you saw him. Without hesitation, you changed your plans to stay longer in Acre just to care for him. Besides putting soothing ointment on his eyes and feeding him your own 'magic potions' to strengthen him, you gave up your personal plans in order to take all of us to the holy sites of Francis's choosing where he found comfort in prayer. You made possible the spiritual refreshment Francis so desperately needed. And now at least he is well enough in spirit if not in body to return to Assisi. And all of us are going home with him – Praise be to God and thanks to you."

Jacoba acknowledged Elias's words with a slight smile and a nod. No further words were shared as the two old friends went back to staring at the sea. They knew what each other was thinking: *Sadly, things would never be the same for Francis…or for themselves.*

ꙮ

Spring was in full bloom when the ship docked in Venice. The brothers traveled to Assisi by land as quickly as they could while still preaching along the way as well as stopping to care for Francis.

During his extended absence, Francis's group of Poor Penitents had grown quickly – too quickly. They now numbered in the thousands. Unfortunately, with the sudden, extreme expansion came chaos and anxiety. In addition, rumors that Francis had died and would, therefore, never return caused various brothers to take matters into their own hands.

Some tried to increase the severity of Francis's already strict fasting rules. Others went in the opposite direction, lacking discipline and not living as austerely as they should. One brother had gone so far as to assemble a group of male and female lepers and set out with them for Rome intent on getting papal approval for a totally new religious order.

The turmoil was noticed by lay people and clerics alike, including the Pope who decided to require a novitiate or probationary period before new brothers were accepted into the order. Upon Francis's return, Honorius instructed him to prepare a formal rule for the order.

ᘓᘐ

Francis soon came to understand the life of poverty and simplicity he and his first followers lived could not continue exactly as it had. A few dozen brothers is much different than 5000. It would take exceptionally strong leadership to maintain the order's focus on poverty and simplicity while accommodating the diverse needs of brothers coming from myriad backgrounds and circumstances. Francis realized he wasn't strong enough physically or emotionally to continue to head the lesser brothers.

At the brothers' major gathering in late summer, Francis announced he was stepping down. Brother Peter Catania took over the leadership role, but died the following spring. The mantle of leadership then fell to Elias who became vicar of the order in spring of 1221.

ᘓᘐ

Jacoba remained in Venice for the summer before returning to Rome where she learned Ugolino had been named official protector of the Poor Penitents and Honorius had required Francis write a formal rule. She was not surprised by Francis's decision to step away from his leadership role.

Chapter XXVI
Blessed Blood
1221 - Rome

For the woman hermit Prassede, time did not exist. She had been living in her tiny stone dwelling for six years but felt like she arrived in Rome yesterday.

Her dank, dark lean-to hugged the back wall of an ancient chapel on Frangipani property abutting the disabitato. It was distant from the city's hustle and bustle, and Prassede was thankful for that. Initially, she longed for her previous life on Mount Subasio. She yearned for its crags and tors, for its exuberant forests and inexhaustible vistas. She couldn't help but see God everywhere and in everything on Subasio.

Rome was different. Prassede had trouble finding the hand of the Divine in the disabitato. Initially she saw only a massive decaying skeleton of a dead civilization – fleshless jagged bones strewn across the landscape. Nature tried its best to cover the marble blocks, and columns with endless varieties of greenery, but the ancient Empire's remains fought all efforts at burial.

Prassede persevered in her quest and eventually discovered abundant life and remarkable beauty hidden amid the eerie ruins. The odd plants and little creatures were much different than the ones on Subasio, but she grew to cherish them.

After a year in the disabitato, Prassede daydreamed less about Mount Subasio. When she did, she would chastise herself for being obstinate and ungrateful. "God apparently wanted me to live in Rome, and I am happy to do His will,"

She would also remind herself the mountain she loved could be heartless at times. She dreaded its brutal winter winds and unpredictable summer storms. There were poisonous plants she kept away from and biting insects she couldn't avoid. She remained on constant alert to steer clear of wild boars, packs of wolves and small biting animals.

She recollected coping with whatever came her way until the incident six summers ago. Her final memory of Subasio involved taking refuge in a small grotto one evening to weather a fast-approaching storm. When she awoke the next morning, a wolf stood at the entrance to her shelter to claim it for himself. His coat was wet and matted. His eyes had a yellow cast, and his jagged teeth were bared. She would have been happy to give it to him, but he didn't give her the opportunity. The wolf mauled her as she tried to get out of his way.

It was providential the attack happened when she and Francis planned to meet. Bloody and half-dead, Prassede staggered down the mountain and through the forest to their rendezvous point outside Assisi's walls. Then she collapsed.

When she came to, Prassede found herself squinting through puffy eyes at the compassionate face of an old woman wiping her brow with a cool, damp cloth.

"The penitent beggar Francis brought you here and charged me to care for you until he returns with a cart and horse."

Prassede couldn't understand the need for a cart and horse. She wanted to ask why, but all she could manage was a fleeting quizzical look before closing her eyes again.

She fell in and out of consciousness for four days. Her only memory was the vague recollection of being given warm broth by the gentle lady. Prassede thought perhaps she was in heaven being fed by an angel because she'd never tasted anything quite so delicious.

After hearing the woman pray aloud and a lot, Prassede wondered if Francis brought her to a nunnery. She knew of such places and wondered what they were like.

Although she appreciated the kindness of the "nun," Prassede grew anxious as she passed in and out of consciousness. Nice as the old woman was, Prassede began to crave the solitude of Mount Subasio.

In light of the "cart and horse" comment, Prassede wondered what lay ahead for her. She recalled Francis expressing concern for her welfare when they met three moons ago. He couldn't meet with her as often because of his itinerant preaching as well as the responsibilities of leading the growing brotherhood of Poor Penitents.

Perhaps he was suggesting she should become a nun. "*But then he would just leave me here. He wouldn't need a cart and a horse.*"

Prassede was aware her physical condition had declined. She had no strength at the moment and wondered whether she would ever heal. Perhaps her earthly life was ending. She rationalized the "cart and horse" were needed to haul her corpse to the "Hill of Hell" where she could rest with her father. Thoughts of death calmed her as she fell back into unconsciousness.

ꕤ

"We are going to Rome, Prassede." Francis's tone was gentle and jovial as he briefly looked over his shoulder and informed her of their travel plans. Her eyes were closed.

Prassede still slept often and deeply while recovering from her injuries. Francis was happy she hadn't awakened at dawn when he and brother Bernardo tenderly positioned her in the back of the cart. The rickety vehicle was borrowed from a merchant Francis befriended in his younger days.

It took Prassede a moment to process what Francis told her. As soon as she recognized the word "Rome," she panicked. Her eyes shot open, and she tried without success to sit up. The realization she was still weak and couldn't escape this "jail on wheels" prompted Prassede to plead with Francis.

"I can't go there. Francis, you know I can't go there. I can't be with people. Why are you doing this to me?" She spoke in an inaudible voice, so Francis didn't hear her. He was concentrating on a curve in the road ahead.

When he eventually turned around and noticed Prassede had opened her eyes, Francis continued.

"Prassede, you will recover, but you cannot return to a mountain or forest. It's too dangerous. You still want to live like a hermit, don't you?"

In her mind Prassede nodded with great enthusiasm but quickly realized what Francis saw was her head go up and down only once, very slowly. The effort of movement was too much for her recuperating body.

"Prassede, you remember Jacoba, don't you?"

Prassede's lips curled upward slightly, and Francis knew her attempt at a smile meant "yes." Jacoba's name as well as Elias's often came up when he and Prassede met. Prassede remained grateful for the kindness they showed her decades earlier on the Hill of Hell.

"Jacoba has arranged for you to have your own place where you won't be with people. No one will know you are there except for Jacoba, one or two of her servants and a priest."

Prassede managed to form a quizzical look, so Francis continued.

"Your new 'cave' will be a simple shed attached to a very small, very old chapel. It's almost a ruin, really. When it was an active church, the priest used to stable his horse in the shed. But that was many years ago. Now no one goes there except Father Antonio who still says Mass sometimes.

"Either he or one of Jacoba's servants will bring you food so you won't have to forage."

Prassede responded to Francis with a weak yet undeniable scowl. He noticed.

"But if you want to forage, Jacoba told me there are lots of edible plants growing in the area where you will live. Come now, my dear friend. I know the adjustment will be hard at first, but it is the will of God." Francis paused a moment before continuing, "And I know you want to follow His will."

Prassede rolled her eyes, then gave a weak smile.

"You are right, Francis. My willfulness; I must work on it." Her voice remained inaudible, but Francis got the gist and smiled.

ꟸ

The years since her departure from Mount Subasio had passed quickly. Prassede tolerated her new surroundings but never liked them. They were too luxurious. Prior to the hermit's arrival, Jacoba ordered a bed and chair be placed in the lean-to along with a small table, a crucifix and a supply of candles. Prassede did not want to appear ungrateful so she kept the furnishings but slept on the dirt floor. She never used the chair, and since she woke at dawn and retired at sunset, she had no need of candles.

She never ate at the table. She treated it like an altar because that's where the small crucifix sat. Accustomed to the rustic crosses she made herself on Mount Subasio, Prassede found the carved image of Christ on the cross deeply inspiring. Although it aided her prayer life, Prassede nevertheless chastised herself for treasuring it too much.

Since her cell once sheltered horses and mules, the hermit occasionally detected faint remains of the animals' scents. The vague odors reminded her of Mount Subasio, and she found them comforting.

Food from the Settesoli kitchens was brought to Prassede on a regular basis until she made clear her preference to eat only wild greens and mushrooms she foraged in the disabitato.

Ultimately, she was grateful to Francis for bringing her to Rome and Jacoba for sheltering her. Prassede believed this must have been God's plan since she could now devote herself entirely to prayer. She no longer wasted time finding shelter or fending off predators.

She attended Mass whenever Father Antonio celebrated it in the adjacent chapel, and she received the Eucharist. She confessed to him at least twice a year. She felt closer to God now than she did on the mountain.

Jacoba visited Prassede often. Initially it was to bring food and check on the hermit's recovery. The two grew close. Prassede considered Jacoba her earthly guardian angel while Jacoba came to regard Prassede as a trusted confidant and spiritual advisor.

On one occasion Jacoba presented Prassede with a small folio of prayers from her family's library along with blank parchment, a writing quill and ink.

"Francis once told me you enjoyed reading and writing. I thought you might appreciate these." Jacoba smiled as she handed the items to Prassede whose eyes grew wide with excitement when she saw the gift then shifted to something else.

"You're very generous, but I'm sorry I can't accept this." Prassede looked at the floor as she passed the gift back to Jacoba. Tears flooded her eyes.

"What's wrong, Prassede? Why do you reject my gift?"

"I like it too much." Prassede's head was still downcast. She sighed. "I already feel my life here is too easy. My surroundings are too lavish." She looked up, and her eyes scanned the tiny cell.

Jacoba looked around, too. "You haven't slept in the bed since you recovered, have you, Prassede? There was exasperation in her voice. "Would you like me to have it taken out of here?"

Prassede nodded. A slight smile crossed her face as she motioned to Jacoba to sit down on the lone chair while she positioned herself on the dirt floor.

"I will have it removed and given to a poor family, but there's one condition," Jacoba sounded amiable but uncompromising. "You must accept these things I've brought for you."

"I can't. I want to live like Francis and the Poor Penitents. I want to own nothing!" Prassede was vehement.

Jacoba response was equally forceful. "Our Francis may own nothing, but he doesn't live a hermit's life like you. You're already poorer than he is. Francis has companionship. He prays and writes, and travels all over, too." Then she inhaled deeply, let out her breath and continued.

"I'm sorry, Prassede. I didn't mean to snap at you." Jacoba's voice hinted of exasperation. "It's just that our situations are not the same as Brother Francis, and I think God puts us where He wants us.

"You are one of the holiest people I know, and this gift is meant to help you and a lot of other people grow holier, including myself. Don't you see God is working through you, Prassede? You've touched the lives of Francis and me and Father Antonio. You have a gift. And you could help even more people if you would write down your inspirations and let me share them with others. Don't you think it's selfish of you *not* to accept these things … and use them to serve God?" Jacoba paused, waiting for Prassede to respond. When the hermit just stared at the dirt floor, Jacoba continued.

"You are thinking being poor means owning 'no thing,' but there is poverty as wretched as having no material goods. It's a poverty of the spirit. It's not knowing God or sometimes it's knowing God but choosing not to do what is right.

"I've seen it. I've been close to living it. Power and wealth have become gods for so many Romans these days. It saddens me greatly. If it were not for Christ's love and the saintly people in my life like you and Brother Francis, I believe I may have surrendered to more temptations than I already have.

"I will always be in danger of succumbing to worldly things because I am weak. I think I could be holier if I left Rome with all its intrigues and attractions. I'd be better off if I gave away all my lands. But I can't. It's not really my choice to make, at least not for now. I can't abandon my children or vassals. People's livelihoods and very lives are in my hands. As much as I'd like to forsake my worldly responsibilities, I just can't. God put me right here right now, and I don't have the 'luxury' of choosing a different life.

"What I'm trying to say, Prassede, is that besides your prayers, I need your wisdom and guidance and so do other people."

Both women sat in uncomfortable silence until Jacoba again spoke.

"I think it's time for me to leave." Jacoba got up and began gathering the things she had brought for the hermit.

Prassede rose from the floor and stood with outstretched hands, palms up in front of Jacoba.

"Maybe you're right. I will accept your gift after all. I'm sorry for my stubbornness. Forgive me." Prassede's contrition was genuine.

"There's nothing to forgive. I'm glad you changed your mind. By the way, I forgot to tell you Francis will be here before the next full moon, and I know he will want to see you."

"It's been a long time. I look forward to seeing him and will pray for his safe travels."

"Now it is time for me to get back to the Septizonium. Will you bless me, Prassede?" Jacoba knelt before the hermit.

Prassede placed her hands on Jacoba's head and whispered a brief blessing that ended when she traced a cross with her thumb on the noblewoman's forehead.

"Thank you for the gift." Prassede's words were heartfelt. She smiled quickly adding, "And you will remember to give my bed to someone who can use it, won't you?"

Jacoba returned the smile. "It will be gone tomorrow."

ഇരു

As promised, Francis visited Prassede a few weeks later. Jacoba was with him. Three Frangipani guards were also nearby but kept themselves out of sight so neither Francis nor the hermit knew of their presence.

Prassede offered her guests freshly picked wild parsley and some unidentified greens along with well chosen mushrooms. The trio made themselves comfortable on her dirt floor, and Francis offered a prayer before they ate. Jacoba brought wine which they shared.

Francis had placed a parcel on Prassede's chair when they arrived. After their meager meal, he grabbed the bundle and removed a folded parchment tucked under the cord that was wrapped around the package.

"This is for you, Sister Prassede," Francis said as he put the parcel into her hands. "Jacoba has been writing to me about your life here. She told me of your wish to live in poverty as I and the other Poor Penitents do. I'm here to tell you the sacrifices you endure living as a hermit are greater than mine or those of my brothers. You anonymously serve others through prayer and writing. You seek no material goods. You interact with no one save Jacoba, Father Antonio and myself. The total focus of your life is God and prayer. If anyone deserves to wear the symbol of the poor penitent, it is you."

"And this is for you, Brother Jacoba." He handed her the parchment. "It has been too long in coming."

Jacoba gave him a quizzical look as she unfolded the document, so Francis explained.

"I've finally written the rule for you and other faithful people who cannot abandon their worldly responsibilities. I hope it will help you grow closer to God."

Jacoba began reading the document to herself as Prassede slipped the cord from the bundle and unfurled the coarse brown poor penitent tunic. Both women had tears in their eyes.

As Jacoba pored over the document and her mind began digesting its contents, she sobbed so hard her body shook. Francis's Rule of Life for the laity. Jacoba knew her own life would change because of his words, but she had no way of knowing the parchment's contents would yield unimaginable spiritual fruit for countless other lay people for centuries to come.

Prassede changed into her uncomfortable, scratchy new tunic after Francis and Jacoba left her dwelling. A week later, the strange, holy hermit formally confessed to Father Antonio that she had sinned because she not only enjoyed wearing the shabby tunic, but it had also become a source of pride for her. The priest smiled, absolved her and gave her one "Our Father" as her penance.

ᘓᘐ

Prassede would wear the same rough garment for the next 37 years until she died at the age of 81. The inspirational tracts she wrote and shared with others have been lost over time. Perhaps in the future, some may be discovered.

Prassede never saw Francis again while he lived. However, she credited him with a miracle after his death.

Late one evening, Prassede had climbed up to the roof of her lean-to because an injured bird had fallen from its nest under the eaves of the adjacent chapel. It flew away as she reached out to rescue it. She lost her footing and fell to the ground, landing hard on her left side. The fracture below her left knee was ugly. Not only was the leg going in a direction that was unnatural, but a bit of bone was jutting out from the skin. Her foot was also broken, and she dislocated her shoulder.

After pulling herself along the ground into her cell, then she saw him. Francis was standing there. He wasn't his disheveled self. His tunic was a light color, fresh and bright. He no longer looked wan or unhealthy. His skin was radiant. She knew it was definitely Francis when he spoke to her in a gentle, unmistakable voice.

"Stand up, Prassede. There's no need to be fearful. You can do this." He took her hand and helped her up.

Then, he disappeared.

She was totally mystified, somewhat terrified and began screaming.

Already dark, Two Frangipane guards making nightly rounds on the perimeter of the Settesoli property rushed to the shed. When they thrust a lantern into the shed and looked inside, they saw Prassede standing there. She didn't speak.

She looked up at them as if in a daze and started examining herself in the light they provided. Her right hand rubbed her left shoulder. Then she used both hands to feel her left leg below her knee to make sure she wasn't imagining it. She wiggled her foot, too.

"I am healed. It was Francis."

Chapter XXVII
Sainted Blood

October, 1226 – Assisi, The Porziuncola

"Is that you, Brother Jacoba?" The question floated up from the naked, emaciated body lying on the ground.

"Yes, Francis. I'm here." Jacoba stood in the doorway of the tiny chapel. She bit down on her lower lip but couldn't disguise the heartache in her voice. She walked toward him. *At least he won't see my tears.*

"I brought your favorite almond treats." Her attempt at sounding nonchalant was unsuccessful.

"Come, touch one to my mouth." Francis's voice was barely audible. Jacoba knelt down next to him and gently pressed a cookie to his lips. With great effort Francis stuck out the tip of his tongue to taste it. She withdrew the small sweet cake to end his struggle and seated herself on the floor close to him.

"I hope heaven has your recipe." Francis tried to put Jacoba at ease. His words came out slowly and softly. "I'm glad you came. It's been a while. Does my appearance shock you?" His eyes were wide open, staring at nothing. "I'd like to say it's nice to see you, but Elias must have told you my sight is gone. Total blackness. Praise the Lord; I'll have eternal light soon." Francis's voice grew stronger at mention of the Lord.

"I knew of your blindness, but I had no idea…" Jacoba couldn't complete the sentence. There weren't words to express what she saw. Francis's body was withered beyond description. What shocked her was the blood. It seeped from his hands, his side, his feet. His hair was matted with more than sweat: puss oozed from wounds around his temples – remnants of recent cauterization treatments to his eyes. His bodily fluids were mixing with ashes that had been sprinkled on him at his request. *Dust to dust* he told Brother Leo.

Before she could say another word, Francis spoke.

"You know you will have quite a job cleaning me up when the time comes!" Francis's voice sounded almost normal. "I probably should have taken better care of 'Brother Ass.' After all, this body is one of God's creations, too. I didn't treat it as kindly as I should have."

Jacoba stroked the hair on Francis's head and said nothing. Francis closed his eyes. His face was peaceful.

After a few minutes, his eyes opened. His body tensed. "You *will* stay and prepare this body for burial, won't you?"

"Of course, Francis. I brought the veil for your face along with candles. She continued to stroke his hair. She didn't tell him she brought incense, too. He would think it too lavish.

"Francis closed his eyes again. Jacoba could tell he was more relaxed.

"You always had the touch of a healer. Did you remember cloth for my shroud?" Francis's voice was calm and soft.

"I already gave it to Elias. The wool is from the lamb you gave us. Little Giacoma wanted you to know she helped card it. I also brought a tunic and cap." Jacoba's voice grew sweetly stern, "Francis, I'm *lending* the clothes to you. You understand you have *no* ownership with regard to them; so, you may *not* give them away. They belong to me. I would be greatly offended if you don't use them." She did not tell him that she also brought two large cloths embroidered with bird and flowers should they be needed for his funeral. The dossals featured gold threads which he would have found offensive.

Jacoba knew Francis's zeal for absolute poverty. He wanted to die with no possessions. Not even an old patched-up habit of his own. It was why he lay unclothed on the ground. She hoped he would allow Elias to move him to a bed, but she doubted that would happen

Both remained silent for several minutes as she continued to delicately massage his forehead. She thought he had fallen asleep until he spoke once more.

"I thank God for you, Brother Jacoba of the Seven Suns. Who would have taken care of me and the brothers in Rome? Who would have helped me see the Pope? You gave me so much."

"Francis, you've given me more."

"Did Elias tell you about what I wrote?

"Not yet. He's so busy being vicar, we haven't had a chance to really talk.

"I wrote a song to praise God. I call it 'Canticle of the Sun.' Our summer together so long ago was its inspiration. Remember how we would run around in the fields outside the city walls and how we played in Subasio's forests? I thought of you and Elias when I composed it."

"That was the best summer of my life, Francis."

"I thought of Clare, too. You're Brother Sun, and she's Sister Moon. If you and I had married we would have had a daughter just like Clare. She has your beauty, nobility and fortitude and my tenacity. You'll recognize Elias and Prassede in it. Tell Elias he has to get one of the brothers to make a copy for you."

"I'm looking forward to it." Jacoba hesitated, then said, "Francis, would you do something for me: would you bless me?"

Francis's strength was ebbing. He tried to raise his right arm to bless her but only managed to lift his hand an inch above the ground. Jacoba slipped her hand under his. He slowly moved his finger tips over her hand until they touched the ring on her third finger. Jacoba noticed his brows move slightly indicating surprise or uncertainty. His forefinger further examined the incised stone that his eyes couldn't see.

"Is this what I think it is?" Francis smiled. "You've continued to wear it?"

"I've been wearing it since San Leo. I still wear Gratien's ring on my other hand." Jacoba's tone was wistful.

"We spoke no vows when I first put it on you a lifetime ago, but you knew I wanted you for my wife, didn't you?" Francis used all his strength to get the words out.

"It was Divine Intervention, Francis. God didn't want us to wed in the flesh because he needed *you* to 'father' *spiritual* children for Him. You certainly must have exceeded His expectations. As for the two of us," Jacoba paused a moment. "He did allow our souls to marry, didn't He? That kind of love is deep and never dies."

Francis responded by smiling as broadly as a dying man could. "Now for your blessing."

Jacoba bowed her head. Resting his hand on Jacoba's, Francis's tone was solemn. *"Farewell my brother, Jacoba, my love. As I hasten to the Lord, I ask Him to hold you close always. May the King of all bless you. I bless you and ask God to be mindful of your good works. May you share in His reward of the just. May you find every blessing you desire, and may whatever you ask worthily be granted. Jacoba, my wife in spirit, I have done what was mine to do; may Christ teach you what you are to do."*

"Thank you." Sobs smothered her words, and tears streamed down her face. The realization this was her last moment with Francis pierced her. She didn't want to leave his side. Not now. Not ever.

A commotion in the doorway made her look up. Elias glowered there summoning her with his hand as he loudly cleared his throat. She read his thoughts through the expression on his face: *Woman, you're not even supposed to be here. You've already spent too much time with him. One of your hands is under his, and the other is grazing his hair. What if someone sees this? They wouldn't understand the way I do.*

Elias was right, as usual, but Jacoba nevertheless took a few more silent moments with Francis. Finally, she leaned over him, tenderly kissed his forehead and whispered, "Goodbye, my beloved, until we meet in heaven."

ꕥ

Sobbing uncontrollably, Jacoba made her way to the door. Elias stood just outside, his arms folded across his chest and his foot impatiently tapping the ground.

His scowl softened when he noticed Jacoba's anguish. He unfolded his arms and wanted to pull her close. Instead, he took a step back. "I'm sorry. I know you wanted to stay with him, but the bishop needs to see him now. He's been waiting quite awhile. There's a line of brothers who want to see him, too. I hate to let anyone in. Is he still refusing to put on his tunic?" Elias was flustered, preoccupied with the myriad tasks in preparation for the approaching funeral.

"I think he may let you dress him. I assured him he will die owning nothing. The clothes I *loaned* him are over there and so is 'my' sackcloth in case he refuses the soft tunic." Jacoba pointed to a small parcel just inside the chapel's entrance.

"Bless you, Jacoba." Elias sounded relieved. He started toward the bundle but quickly stopped and faced her.

"The 'Poverello' stayed faithful to 'Lady Poverty' all right. Wouldn't dirty his hands with money or 'things,' but he never renounced beauty. He found it everywhere and in everyone, even where none of us could see it. I still don't think I could hold lepers the way he did. Elias shook his head back and forth. Jacoba noticed tears forming in his eyes, something she'd never seen in the years she'd known him.

"He loved you in a special way, didn't he?" Elias spoke as he looked into Jacoba's eyes. She sensed a subtle sharpness in his voice not present earlier. "I always knew there was something going on between you two. I could tell from the first time you laid eyes on each other in his father's shop. He owns a piece of your heart, doesn't he?" Elias gave Jacoba no time to respond to the question even if she wanted to. Surprisingly, he sighed, "I loved him, too.

"He owns so many hearts and has so many spiritual children, he's wealthier than a king. Who knew when we were gallivanting around Assisi that summer he'd grow up to be a saint? You *will* help us get the Pope to canonize him, won't you?"

Elias sniffed and used the sleeve of his tunic to wipe his nose. "I'll talk to you about it later. Right now, I'd better get him dressed. I see the bishop is walking toward us and doesn't look pleased." Elias hurried past Jacoba into the Porziuncola to prepare Francis for his last hours on earth.

Jacoba walked back silently to the grove where her sons were waiting with a sizeable entourage. The group wordlessly made its way to a palazzo in upper Assisi where they would stay until after the funeral.

ꙮ

Francis died after sunset on Saturday, October 3, 1226. One of the brothers brought the news to Jacoba's household within an hour of the event. Elias made clear to the brothers it was Francis's wish Jacoba prepare his body for burial. So, by lantern light, she, her son Giovanni and several guards and servants made their way through the darkness back to the Porziuncola where Elias was waiting for them.

Francis's corpse was still on the floor. A dozen friars had gathered around it. Some chanted softly while others silently prayed. When they saw Jacoba enter with Elias, they quietly filed out of the tiny church.

Jacoba's eyes tried to focus on the corpse lying before her. She had begun to cry enroute to the Porziuncola, and by the time she arrived her tears were flowing uncontrollably.

"You loved him in life, and you shall hold him in your arms in death." Elias motioned to Jacoba to sit on the ground. After placing Francis's body in her arms, he began walking toward the door. As an afterthought, he stopped and turned. "You won't have much time alone. We have to take his body to San Damiano so Clare and the poor ladies can say good-bye. Then we process through Assisi. I hear crowds are already lining the streets. I'll be right outside the door if you need my help. I'd like to talk with your son."

Jacoba removed the veil from Francis's face and loosened the cloth that covered him. She began kissing him, and her hot tears streamed over his lifeless body. She never grieved so deeply for anyone, not even her husband. She wanted to grieve for Gratien, but she couldn't. It wasn't lack of devotion: it was lack of finality. Gratien's body was never found. To her, his death felt like desertion, and she nurtured a fading hope he might someday show up alive.

Francis's death was absolute. The corpse she embraced confirmed no hope of any earthly reunion. She gently returned Francis's frail body to the floor. Wiping her eyes with the backs of her hands, Jacoba prepared to begin the cleansing ritual. When she initially unwrapped his body, it looked as it did the day before – bloody, beat-up, broken down.

No longer blinded by tears, Jacoba realized as she cleansed the corpse, it was not that of the man who blessed her the previous day. That body was dark and shriveled. This one had the skin of a child. And its muscles were pliable, not rigid like other corpses. What most astonished her was the way his hands, feet and side looked after she wiped away the blood and puss. She shrieked in amazement.

Elias was at her side before she got out his name. "Elias, did you know what was on his hands and feet under the blood and ashes?"

"I had an idea. We all had thoughts about his 'injuries,' but we never talked about it."

"Look at them! Look at him! You need to tell people! It truly is the work of the Almighty, and it must be shared with the world." Jacoba was adamant. "Giovanni, come here." She shouted to her son who had been standing outside with Elias.

Elias and Giovanni were as amazed as Jacoba to see that yesterday's bloody holes in the middle of Francis's hands and feet were now gone. In their place appeared the nails themselves, black as iron, formed by his own flesh mingled with the dried blood and ashes. The wound on Francis's side, however, was still red and weepy. It was almost as if his blood hadn't dried at all.

Other brothers noticed the commotion, and Elias reluctantly waved them in to see the stigmata. Most wept and all marveled.

"He looks so beautiful…like an angel."

"It's like he's still living."

"Those are Christ's nails in his hands and feet."

"They are exquisite, like little black stones set in a white pavement."

Those who kissed his hands and feet and even those who were only permitted to see them felt they had been granted a wonderful gift.

While the attention was on Francis's stigmata, Elias pulled Jacoba away from her entourage.

"We have a problem with Francis's interment." He looked around to make sure no one else was within earshot. "You know there's already been a lot of talk about building a new church to house his remains. That means we have to find a temporary location."

"Why is that a problem?" Jacoba looked puzzled. "I'm sure any parish in Assisi would gladly inter him for a few years until his permanent tomb is finished."

"The problem is Perugia. We got word some nobles there are planning to steal his corpse and sell pieces of it as relics. They don't even care about the money. They just hate Assisi. They'll know a temporary tomb won't be as secure as his final resting place.

"I and a couple of the other brothers came up with a plan, and we need your help. Everyone thinks Francs will be interred at San Rufino. We want to keep it that way. His remains will actually be kept in the crypt of the Church of San Giorgio. Can you loan us your son Giovanni and some of your soldiers to help? I'll work directly with Giovanni on the details. I mentioned it to him last night."

On the spot Jacoba instructed several Frangipane soldiers to stand guard at the Porziuncola, remain near the coffin as the cortege moved up to Assisi, and follow Elias's orders to the letter.

ഗ്ദ

The day of the funeral, many of the same Assisians who jeered at Francis two decades earlier when his father dragged him through the streets now paid tribute with hymns, praises and sounding trumpets.

Elias and the bishop opened the lid of the wooden coffin several times along the route for the faithful to view Francis's corpse and be inspired by his stigmata. Jacoba had ordered additional Frangipane soldiers to protect it on its way to San Giorgio.

Everyone was told the procession would stop momentarily at Francis's old parish on its way to San Rufino. Elias and the bishop allowed those present a final viewing before placing a crimson dossal of richly embroidered brocade over the coffin.

No one would be allowed in the church since it would delay the cortege and interment. The beautifully draped box disappeared into the church. Its doors were closed for no more than five minutes when the coffin reappeared, and the procession continued.

What onlookers did not know was Francis's coffin now contained merely stones and rags. His body had been rapidly transferred to an ancient stone animal trough in a crypt below San Giorgio Church. The only people who knew of the subterfuge besides San Giorgio's pastor, Elias, Jacoba, and four trusted Frangipane guards were the two brothers who helped plan it. Elias said he would inform the bishop after the burial place was secure.

Before the guards lifted the heavy stone slab to cover the makeshift sarcophagus, Jacoba asked a moment for her final goodbye. Eyes now red from crying, she slipped off the silver ring on her finger. She leaned over the edge of the trough to kiss Francis's forehead and placed the ring under his hand. "Remember me, Francis. Remember us," she whispered.

"This is from little Giacoma." She laid her daughter's favorite necklace next to his arm.

Elias was looking at her, but she couldn't read his expression.

"I'm not sure we should be doing this," He said. Then he asked her for some coins to put in the makeshift sarcophagus. "If something happens and they don't find his body for a hundred years, it would be good to have some way to date it."

Elias reached inside his tunic and took out what looked like a small iron nail caked with rust. He fingered it lovingly, then put it into the sarcophagus near Jacoba's ring. She gave him a puzzled look.

"It's part of an ancient Roman fibula. My only possession other than my cap and tunic. I treasured that little piece of worthless metal. I knew it was wrong to keep anything once I joined the Poor Penitents, but I just couldn't part with it. It was the first 'artifact' we found on the Hill of Hell. Francis was actually the one who found it, but he could tell I really wanted it. So he *gave it to me*. He was so kind-hearted – even when we were kids. I kept it all these years. I always meant to give it back. Now I did."

Jacoba was sure Francis was with God and where he wanted to be, but she missed him greatly nonetheless.

A Letter from Jacoba

To Elias

1227

My Most Dear Elias,

Here is the silk brocade cover for the pillow our beloved Francis used during his final sickness. As you see, it was made from pieces of the large cloth that covered his coffin. I hope its quality will help preserve the delicate relic as well as conceal the various blood and fluid stains on it.

I noticed that the soft, little pillow was no longer under his head when he died. I assumed he gave it away like everything else. I should never have given it to him: I should have assured him he was only borrowing it.

I'm glad you retrieved it from whichever brother had it. Have you determined where this relic will be housed? Francis was dearly loved in so many other cities, I think it would be good to share some of his sacred remembrances beyond Assisi.

As you well know, Francis found great peace in the raw beauty of Le Celle on the outskirts of Cortona. Perhaps the good people there would be willing to build a chapel or church to honor Francis if they knew his pillow would be housed there. It's something to think about.

I've already made plans to donate one of the paintings I commissioned from Margaritone D'Arezzo to the hermitage at Greccio. The painting was completed before Francis was given his holy wounds. So, I told the artist to add the stigmata before delivering it to Greccio. My family and I are planning to go to Greccio to celebrate Christmas in memory of Francis. Perhaps you can join us and see the painting. I think you will like it.

I should also let you know I've asked Giunta Pisano to paint a crucifix to hang in the Porziuncola since I'm sure Francis's favorite little church will soon become an important pilgrimage site. I expect it will take Giunta a few years to complete it since he's working on so many projects right now. This cross will be more sorrowful in depiction than many but somewhat less grisly than Francis may have wished. I want the children who see it to be inspired not frightened.

I've asked the brothers at San Biagio in Rome to gather items Francis used when he stayed with them. I suggested they hide these relics in a safe place until a permanent home for them is determined. It will be difficult to get the brothers there to part with any of the objects in their possession. Apparently, Francis used a stone for a pillow whenever he slept there. The brothers said they've been taking turns sleeping on it since he died. So, I'm sure at least that relic will be quite secure where it is.

As soon as Francis's sainthood is formalized, I will move forward on enlarging San Biagio's as well as renaming it in memory of Francis. I believe pilgrims visiting Rome as well as Roman citizenry will want to visit "St. Francis Church at the River" to pray and see his stone pillow and other relics. Don't you agree?

I plan to help you and the brothers with designing, building and financing the church in Assisi in whatever ways I can. However, I will need you to promise one thing. When I die, my remains must be interred near those of Francis. My husband's body was never found, so I am not able to be entombed with him. And I'm now in the lengthy process of dissolving ties with Rome and Marino; so, there will be nothing in those places for me or my children. I believe Gratien would want me to be close to Francis since he loved him too. Now that Cardinal Ugolino is Pope, I'm confident I can get any special permission or dispensation required for my burial stipulation.

I can't thank you enough, Elias, for finding a more permanent residence in Assisi for me and what remains of my family. I will still need to make many trips to Rome and Marino to handle business matters, but from now on I will consider Assisi my home. Francis and you have dramatically impacted not only my life but also the lives of my children.

I have not seen my daughter Johanna since she joined the poor ladies in Orvieto five years ago. You never really got to know Johanna. She always had a mind of her own. Whenever Francis visited our family in Rome, Johanna was the one who sat at his feet and listened intently for as long as he talked. Then she would bombard him with questions.

When he told her about Clare and the poor ladies, she wanted to immediately join them. I approved but told her she had to wait for at least two years. After only a year she convinced me she was ready for that life. Francis told her there was a place for her in the little community at Orvieto, and she jumped at the opportunity. I miss her greatly but take solace in knowing she is probably finding great joy in her way of life. I received word recently she has been named abbess of the poor ladies there.

"Losing" Johanna to the poor ladies was much easier on me than losing Jacob. You pray none of your children die before you do. He was my oldest and most like Gratien in every good way. I know he is with God, but it still makes me sad to know I will never again see him in my earthly life.

I had been counting on Jacob to take over our family's affairs after returning from the Crusades. While I always feared he would be killed in battle, I never dreamed he would die of fever in Ancona. I will be making a journey there within the next several months to visit his widow and their son. Perhaps I can convince them to come to Assisi to live with me.

Giovanni is of age now and helping with our family's many holdings. However, he recently informed me he is considering renouncing his inheritance in order to live a simpler life.

My son Gratien and daughter Giacoma are still too young to leave home, but both have already given me reason to think they will follow in Francis's footsteps in some manner when they are of age. They seem very pleased about our upcoming move to Assisi.

I look forward to seeing you soon. May God bless you in your leadership of the Friars Minor. My children and I thank you for the kindness you have shown us.

Pax et bonum.
Your Brother in Christ,
Jacoba

AUTHOR'S NOTE

This book is fiction based upon several undisputed facts: Jacoba's remains do share the crypt of St. Francis. She was indeed a wealthy Roman noble who married into the branch of the famous Frangipane Family that lived in the Septizonium. She attended the saint at his death. Her ties to Trastevere, Marino, and Assisi are documented.

Few other details of her life are known such as the number of children she bore and the exact year of her birth. The years most often cited for her death are decades apart.

My research included spending time in Marino and Rome with an archaeologist who grew up there and whose post-graduate specialization was Early Christian and Medieval Archaeology. She provided insight while somewhat apologetically explaining historical records related to 12th and 13th Century Rome are limited. She said most archaeologists and historians prefer digging for artifacts and delving for information related to Ancient and Renaissance Rome instead of Rome in the Middle Ages.

In my multi-year search for background for this novel, I used a variety of resources ranging from the writings of St. Francis himself and his early biographers to obscure material no longer in print such as a booklet I discovered years ago on a web search of the Vatican Library. (A list of print and e-sources appears after "Acknowledgments.")

I also traveled to more than a dozen cities and towns in Italy where I scoured famous and obscure museums; visited medieval churches, palaces, and ruins; and talked with locals to learn whatever I could about the book's characters and medieval life. (A list of those places appears below.)

I gathered considerable factual information and used it wherever possible. However, I am a fiction writer and took poetic license inventing characters and situations. If anything is incorrect, offensive, or obtuse; please blame me – not my sources or editors.

I'm not an academic, and my book isn't a biography. However, I wrote this story in the hope that shining a light on Jacoba may inspire a genuine scholar to uncover the truth of her life and her relationship to St. Francis.

More than one source indicated nearly all documents related to Jacoba disappeared soon after Francis's death. He was on a fast track to sainthood, and revealing an uncharacteristically close relationship with a secular woman may have greatly slowed or even halted the process.

Some claim the records were destroyed…but possibly not. Maybe they are waiting somewhere to be discovered – perhaps in one of the 1,200 caves under the city of Orvieto or within the Vatican's vaults. After all, the Church apparently had enough information to consider Jacoba "Blessed" and set her feast day as February 8.

Finally, I apologize for my overuse of ellipses. They are a remnant from my work in the electronic media, and I'm still very fond of them.

꧁꧂

Assisi	Lago Trasimeno	Ninfa	Sorrento
Cortona	Monte La Verna	Orvieto	Subiaco
Florence	Monte Subasio	Rome	Venice
Greccio	Marino	Sermoneta	
Ischia	Naples	Sicily	

ACKNOWLEDGMENTS

Although I've been writing professionally for decades, this is my first novel. To acknowledge everyone in my lifetime who helped me get here would require a tome. Instead, I offer this extremely abridged list:

- My spouse, MDW, who loves, encourages, and (with my utmost gratitude) edits me.
- My children, grandchildren, and extended family who love, encourage and don't edit me.
- My parents, Roy & LaVerne, who gave me faith in God and in myself…and nurtured both throughout my life.
- My great-grandmother (a secular Franciscan), my grandparents, other relatives and friends who influenced me growing up and as an adult.
- My many editors including those at the daily newspaper where I got my professional start; those in corporate communications where I worked for much of my life; and Kenneth Fleurant, PhD, for his help with this book.
- The professionals who helped me in Italy particularly Archaeologist Flavia Vitucci in Rome & Marino and the staff of the Treasure Museum of the Basilica of Saint Francis in Assisi.
- Hospital Sisters of St. Francis, Springfield, IL, who introduced me to Jacoba and took me on pilgrimage to Assisi.
- Sr. Joanne Schatzlein, OSF, who sparked my interest in Jacoba and connected me to key resources.
- Authors, especially Vicky Meawasige Reed, who helped a neophyte novelist navigate the publishing process.

PRINT & E-SOURCES

Anonymous. *The Deeds of Pope Innocent III* (translated by James M. Powell). Washington, D. C.: The Catholic University Press of America, 2007. Print.

Armeni, Elisa. *Giacomina de' Settesoli.* Florence, Italy: Unione Francescana, 1938. Print.

Brooke, Christopher. *Europe in the Central Middle Ages 962-1154, Second Edition.* New York: Longman Inc, 1987. Print.

Cantor, Norman F. *Medieval History – the Life and Death of a Civilization.* New York: The Macmillan Company, 1966. Print.

Catholic Encyclopedia: Home. Web. 25 January 2019. http://www.newadvent.org/cathen/

Cipiciani, Maria Letizia. *Assisi 1182 - Francis's Home.* Perugia, Italy: MLC Libri di Viaggio, 2015. Print.

Cooper, OFM Cap, John. OFS – Conference of National Spiritual Assistants – Monthly Spiritual Messages. Web. January 2016 – May 2017. http://www.ofsaustralia.org.au/LiteratureRetrieve.aspx?ID=157825

Cowan, James. *A Saint's Way*. Liguori, Missouri: Liguori/Triumph, 2001. Print

Cunningham, Lawrence, and Dennis Stock. *St. Francis of Assisi.* San Francisco: Harper & Row, 1989. Print.

Cuthbert, O.S.F.C., Father. *Life of Francis of Assisi.* London/New York/Bombay/Calcutta: Longmans, Green and Co., 1914. Print

Duby, Georges (Editor). *A History of Private Life – II – Revelations of the Medieval World.* Cambridge, Massachusetts: The Belknap Press of Harvard University Press, 1988. Print.

Englebert, Omer. *St. Francis of Assisi: A Biography.* Ann Arbor, Michigan: Servant Books, 1965. Print.

Evans, Joan. *Life in Medieval France.* London: Phaidon Press, 1957. Print.

Franciscan Pilgrimage Programs. *Pilgrim's Companion to Franciscan Places.* Assisi, Italy: Editrice Minerva Assisi, 2002. Print

Gasnick OFM, Roy M. *The Francis Book - 800 Years with the Saint from Assisi.* New York: Macmillan Publishing Co, Inc. 1980. Print.

Gies, Joseph and Frances. *Life in a Medieval City.* New York: Harper Perennial, 1980. Print.

Gies, Frances & Joseph. *Daily Life in Medieval Times – A Vivid, Detailed Account of Birth, Marriage and Death; Food, Clothing and Housing; Love and Labor in the Middle Ages.* New York: Barnes & Noble Books, 1990. Print.

Gregorovius, Ferdinand. *Rome and Medieval Culture – Selection from History of the City of Rome in the Middle Ages.* Chicago: The University of Chicago Press, 1971. Print.

Habig, Marion A. (Editor). *St. Francis of Assisi, Writings and Early Biographies: English Omnibus of the Sources for the Life of St. Francis.* Chicago: Franciscan Herald Press, 1973. Print.

Hare, Augustus J.C. Walks in Rome, Vol. 1. London: George Allen, 1871. Print.

Hernandez, Reverend Antonio. *My Kingdom for a Crown: An Around-the-World History of the Skullcap and its Modern Socio-Political Significance.* Web. 1 January 2019. http://www.dieter-philippi.de/files/literatur/1968_antonio_hernandez_-_history_of_the_skullcap.pdf

Hetherington, Paul. *Medieval Rome – A Portrait of the City and its Life.* New York, St. Martin's Press, 1994. Print.

Hollister, C. Warren. *Medieval Europe – A Short History, Fifth Edition.* New York: John Wiley & Sons, Inc., 1982. Print.

"Women in World History: A Biographical Encyclopedia. Web. 2 Feb.2019. https://www.encyclopedia.com

Jacopa dei Settesoli, News. Cenni storici e biografici. Web. 10 Jan. 2012. http://www.assisiofm.it/Jacopa-dei-settesoli-2347-1.html

Johnson, Paul. *The Papacy.* New York: Barnes & Noble Books, 1997. Print.

Kessler, Herbert L. and Johanna Zacharias. *Rome 1300 – On the Path of the Pilgrim.* New Haven and London: Yale University Press, 2000. Print.

Key to Umbria. Web. 23 Jan. 2019. http://www.keytoumbria.com/Assisi/Home.html

Lacroix, Paul. *The Arts in the Middle Ages and the Renaissance.* London: Random House UK Ltd, 1996. Print.

Lindberg, David C. *The Beginnings of Western Science – The European Scientific Tradition in Philosophical, Religious, and Institutional Context, 600 B.C. to A. D. 1450.* Chicago: The University of Chicago Press, 1992. Print.

MacDonell, Anne. *Sons of Francis.* London/New York: J. M. Dent/G.P. Putnam's Sons, 1902. Print.

McCall, Andrew. *The Medieval Underworld.* London: Hamish Hamilton, 1979. Print.

McEvedy, Colin. *The New Penguin Atlas of Medieval History.* London: Penguin Books, 1992. Print.

Morton, H.V. *A Traveller in Rome.* New York: Dodd, Mead & Company, 1957. Print.

Nichols, Francis Morgan (Editor and Translator). *The Marvels of Rome – Mirabilia Urbis Romae.* New York: Italica Press, 1986. Print.

Phillips, Jonathan. *The Fourth Crusade and the Sack of Constantinople.* New York: Viking Penguin, 2004. Print.

Picard, OFM, Cap., Marc. *The Icon of the Christ of San Damiano.* Assisi, Italy: Casa Editrice Francescana Frati Minori Conventuali. Print.

Power, Eileen. *Medieval Women.* Cambridge, Great Britain: Cambridge University Press, 1997. Print.

Rowling, Marjorie. *Life in Medieval Times.* New York: G.P. Putnam's Sons, 1979. Print.

Sabatier, Paul. *The Road to Assisi – The Essential Biography of St. Francis.* Brewster, Massachusetts: Paraclete Press, 2005. Print.

Spoto, Donald. *Reluctant Saint – The Life of Francis of Assisi.* New York: Penguin Group (USA) Inc., 2003. Print.

Urner, Carol Reilley. *The Search for Brother Jacopa: A Study on Jacopa Dei Settesoli, Friend of Francis of Assisi and His Movement. A Thesis Presented to the Faculty of the Graduate School Ateneo de Manila University.* St. Bonaventure, New York: The Franciscan Institute, 1980.Print.

DISCUSSION QUESTIONS

1. What if anything did you gain by reading this book?
2. Who was your favorite character? Why?
3. Which character most surprised you? Why?
4. Why did you select this book?
5. Did this book change your thinking about what it means to be a Catholic saint?
6. If this book were to be made into a movie, who would you cast in leading roles?
7. If you could invite one of the characters to your house for dinner, who would it be?
8. What do you think would have happened if Jacoba hadn't married Gratien?
9. If you could pose a question to one character: Who would it be? What would you ask?

ABOUT THE AUTHOR

I'm a Baby Boomer–born and bred in the Midwest–with a brief stint in New York City.

As a young teen, I began writing professionally for a daily newspaper and received various writing awards including national recognition for the youth section I edited.

My bachelor's degree in journalism is from the University of Wisconsin-Madison. I have also worked professionally in television, radio, and in corporate communications where I edited a regional magazine.

My Faith and family are most important in my life. I like to spend time at home…or somewhere in Italy. I enjoy reading. I occasionally draw or paint. And I have a like-dislike relationship with golf.

My words to live by:

"Thy Will be done."

-- H.G. Watts

If you like this book, please consider a review.

Amazon.com

Goodreads.com

BN.com

Made in the USA
Columbia, SC
24 December 2019

85468280R00212